"The tools Hunter S. Thompson would use in the years ahead—bizarre wit, mockery without end, redundant excess, supreme self-confidence, the narrative of the wounded meritorious ego, and the idiopathic anger of the righteous outlaw—were all there in his precocious imagination in San Juan. There, too were the beginnings of his future as a masterful prose stylist."

—William Kennedy, Pulitzer Prize–winning author of *Ironweed*

"*The Rum Diary* shows a side of human nature that is ugly and wrong. But it is a world that Hunter Thompson knows in the nerves of his neck. This is a brilliant tribal study and a bone in the throat of all decent people."

—Jimmy Buffett

the rum diary

a novel

Hunter S. Thompson

Simon & Schuster Paperbacks

new york london toronto sydney new delhi

SIMON & SCHUSTER PAPERBACKS
A Division of Simon & Schuster, Inc.
1230 Avenue of the Americas
New York, NY 10020

This Simon & Schuster trade paperback edition October 2011.

SIMON & SCHUSTER PAPERBACKS and colophon are registered trademarks of Simon & Schuster Inc.

For information about special discounts for bulk purchases, please contact Simon & Schuster Special Sales at 1-800-456-6798 or business@simonandschuster.com.v

DESIGNED BY ROBERT BULL DESIGN

Map copyright © 1998 by Anita Karl and Jim Kemp
Palm tree photograph copyright © 1998 by Corbis/Bettmann

Manufactured in the United States of America

1   3   5   7   9   10   8   6   4   2

The Library of Congress has catalogued the hardcover edition as follows:
Thompson, Hunter S.
The rum diary : the long lost novel / Hunter S. Thompson.
p.   cm.
I. Title.
PS3570.H62R86   1998
813'.54—dc21   98-34128

ISBN 978-0-684-85521-9
ISBN 978-1-4516-5971-9 (pbk)
ISBN 978-1-4516-6927-5 (ebook)

To Heidi Opheim, Marysue Rucci and Dana Kennedy

the rum diary

My rider of the bright eyes,
What happened you yesterday?
I thought you in my heart,
When I bought you your fine clothes,
A man the world could not slay.
—Dark Eileen O'Connell, 1773

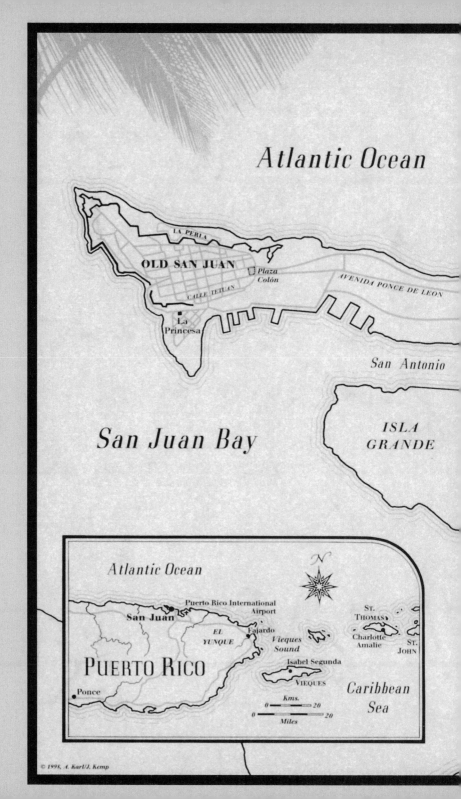

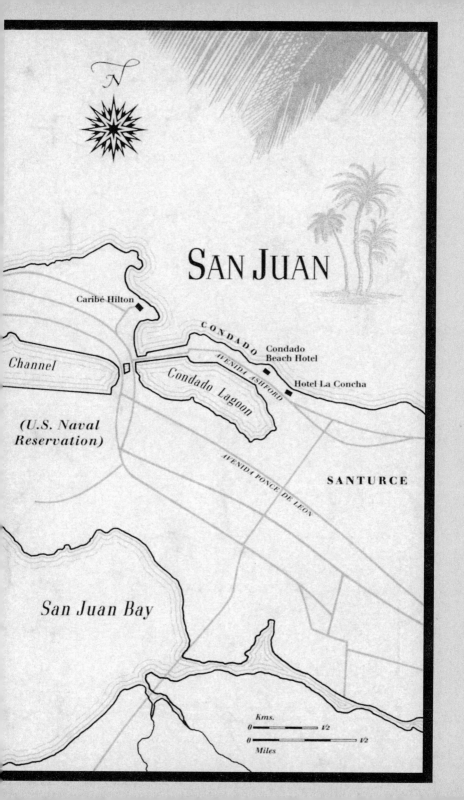

SAN JUAN

Caribé Hilton

CONDADO

Channel

Condado Lagoon

AVENIDA ASHFORD

Condado Beach Hotel

Hotel La Concha

(U.S. Naval Reservation)

AVENIDA PONCE DE LEÓN

SANTURCE

San Juan Bay

Kms.
0   1/2
0   1/2
Miles

San Juan, Winter of 1958

I N the early Fifties, when San Juan first became a tourist town, an ex-jockey named *Al Arbonito* built a bar in the patio behind his house on Calle O'Leary. He called it *Al's Backyard* and hung a sign above his doorway on the street, with an arrow pointing between two ramshackle buildings to the patio in back. At first he served nothing but beer, at twenty cents a bottle, and rum, at a dime a shot or fifteen cents with ice. After several months he began serving hamburgers, which he made himself.

It was a pleasant place to drink, especially in the mornings when the sun was still cool and the salt mist came up from the ocean to give the air a crisp, healthy smell that for a few early hours would hold its own against the steaming, sweaty heat that clamps San Juan at noon and remains until long after sundown.

It was good in the evenings, too, but not so cool. Sometimes there would be a breeze and *Al's* would usually catch it because of the fine location—at the very top of *Calle O'Leary* hill, so high that if the patio had windows you could look down on the whole city. But there is a thick wall around the patio, and all you can see is the sky and a few plantain trees.

As time passed, *Al* bought a new cash register, then he bought wood umbrella-tables for the patio; and finally moved his family out

1

of the house on Calle O'Leary, out in the suburbs to a new urbanización near the airport. He hired a large negro named Sweep, who washed the dishes and carried hamburgers and eventually learned to cook.

He turned his old living room into a small piano bar, and got a pianist from Miami, a thin, sad-faced man called Nelson Otto. The piano was midway between the cocktail lounge and the patio. It was an old baby-grand, painted light grey and covered with special shellac to keep the salt air from ruining the finish—and seven nights a week, through all twelve months of the endless Caribbean summer, Nelson Otto sat down at the keyboard to mingle his sweat with the weary chords of his music.

At the Tourist Bureau they talk about the cooling trade winds that caress the shores of Puerto Rico every day and night of the year—but Nelson Otto was a man the trade winds never seemed to touch. Hour after muggy hour, through a tired repertoire of blues and sentimental ballads, the sweat dripped from his chin and soaked the armpits of his flowered cotton sportshirts. He cursed the "goddamn shitting heat" with such violence and such hatred that it sometimes ruined the atmosphere of the place, and people would get up and walk down the street to the Flamboyan Lounge, where a bottle of beer cost sixty cents and a sirloin steak was three-fifty.

When an ex-communist named Lotterman came down from Florida to start the San Juan Daily News, *Al's Backyard became the English-language press club, because none of the drifters and the dreamers who came to work for Lotterman's new paper could afford the high-price "New York" bars that were springing up all over the city like a rash of neon toadstools. The day-shift reporters and deskmen straggled in about seven, and the night-shift types—sports people, proofreaders and make-up men—usually arrived en masse around midnight. Once in a while someone had a date, but on any normal night a girl in Al's Backyard was a rare and erotic sight. White girls were not plentiful in San Juan, and most of them were either tourists, hustlers or airline stewardesses. It was not surprising that they preferred the casinos or the terrace bar at the Hilton.*

All manner of men came to work for the News: *everything from wild young Turks who wanted to rip the world in half and start all over again—to tired, beer-bellied old hacks who wanted nothing* more than to live out their days in peace before a bunch of lunatics ripped the world in half.

They ran the whole gamut from genuine talents and honest men, to degenerates and hopeless losers who could barely write a post-card—loons and fugitives and dangerous drunks, a shoplifting Cuban who carried a gun in his armpit, a half-wit Mexican who molested small children, pimps and pederasts and human chancres of every description, most of them working just long enough to make the price of a few drinks and a plane ticket.

On the other hand, there were people like Tom Vanderwitz, who later worked for the Washington Post and won a Pulitzer Prize. And a man named Tyrrell, now an editor of the London Times, who worked fifteen hours a day just to keep the paper from going under.

When I arrived the News was three years old and Ed Lotterman was on the verge of a breakdown. To hear him talk you would think he'd been sitting at the very cross-corners of the earth, seeing himself as a combination of God, Pulitzer and the Salvation Army. He often swore that if all the people who had worked for the paper in those years could appear at one time before the throne of The Almighty— if they all stood there and recited their histories and their quirks and their crimes and their deviations—there was no doubt in his mind that God himself would fall down in a swoon and tear his hair.

Of course Lotterman exaggerated; in his tirade he forgot about the good men and talked only about what he called the "wineheads." But there were more than a few of these, and the best that can be said of that staff is that they were a strange and unruly lot. At best they were unreliable, and at worst they were drunk, dirty and no more dependable than goats. But they managed to put out a paper, and when they were not working a good many of them passed the time drinking in Al's Backyard.

They bitched and groaned when—in what some of them called "a fit of greed"—Al jacked the price of beer up to a quarter; and they kept on bitching until he tacked up a sign listing beer and drink prices at the Caribé Hilton. It was scrawled in black crayon and hung in plain sight behind the bar.

Since the newspaper functioned as a clearing-house for every writer, photographer and neo-literate con man who happened to find himself in Puerto Rico, Al got the dubious benefit of this trade *too. The drawer beneath the cash register was full of unpaid tabs and letters from all over the world, promising to "get that bill squared away in the near future." Vagrant journalists are notorious welshers, and to those who travel in that rootless world, a large unpaid bar tab can be a fashionable burden.*

There was no shortage of people to drink with in those days. They never lasted very long, but they kept coming. I call them vagrant journalists because no other term would be quite as valid. No two were alike. They were professionally deviant, but they had a few things in common. They depended, mostly from habit, on newspapers and magazines for the bulk of their income; their lives were geared to long chances and sudden movement; and they claimed no allegiance to any flag and valued no currency but luck and good contacts.

Some of them were more journalists than vagrants, and others were more vagrants than journalists—but with a few exceptions they were part-time, freelance, would-be foreign correspondents who, for one reason or another, lived at several removes from the journalistic establishment. Not the slick strivers and jingo parrots who staffed the mossback papers and news magazines of the Luce empire. Those were a different breed.

Puerto Rico was a backwater and the Daily News *was staffed mainly by ill-tempered wandering rabble. They moved erratically, on the winds of rumor and opportunity, all over Europe, Latin America and the Far East—wherever there were English-language newspapers, jumping from one to another, looking always for the big break, the crucial assignment, the rich heiress or the fat job at the far end of the next plane ticket.*

In a sense I was one of them—more competent than some and more stable than others—and in the years that I carried that ragged banner I was seldom unemployed. Sometimes I worked for three newspapers at once. I wrote ad copy for new casinos and bowling alleys. I was a consultant for the cockfighting syndicate, an utterly corrupt high-end restaurant critic, a yachting photographer and a routine victim of police brutality. It was a greedy life and I was good at it. I made some interesting friends, had enough money to get around, and learned a lot about the world that I could never have learned in any other way.

Like most of the others, I was a seeker, a mover, a malcontent, and at times a stupid hell-raiser. I was never idle long enough to do much thinking, but I felt somehow that my instincts were right. I shared a vagrant optimism that some of us were making real progress, that we had taken an honest road, and that the best of us would inevitably make it over the top.

At the same time, I shared a dark suspicion that the life we were leading was a lost cause, that we were all actors, kidding ourselves along on a senseless odyssey. It was the tension between these two poles—a restless idealism on one hand and a sense of impending doom on the other—that kept me going.

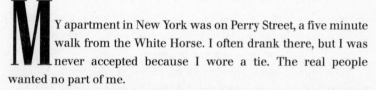

One

MY apartment in New York was on Perry Street, a five minute walk from the White Horse. I often drank there, but I was never accepted because I wore a tie. The real people wanted no part of me.

I did some drinking there on the night I left for San Juan. Phil Rollins, who'd worked with me, was paying for the ale, and I was swilling it down, trying to get drunk enough to sleep on the plane. Art Millick, the most vicious cab driver in New York, was there. So was Duke Peterson, who had just come back from the Virgin Islands. I recall Peterson giving me a list of people to look up when I got to St. Thomas, but I lost the list and never met any of them.

It was a rotten night in the middle of January, but I wore a light cord coat. Everyone else had on heavy jackets and flannel suits. The last thing I remember is standing on the dirty bricks of Hudson Street, shaking hands with Rollins and cursing the freezing wind that blew in off the river. Then I got in Millick's cab and slept all the way to the airport.

I was late and there was a line at the reservations desk. I fell in behind fifteen or so Puerto Ricans and one small blonde girl a few places ahead of me. I pegged her for a tourist, a wild young secretary going down to the Caribbean for a two week romp. She had a fine little body and an impatient way of standing that indicated a mass of stored-up energy. I watched her intently, smiling, feeling the ale in my veins, waiting for her to turn around for a swift contact with the eyes.

She got her ticket and walked away toward the plane. There were still three Puerto Ricans in front of me. Two of them did their business and passed on, but the third was stymied by the clerk's refusal to let him carry a huge cardboard box on the plane as hand baggage. I gritted my teeth as they argued.

Finally I broke in. "Hey!" I shouted. "What the hell is this? I have to get on that plane!"

The clerk looked up, disregarding the shouts of the little man in front of me. "What's your name?"

I told him, got my ticket, and bolted for the gate. When I got to the plane I had to shove past five or six people waiting to board. I showed my ticket to the grumbling stewardess and stepped inside to scan the seats on both sides of the aisle.

Not a blonde head anywhere. I hurried up to the front, thinking that she might be so small that her head wouldn't show over the back seat. But she wasn't on the plane and by this time there were only two double seats left. I fell into one on the aisle and put my typewriter on the one next to the window. They were starting the engines when I looked out and saw her coming across the runway, waving at the stewardess who was about to close the door.

"Wait a minute!" I shouted. "Another passenger!" I watched until she reached the bottom of the steps. Then I turned around to smile as she came on. I was reaching for my typewriter, thinking to put it on the floor, when an old man shoved in front of me and sat down in the seat I was saving.

"This seat's taken," I said quickly, grabbing him by the arm.

He jerked away and snarled something in Spanish, turning his head toward the window.

I grabbed him again. "Get up," I said angrily.

He started to yell just as the girl went by and stopped a few feet up the aisle, looking around for a seat. "Here's one," I said, giving the old man a savage jerk. Before she could turn around the stewardess was on me, pulling at my arm.

"He sat on my typewriter," I explained, helplessly watching the girl find a seat far up at the front of the plane.

The stewardess patted the old man's shoulder and eased him back to the seat. "What kind of a bully are you?" she asked me. "I should put you off!"

I grumbled and slumped back in the seat. The old man stared straight ahead until we got off the ground. "You rotten old bastard," I mumbled at him.

He didn't even blink, and finally I shut my eyes and tried to sleep. Now and then I would glance up at the blonde head at the front of the plane. Then they turned out the lights and I couldn't see anything.

It was dawn when I woke up. The old man was still asleep and I leaned across him to look out the window. Several thousand feet below us the ocean was dark blue and calm as a lake. Up ahead I saw an island, bright green in the early morning sun. There were beaches along the edge of it, and brown swamps further inland. The plane started down and the stewardess announced that we should all buckle our safety belts.

Moments later we swept in over acres of palm trees and taxied to a halt in front of the big terminal. I decided to stay in my seat until the girl came past, then get up and walk with her across the runway. Since we were the only white people on the plane, it would seem quite natural.

The others were standing now, laughing and jabbering as they waited for the stewardess to open the door. Suddenly the old man jumped up and tried to scramble over me like a dog. Without thinking, I slammed him back against the window, causing a thump that silenced the crowd. The man appeared to be sick and tried to scramble past me again, shouting hysterically in Spanish.

"You crazy old bastard!" I yelled, shoving him back with one hand and reaching for my typewriter with the other. The door was open now and they were filing out. The girl came past me and I tried to smile at her, keeping the old man pinned against the window until I could back into the aisle. He was raising so much hell, shouting and waving his arms, that I was tempted to belt him in the throat to calm him down.

Then the stewardess arrived, followed by the co-pilot, who demanded to know what I thought I was doing.

"He's been beating that old man ever since we left New York," said the stewardess. "He must be a sadist."

They kept me there for ten minutes and at first I thought they meant to have me arrested. I tried to explain, but I was so tired and confused that I couldn't think what I was saying. When they finally let me go I slunk off the plane like a criminal, squinting and sweating in the sun as I crossed the runway to the baggage room.

It was crowded with Puerto Ricans and the girl was nowhere in sight. There was not much hope of finding her now and I was not optimistic about what might happen if I did. Few girls look with favor on a man of my stripe, a brutalizer of old people. I remembered the expression on her face when she saw me with the old man pinned against the window. It was almost too much to overcome. I decided to get some breakfast and pick up my baggage later on.

The airport in San Juan is a fine, modern thing, full of bright colors and suntanned people and Latin rhythms blaring from speakers hung on naked girders above the lobby. I walked up a long ramp, carrying my topcoat and my typewriter in one hand, and a small leather bag in the other. The signs led me up another ramp and finally to the coffee shop. As I went in I saw myself in a mirror, looking dirty and disreputable, a pale vagrant with red eyes.

On top of my slovenly appearance, I stank of ale. It hung in my stomach like a lump of rancid milk. I tried not to breathe on anyone as I sat down at the counter and ordered sliced pineapple.

Outside, the runway glistened in the early sun. Beyond it a thick palm jungle stood between me and the ocean. Several miles out at sea a sailboat moved slowly across the horizon. I stared for several moments and fell into a trance. It looked peaceful out there, peaceful and hot. I wanted to go into the palms and sleep, take a few chunks of pineapple and wander into the jungle to pass out.

Instead, I ordered more coffee and looked again at the cable that had come with my plane ticket. It said I had reservations at the Condado Beach Hotel.

It was not yet seven o'clock, but the coffee shop was crowded.

Groups of men sat at tables beside the long window, sipping a milky brew and talking energetically. A few wore suits, but most of them had on what appeared to be the uniform of the day—thick-rimmed sunglasses, shiny dark pants and white shirts with short sleeves and ties.

I caught snatches of conversation here and there: ". . . no such thing as cheap beach-front anymore . . . yeah, but this ain't Montego, gentlemen . . . don't worry, he has plenty, and all we need is . . . sewed up, but we gotta move quick before Castro and that crowd jumps in with . . ."

After ten minutes of half-hearted listening I suspected I was in a den of hustlers. Most of them seemed to be waiting for the seven-thirty flight from Miami, which—from what I gathered of the con-versations—would be bulging at the seams with architects, strip-men, consultants and Sicilians fleeing Cuba.

Their voices set my teeth on edge. I have no valid complaint against hustlers, no rational bitch, but the act of selling is repulsive to me. I harbor a secret urge to whack a salesman in the face, crack his teeth and put red bumps around his eyes.

Once I was conscious of the talk I couldn't hear anything else. It shattered my feeling of laziness and finally annoyed me so much that I sucked down the rest of my coffee and hurried out of the place.

The baggage room was empty. I found my two duffel bags and had a porter carry them out to the cab. All the way through the lobby he favored me with a steady grin and kept saying: "Sí, Puerto Rico está bueno . . . ah, sí, muy bueno . . . mucho ha-ha, sí . . ."

In the cab I leaned back and lit a small cigar I'd bought in the coffee shop. I was feeling better now, warm and sleepy and ab-solutely free. With the palms zipping past and the big sun burning down on the road ahead, I had a flash of something I hadn't felt since my first months in Europe—a mixture of ignorance and a loose, "what the hell" kind of confidence that comes on a man when the wind picks up and he begins to move in a hard straight line toward an unknown horizon.

We were speeding along a four-lane highway. Stretching off on both sides was a vast complex of yellow housing developments, laced with tall cyclone fences. Moments later we passed what looked like a new subdivision, full of identical pink and blue houses. There was a billboard at the entrance, announcing to all travelers that they were passing the El Jippo Urbanización. A few yards from the billboard was a tiny shack made of palm fronds and tin scraps, and beside it was a hand-painted sign saying "Coco Frío." Inside, a boy of about thirteen leaned on his counter and stared out at the passing cars.

Arriving half-drunk in a foreign place is hard on the nerves. You have a feeling that something is wrong, that you can't get a grip. I had this feeling, and when I got to the hotel I went straight to bed.

It was four-thirty when I woke up, hungry and dirty and not at all sure where I was. I walked out on my balcony and stared down at the beach. Below me, a crowd of women, children and pot-bellied men were splashing around in the surf. To my right was another hotel, and then another, each with its own crowded beach.

I took a shower, then went downstairs to the open-air lobby. The restaurant was closed, so I tried the bar. It showed every sign of having been flown down intact from a Catskill mountain resort. I sat there for two hours, drinking, eating peanuts and staring out at the ocean. There were roughly a dozen people in the place. The men looked like sick Mexicans, with thin little mustaches and silk suits that glistened like plastic. Most of the women were Americans, a brittle-looking lot, none of them young, all wearing sleeveless cocktail dresses that fit like rubber sacks.

I felt like something that had washed up on the beach. My wrinkled cord coat was five years old and frayed at the neck, my pants had no creases and, although it had never occurred to me to wear a tie, I was obviously out of place without one. Rather than seem like a pretender, I gave up on rum and ordered a beer. The bartender eyed me sullenly and I knew the reason why—I was wearing nothing that glistened. No doubt it was the mark of a bad apple. In order to make a go of it here, I would have to get some dazzling clothes.

At six-thirty I left the bar and walked outside. It was getting dark and the big Avenida looked cool and graceful. On the other side were homes that once looked out on the beach. Now they looked out on hotels and most of them had retreated behind tall hedges and walls that cut them off from the street. Here and there I could see a patio or a screen porch where people sat beneath fans and drank rum. Somewhere up the street I heard bells, the sleepy tinkling of Brahms' Lullaby.

I walked a block or so, trying to get the feel of the place, and the bells kept coming closer. Soon an ice-cream truck appeared, moving slowly down the middle of the street. On its roof was a giant popsicle, flashing on and off with red neon explosions that lit up the whole area. From somewhere in its bowels came the clanging of Mr. Brahms' tune. As it passed me, the driver grinned happily and blew his horn.

I immediately hailed a cab, telling the man to take me to the middle of town. Old San Juan is an island, connected to the mainland by several causeways. We crossed on the one that comes in from Condado. Dozens of Puerto Ricans stood along the rails, fishing in the shallow lagoon, and off to my right was a huge white shape beneath a neon sign that said Caribé Hilton. This, I knew, was the cornerstone of The Boom. Conrad had come in like Jesus and all the fish had followed. Before Hilton there was nothing; now the sky was the limit. We passed a deserted stadium and soon we were on a boulevard that ran along a cliff. On one side was the dark Atlantic, and, on the other, across the narrow city, were thousands of colored lights on cruise ships tied up at the waterfront. We turned off the boulevard and stopped at a place the driver said was Plaza Colón. The fare was a dollar-thirty and I gave him two bills.

He looked at the money and shook his head.

"What's wrong?" I said.

He shrugged. "No change, señor."

I felt in my pocket—nothing but a nickel. I knew he was lying, but I didn't feel like taking the trouble to get a dollar changed. "You goddamn thief," I said, tossing the bills in his lap. He shrugged again and drove off.

The Plaza Colón was a hub for several narrow streets. The buildings were jammed together, two and three stories high, with balconies that hung out over the street. The air was hot, and a smell of sweat and garbage rode on the faint breeze. A chatter of music and voices came from open windows. The sidewalks were so narrow that it was an effort to stay out of the gutter, and fruit vendors blocked the streets with wooden carts, selling peeled oranges for a nickel each.

I walked for thirty minutes, looking into windows of stores that sold "Ivy Liga" clothes, peering into foul bars full of whores and sailors, dodging people on the sidewalks, thinking I would collapse at any moment if I didn't find a restaurant.

Finally I gave up. There seemed to be no restaurants in the Old City. The only thing I saw was called the New York Diner, and it was closed. In desperation, I hailed a cab and told him to take me to the *Daily News*.

He stared at me.

"The newspaper!" I shouted, slamming the door as I got in.

"Ah, sí," he murmured. "*El Diario*, sí."

"No, goddamnit," I said. The *Daily News*—the American news-paper—El *News*."

He had never heard of it, so we drove back to Plaza Colón, where I leaned out the window and asked a cop. He didn't know either, but finally a man came over from the bus stop and told us where it was.

We drove down a cobblestone hill toward the waterfront. There was no sign of a newspaper, and I suspected he was bringing me down here to get rid of me. We turned a corner and he suddenly hit his brakes. Just ahead of us was some kind of a gang-fight, a shout-ing mob, trying to enter an old greenish building that looked like a warehouse.

"Go on," I said to the driver. "We can get by."

He mumbled and shook his head.

I banged my fist on the back of the seat. "Get going! No move—no pay."

He mumbled again, but shifted into first and angled toward the far side of the street, putting as much distance as possible between us and the fight. He stopped as we came abreast of the building and I saw that it was a gang of about twenty Puerto Ricans, attacking a tall American in a tan suit. He was standing on the steps, swinging a big wooden sign like a baseball bat.

"You rotten little punks!" he yelled. There was a flurry of movement and I heard the sound of thumping and shouting. One of the attackers fell down in the street with blood on his face. The large fellow backed toward the door, waving the sign in front of him. Two men tried to grab it and he whacked one of them in the chest, knocking him down the steps. The others stood away, yelling and shaking their fists. He snarled back at them: "Here it is, punks— come get it!"

Nobody moved. He waited a moment, then lifted the sign over his shoulder and threw it into their midst. It hit one man in the stomach, driving him back on the others. I heard a burst of laughter, then he disappeared into the building.

"Okay," I said, turning back to the driver. "That's it—let's go."

He shook his head and pointed at the building, then at me. "Sí, está *News*." He nodded, then pointed again at the building. "Sí," he said gravely.

It dawned on me that we were sitting in front of the *Daily News*— my new home. I took one look at the dirty mob between me and the door, and decided to go back to the hotel. Just then I heard another commotion. A Volkswagen pulled up behind us and three cops got out, waving long billyclubs and yelling in Spanish. Some of the mob ran, but others stayed to argue. I watched for a moment, then gave the driver a dollar and ran into the building.

A sign said the *News* editorial office was on the second floor. I took an elevator, half expecting to find myself lifted into the midst of more violence. But the door opened on a dark hall, and a little to my left I heard the noise of the city room.

The moment I got inside I felt better. There was a friendly messiness about the place, a steady clatter of typewriters and wire machines, even the smell was familiar. The room was so big that it looked empty, although I could see at least ten people. The only one not working was a small, black-haired man at a desk beside the door. He was tilted back in a chair, staring at the ceiling.

I walked over and as I started to speak he jerked around in the chair. "All right!" he snapped. "What the fuck are you after?"

I glared down at him. "I start work here tomorrow," I said. "My name's Kemp, Paul Kemp."

He smiled faintly. "Sorry—thought you were after my film."

"What?" I said.

He grumbled something about being "robbed blind," and "watching it like a hawk."

I glanced around the room. "They look normal."

He snorted. "Thieves—packrats." He stood up and held out his hand. "Bob Sala, staff photographer," he said. "What brings you in tonight?"

"I'm looking for a place to eat."

He smiled. "You broke?"

"No, I'm rich—I just can't find a restaurant."

He dropped back in his chair. "You're lucky. The first thing you learn here is to avoid restaurants."

"Why?" I said. "Dysentery?"

He laughed. "Dysentery, crabs, gout, Hutchinson's Disease—you can get anything here, anything at all." He looked at his watch. "Wait about ten minutes and I'll take you up to Al's."

I moved a camera out of the way and sat down on his desk. He leaned back and stared again at the ceiling, scratching his wiry head from time to time and apparently drifting off to some happier land where there were good restaurants and no thieves. He looked out of place here—more like a ticket-taker at some Indiana carnival. His teeth were bad, he needed a shave, his shirt was filthy, and his shoes looked like they'd come from the Goodwill.

We sat there in silence until two men came out of an office on the other side of the room. One was the tall American I'd seen fighting in the street. The other was short and bald, talking excitedly and gesturing with both hands.

"Who's that?" I asked Sala, pointing at the tall one.

He looked. "The guy with Lotterman?"

I nodded, presuming the short one to be Lotterman.

"His name's Yeamon," said Sala, turning back to the desk. "He's new—got here a few weeks ago."

"I saw him fighting outside," I said. "A bunch of Puerto Ricans jumped him right in front of the building."

Sala shook his head. "That figures—he's a nut." He nodded. "Probably mouthed off at those union goons. It's some kind of a wildcat strike—nobody knows what it means."

Just then Lotterman called across the room: "What are you doing, Sala?"

Sala didn't look up. "Nothing—I'm off in three minutes."

"Who's that with you?" Lotterman asked, eyeing me suspiciously.

"Judge Crater," Sala replied. "Might be a story."

"Judge who?" said Lotterman, advancing on the desk.

"Never mind," said Sala. "His name is Kemp and he claims you hired him."

Lotterman looked puzzled. "Judge Kemp?" he muttered. Then he smiled broadly and held out both hands. "Oh yes—Kemp! Good to see you, boy. When did you get in?"

"This morning," I said, getting off the desk to shake hands. "I slept most of the day."

"Good!" he said. "That's very smart." He nodded emphatically. "Well, I hope you're ready to go."

"Not right now," I said. "I have to eat."

He laughed. "Oh no—tomorrow. I wouldn't put you to work tonight." He laughed again. "No, I want you boys to eat." He smiled down at Sala. "I suppose Bob's going to show you the town, *eh?*"

"Sure I am," said Sala. "Do it on the old expense account, *eh?*"

Lotterman laughed nervously. "You know what I mean, Bob—let's try to be civil." He turned and waved at Yeamon, who was standing in the middle of the room, examining a rip in the armpit of his coat.

Yeamon came toward us with a long bow-legged stride, smiling politely when Lotterman introduced me. He was tall, with a face that was either arrogant or something else that I couldn't quite place.

Lotterman rubbed his hands together. "Yessir, Bob," he said with a grin. "We're getting a real team together, eh?" He slapped Yeamon on the back. "Old Yeamon just had a scrape with those communist bastards outside," he said. "They're savage—they should be locked up."

Sala nodded. "They'll kill one of us pretty soon."

"Don't say that, Bob," said Lotterman. "Nobody's going to be killed."

Sala shrugged.

"I called Commissioner Rogan about it this morning," Lotterman explained. "We can't tolerate this sort of thing—it's a menace."

"Damn right it is," Sala replied. "To hell with Commissioner Rogan—we need a few Lugers." He stood up and pulled his coat off the back of the chair. "Well, time to go." He looked at Yeamon. "We're going up to Al's—you hungry?"

"I'll be up later on," Yeamon replied. "I want to check by the apartment and see if Chenault's still asleep."

"Okay," said Sala. He waved me toward the door. "Come on. We'll go out the back way—I don't feel like a fight."

"Be careful, boys," Lotterman called after us. I nodded and followed Sala into the hall. At the rear of the building a stairway led down to a metal door. Sala poked at it with a pocket knife and it swung open. "Can't do it from outside," he explained as I followed him into the alley.

His car was a tiny Fiat convertible, half eaten away by rust. It wouldn't start and I had to get out and push. Finally it kicked over and I jumped in. The engine roared painfully as we started up the hill. I didn't think we'd make it, but the little car staggered manfully over the crest and started up another steep hill. Sala seemed unconcerned with the strain, riding the clutch whenever we threatened to stall.

We parked in front of Al's and went back to the patio. "I'm getting three hamburgers," said Sala. "That's all he serves."

I nodded. "Anything—I need bulk."

He called to the cook and told him we wanted six hamburgers. "And two beers," he added. "Real quick."

"I'll have rum," I said.

"Two beers and two rums," Sala shouted. Then he leaned back in his chair and lit a cigarette. "You a reporter?"

"Yeah," I said.

"What brings you down here?"

"Why not?" I replied. "A man could do worse than the Caribbean."

He grunted. "This isn't the Caribbean—you should have kept on going south."

The cook shuffled across the patio with our drinks. "Where were you before this?" Sala asked, lifting his beers off the tray.

"New York," I said. "Before that, Europe."

"Where in Europe?"

"All over—mainly Rome and London."

"*Daily American*?" he asked.

"Yeah," I said. "I had a fill-in job for six months."

"You know a guy named Fred Ballinger?" he asked.

I nodded.

"He's here," Sala said. "He's getting rich."

I groaned. "Man, what a jackass."

"You'll see him," he said with a grin. "He hangs around the office."

"What the hell for?" I snapped.

"Sucks up to Donovan." He laughed. "Claims he was sports editor of the *Daily American*."

"He was a pimp!" I said.

Sala laughed. "Donovan threw him down the stairs one night—he hasn't been around for a while."

"Good," I said. "Who's Donovan—the sports editor?"

He nodded. "A drunkard—he's about to quit."

"Why?"

He laughed. "Everybody quits—you'll quit. Nobody worth a shit can work here." He shook his head. "People dropping out like flies. I've been here longer than anybody—except Tyrrell, the city editor, and he's going soon. Lotterman doesn't know it yet—that'll be it— Tyrrell's the only good head left." He laughed quickly. "Wait till you meet the managing editor—can't even write a headline."

"Who's that?" I said.

"Segarra—Greasy Nick. He's writing the governor's biography. Any time of the day or night he's writing the governor's biography—can't be disturbed."

I sipped my drink. "How long have you been here?" I asked him.

"Too long, more than a year."

"Couldn't be too bad," I said.

He smiled. "Hell, don't let me throw you off. You may like it— there's a type that does."

"What type is that?" I asked.

"Bagmasters," he replied. "The wheelers and the dealers—they love it here."

"Yeah," I said. "I got that feeling at the airport." I looked over at him. "What keeps you here? It's only forty-five dollars to New York."

He snorted. "Hell, I make that much in an hour—just for punching a button."

"You sound greedy," I said.

He grinned. "I am. There's nobody on the island greedier than me. Sometimes I feel like kicking myself in the balls."

Sweep arrived with our hamburgers. Sala grabbed his off the tray and opened them up on the table, throwing the lettuce and tomato slices into the ashtray. "You brainless monster," he said wearily. "How many times have I told you to keep this garbage off my meat?"

The waiter stared down at the garbage.

"A thousand times!" Sala shouted. "I tell you every stinking day!"

"Man," I said with a smile. "You *should* leave—this place is getting to you."

He gobbled one of his hamburgers. "You'll see," he muttered. "You and Yeamon—that guy's a freak. He won't last. None of us will last." He slammed his fist on the table. "Sweep—more beer!"

The waiter came out of the kitchen and looked at us. "Two beers!" Sala yelled. "Hurry!"

I smiled and leaned back in the chair. "What's wrong with Yeamon?"

He looked at me as if it were incredible that I should have to ask. "Didn't you see him?" he said. "That wild-eyed sonofabitch! Lotterman's scared shitless of him—couldn't you see it?"

I shook my head. "He looked okay to me."

"Okay?" he shouted. "You should have been here a few nights ago! He flipped this table for no reason at all—this very table." He slapped our table with his palm. "No damn reason," he repeated. "Knocked all our drinks in the dirt and flipped the table on some poor bastard who didn't know what he was saying—then threatened to stomp him!" Sala shook his head. "I don't know where Lotterman found that guy. He's so scared of him that he lent him a hundred dollars and Yeamon went out and blew it on a motorscooter." He laughed bitterly. "Now he's brought some girl down here to live with him."

The waiter appeared with the beers and Sala snatched them off the tray. "No girl with any brains would come here," he said. "Just virgins—hysterical virgins." He shook his finger at me. "You'll turn queer in this place, Kemp—mark my words. This place will turn a man queer and crazy."

"I don't know," I said. "A fine young thing came down on the plane with me." I smiled. "I think I'll look around for her tomorrow. She's bound to be on the beach somewhere."

"She's probably a lesbian," he replied. "This place is full of them." He shook his head. "It's the tropic rot—this constant sexless drinking!" He slumped back in his chair. "It's driving me wild—I'm cracking up!"

Sweep came hurrying out with two more beers and Sala grabbed them off the tray. Just then Yeamon appeared in the doorway; he saw us and came over to the table.

Sala groaned miserably. "Oh god, here he is," he muttered. "Don't stomp me, Yeamon—I didn't mean it."

Yeamon smiled and sat down. "Are you still bitching about Moberg?" He laughed and turned to me. "Robert thinks I mistreated Moberg."

Sala grumbled something about "nuts."

Yeamon laughed again. "Sala's the oldest man in San Juan. How old are you, Robert—about ninety?"

"Don't give me your crazy shit!" Sala shouted, springing up from his chair.

Yeamon nodded. "Robert needs a woman," he said gently. "His penis is pressing on his brain and he can't think."

Sala groaned and shut his eyes.

Yeamon tapped on the table. "Robert, the streets are full of whores. You should look around sometime. I saw so many on the way up here that I wanted to grab about six and fall down naked and let them crawl all over me like puppies." He laughed and signaled for the waiter.

"You bastard," Sala muttered. "That girl hasn't been here a day and you're already talking about having whores crawl on you." He nodded wisely. "You'll get the syphilis—you keep on whoring and stomping around and pretty soon you'll stomp in shit."

Yeamon grinned. "Okay, Robert. You've warned me."

Sala looked up. "Is she still asleep? How long before I can go back to my own apartment?"

"Soon as we leave here," Yeamon replied. "I'll take her on out to the house." He nodded. "Of course I'll have to borrow your car—too much luggage for the scooter."

"Jesus," Sala muttered. "You're a plague, Yeamon—you'll suck me dry."

Yeamon laughed. "You're a fine Christian, Robert. You'll get your reward." He ignored Sala's snort and turned to me. "Did you come in on the morning plane?"

"Yeah," I said.

He smiled. "Chenault said there was some young guy beating up an old man on the plane with her—was that you?"

I groaned, feeling the web of sin and circumstance close down on the table. Sala eyed me suspiciously.

I explained that I'd been sitting next to an aged lunatic who kept trying to crawl over me.

Yeamon laughed. "Chenault thought *you* were the lunatic—claimed you kept staring at her, then ran amok on the old man—you were still beating him when she got off the plane."

"Jesus Christ!" Sala exclaimed, giving me a disgusted look.

I shook my head and tried to laugh it off. The implications were ugly—a crazed masher and a slugger of old men—not the kind of introduction a man wants to make for himself on a new job.

Yeamon seemed amused, but Sala was plainly leery. I called for more drinks and quickly changed the subject.

We sat there for several hours, talking, drinking lazily, killing the time while a sad piano tinkled away inside. The notes floated out to the patio, giving the night a hopeless, melancholy tone that was almost pleasant.

Sala was sure the paper was going to fold. "I'll ride it out," he assured us. "Give it another month." He had two more big photo assignments and then he was off, probably to Mexico City. "Yeah," he said, "figure about a month, then we start packing."

Yeamon shook his head. "Robert wants the paper to fold so he'll have an excuse to leave." He smiled. "It'll last a while. All I need is about three months—enough money to take off down the islands."

"Where?" I asked.

He shrugged. "Anywhere—find a good island, someplace cheap."

Sala hissed. "You talk like a caveman, Yeamon. What you need is a good job in Chicago."

Yeamon laughed. "You'll feel better when you get humped, Robert."

Sala grumbled and drank his beer. I liked him, in spite of his bitching. I guessed he was a few years older than I was, maybe thirty-two or -three, but there was something about him that made me feel like I'd known him a long time.

Yeamon was familiar too, but not quite as close—more like a memory of somebody I'd known in some other place and then lost track of. He was probably twenty-four or -five and he reminded me vaguely of myself at that age—not exactly the way I was, but the way I might have seen myself if I'd stopped to think about it. Listening to him, I realized how long it had been since I'd felt like I had the world by the balls, how many quick birthdays had gone by since that first year in Europe when I was so ignorant and so confident that every splinter of luck made me feel like a roaring champion.

I hadn't felt that way in a long time. Perhaps, in the ambush of those years, the idea that I was a champion had been shot out from under me. But I remembered it now and it made me feel old and slightly nervous that I had done so little in so long a time.

I leaned back in the chair and sipped my drink. The cook was banging around in the kitchen and for some reason the piano had stopped. From inside came a babble of Spanish, an incoherent background for my scrambled thoughts. For the first time I felt the foreignness of the place, the real distance I had put between me and my last foothold. There was no reason to feel pressure, but I felt it anyway—the pressure of hot air and passing time, an idle tension that builds up in places where men sweat twenty-four hours a day.

TWO

I GOT up early the next morning and went for a swim. The sun was hot and I squatted on the beach for several hours, hoping no one would notice my sickly New York pallor.

At eleven-thirty I caught a bus in front of the hotel. It was crowded and I had to stand. The air in the bus was like steam, but no one else seemed to mind. Every window was closed, the smell was unbearable, and by the time we got to the Plaza Colón I was dizzy and soaked with sweat.

As I came down the hill to the *News* building I saw the mob. Some of them carried big signs and others sat on the curbing or leaned against parked cars, shouting from time to time at anyone going in or out. I tried to ignore them, but one man came after me yelling in Spanish and shaking his fist as I hurried into the elevator. I tried to catch him in the door, but he jumped away as it closed.

As I crossed the hall to the newsroom I heard someone yelling inside. When I opened the door I saw Lotterman standing in the middle of the room, waving a copy of *El Diario*. He pointed at a small blond man: "Moberg! You drunken bastard! Your days are numbered! If anything goes wrong with that wire machine I'll have it repaired out of your severance check!"

Moberg said nothing. He looked sick enough to be in a hospital. I later learned that he'd come into the newsroom at midnight, raving drunk, and pissed on the teletype machine. On top of that, we'd been scooped on a waterfront stabbing and Moberg had the police beat. Lotterman cursed him again, then turned on Sala, who had just come in. "Where were you last night, Sala? Why don't we have any pictures of this stabbing?"

Sala looked surprised. "What the hell? I finished at eight—you expect me to work twenty-four hours a day?"

Lotterman mumbled and turned away. Then he caught sight of me and waved me into his office.

"Jesus!" he exclaimed as he sat down. "What's wrong with these bums—sneaking out of the office, pissing on expensive equipment, drunk all the time—it's a wonder I'm not crazy!"

I smiled and lit a cigarette.

He looked at me curiously. "I hope to Christ you're a normal human being—one more pervert around here will be the last straw."

"Pervert?" I said.

"Ah, you know what I mean," he said with a wave of his hand. "General perverts—drunks, bums, thieves—god only knows where they come from.

"Not worth a pound of piss!" he exclaimed. "Sneak around here like weasels, give me the big smile, then disappear without a goddamn word to anybody." He shook his head sadly. "How can I put out a paper with nothing but wineheads?"

"Sounds bad," I said.

"It is," he muttered, "believe me, it is." Then he looked up. "I want you to get acquainted as fast as you can. When we finish here, you go back to the library and dig into the back issues—take some notes, find out what's going on." He nodded. "Later on you can sit down with Segarra, our managing editor. I told him to give you a briefing."

We talked a while longer and I mentioned that I'd heard a rumor that the paper might fold.

He looked alarmed. "You got that from Sala, didn't you? Well don't pay any attention to him—he's crazy!"

I smiled. "Okay—just thought I should ask."

"Too many crazy ones around here," he snapped. "We need some sanity."

On my way back to the library I wondered how long I would last in San Juan—how long before I'd be labeled a "weasel" or a "pervert," before I started kicking myself in the balls or got chopped up by nationalist thugs. I remembered Lotterman's voice when he'd called me in New York; the strange jerkiness and the odd phrasing. I had sensed it then, but now I knew. I could almost see him—gripping the phone with both white-knuckled hands, trying to keep his voice steady while mobs gathered on his doorstep and drunken reporters pissed all over the office—saying tensely: "Sure thing, Kemp, you sound normal enough, just come on down and—"

And here I was, a new face in the snakepit, a pervert yet to be classified, sporting a paisley tie and a button-down shirt, no longer young but not quite over the hump—a man on the brink, as it were, trotting back to the library to find out what was going on.

I had been there about twenty minutes when a thin, handsome Puerto Rican came in and tapped me on the shoulder. "Kemp?" he said. "I'm Nick Segarra—you have a minute?"

I got up and we shook hands. His eyes were tiny and his hair was combed so perfectly that I thought it might be a toupee. He looked like a man who might write the governor's biography—also like a man who would be at the governor's cocktail parties.

As we crossed the newsroom, heading for his desk in the corner, a man who looked like he'd just stepped out of a rum advertisement came through the door and waved at Segarra. He came toward us—graceful, smiling, a solid American face, very much the embassy type with his deep tan and his grey linen suit.

He greeted Segarra warmly and they shook hands. "A charming bunch out there in the street," he said. "One of them spit at me as I came in."

Segarra shook his head. "It's terrible, terrible . . . Ed just keeps antagonizing them . . ." Then he looked over at me. "Paul Kemp," he said. "Hal Sanderson."

We shook hands. Sanderson had a firm, practiced grip and I had a feeling that somewhere in his youth he'd been told that a man was measured by the strength of his handshake. He smiled, then looked at Segarra. "You have time for a drink? I'm on to something that might interest you."

Segarra looked at his watch. "You bet. I was about ready to leave anyway." He turned to me. "We'll talk tomorrow—okay?"

As I turned to go, Sanderson called after me. "Good to have you with us, Paul. One of these days we'll have lunch."

"Sure," I said.

I spent the rest of the day in the library, and left at eight. On my way out of the building I met Sala coming in. "What are you doing tonight?" he asked.

"Nothing," I said.

He looked pleased. "Good. I have to get some pictures at the casinos—want to come along?"

"I guess so," I said. "Can I go like this?"

"Hell yes," he said with a grin. "All you need is a tie."

"Okay," I said. "I'm on my way up to Al's—come on up when you finish."

He nodded. "I'll be about thirty minutes. I have to get this film developed."

The night was hot and the waterfront was alive with rats. Several blocks away a big cruise ship was tied up. Thousands of lights glittered on the deck and music came from somewhere inside. At the bottom of the gangplank was a group of what appeared to be American businessmen and their wives. I passed on the other side of the street, but the air was so still that I could hear them plainly—happy half-tight voices from somewhere in the middle of America, some flat little town where they spent fifty weeks of every year. I stopped and listened, standing in the shadows of an ancient warehouse and feeling like a man with no country at all. They couldn't see me and I watched for several minutes, hearing those voices from Illinois or Missouri or Kansas and knowing them all too well. Then I moved on, still in the shadows as I turned up the hill toward Calle O'Leary.

The block in front of Al's was full of people: old men sitting on steps, women moving in and out of doorways, children chasing each other on the narrow sidewalks, music from open windows, voices murmuring in Spanish, the tinkle of Brahms' Lullaby from an ice-cream truck, and a dim light above Al's door.

I went through to the patio, stopping on the way to order hamburgers and beer. Yeamon was there, sitting alone at the rear table, staring at something he had written in a notebook.

"What's that?" I said, sitting down across from him.

He looked up, shoving the notebook aside. "Ah, it's that goddamn migrant story," he said wearily. "It's supposed to be in on Monday and I haven't even started."

"Something big?" I asked.

He looked down at the notebook. "Well . . . maybe too big for a newspaper." He looked up. "You know—why do Puerto Ricans leave Puerto Rico?" He shook his head. "I kept putting it off all week, and now with Chenault here I can't get a damn thing done at home . . . I'm feeling a little pressed."

"Where do you live?" I asked.

He smiled broadly. "Man, you should see it—right on the beach, about twenty miles out of town. It's too much. You really have to see it."

"Sounds good," I said. "I'd like to get something like that."

"You need a car," he said, "or something like I have—a scooter."

I nodded. "Yeah, I'll start looking around on Monday."

Sala arrived just as Sweep came out with my hamburgers. "Three of those for me," Sala snapped. "Quick as you can—I'm in a hurry."

"You still working?" Yeamon asked.

Sala nodded. "Not for Lotterman—this one's for old Bob." He lit a cigarette. "My agent wants some casino shots. They're hard to come by."

"Why?" I asked.

"Illegal," he said. "When I first got here they caught me shooting at the Caribé—I had to go see Commissioner Rogan." He laughed. "He asked me how I'd feel if I took a shot of some poor bastard at the roulette wheel and it happened to appear in his hometown paper just about the time he applied for a bank loan." He laughed again. "I told him I couldn't care less. I'm a photographer, not a goddamn social worker."

"You're a terror," Yeamon said with a smile.

"Yeah," Sala agreed. "They know me now—so I have to work with this." He showed us a tiny camera no bigger than a cigarette lighter. "Me and Dick Tracy," he said with a grin. "I'll bust 'em all."

Then he looked over at me. "Well, you got through the day—any offers?"

"Offers?"

"Your first day on the job," he said. "Somebody's bound to have offered you a deal."

"No," I said. "I met Segarra . . . and a guy named Sanderson. What does he do?"

"He's a PR man. Works for Adelante."

"The government?"

"In a way," Sala said. "The people of Puerto Rico are paying Sanderson to tidy up their image in the States. Adelante is a big public relations outfit."

"When did he work for Lotterman?" I asked. I had seen Sanderson's byline in some old issues of the *News*.

"He was here from the beginning—worked about a year, then hooked up with Adelante. Lotterman claims they stole him, but it was no loss. He's a phony, a real prick."

"Is that Segarra's buddy?" Yeamon asked.

"Yeah," Sala replied, absently tossing the lettuce and tomatoes off his hamburgers. He ate hurriedly and stood up. "Let's go," he said, looking at Yeamon. "Come on—we may get some action."

Yeamon shook his head. "I have to do this goddamn story, then drive all the way out to the house." He smiled. "I'm a family man now."

We paid our bill and went out to Sala's car. The top was down and it was a fine, fast ride along the Boulevard to Condado. The wind was cool and the roar of the little engine bounced around in the trees above our heads as we swerved in and out of traffic.

The Caribé casino was on the second floor, a big smoky place with dark drapes around the walls. Sala wanted to work alone, so we separated at the door.

I stopped at the blackjack table, but everyone there seemed bored, so I moved on to the craps game. There was more noise here. A group of sailors were yelling around the table as the dice bounced on the green cloth and the croupiers raked chips back and forth like frantic gardeners. Scattered among the sailors were men in dinner jackets and silk suits. Most of them smoked cigars, and when they talked it was with the accent of Ne'Yak. Somewhere in the cloud of smoke behind me I heard a man introduced as the "biggest crook in New Jersey." I turned, slightly curious, and saw the crook smile modestly as the woman beside him burst into wild laughter.

The roulette wheel was surrounded by low rollers, most of them much older than they wanted to look. The light in gambling rooms is not good for aging women. It catches every crease in their faces and every wart on their necks; drops of sweat between fallow breasts, hairs on a nipple momentarily exposed, a flabby arm or a sagging eye. I watched their faces, most of them red with new sunburns, as they stared at the bouncing ball and nervously fingered their chips.

Then I walked back to a table where a young Puerto Rican in a white jacket was giving out free sandwiches. "The fat is in the fire," I said to him.

"Sí," he replied gravely.

As I started back toward the roulette wheel I felt a hand on my arm.

It was Sala. "Ready?" he said. "Let's move on."

We drove up the street to the Condado Beach Hotel, but the casino was almost empty. "Nothing here," he said. "Let's go next door."

Next door was La Concha. The casino here was more crowded, but the atmosphere was the same as the others—a sort of dull frenzy, like taking a pep pill when what you really want to do is sleep.

Somehow, I became involved with a woman who claimed to be from Trinidad. She had large breasts, a British accent, and wore a tight green dress. One moment I was standing next to her at the roulette wheel, and before I realized what was happening we were in the parking lot, waiting for Sala—who, in the same weird way, had found himself with a girl who turned out to be a friend of my date.

After much effort, we fitted ourselves in the car. Sala seemed agitated. "To hell with the rest of the shots," he said. "I'll get them tomorrow." He paused. "Well . . . what now?"

The only place I knew was Al's, so I suggested we go there.

Sala objected. "Those bums from the paper will be there," he said. "They're finishing up about now."

There was a moment of silence—then Lorraine leaned over the seat and suggested we go to the beach. "It's such a beautiful night," she said. "Let's just drive along the dunes."

I couldn't help laughing. "Hell yes," I said. "Let's get some rum and drive on the dunes."

Sala mumbled and started the car. A few blocks from the hotel we stopped at a bodega and he got out. "I'll get a bottle," he said. "They probably won't have any ice."

"Don't worry about it," I said. "Just get some paper cups."

Rather than drive all the way out to the airport, where Sala said the beaches would be deserted, he turned off near the edge of Condado and we stopped on a beach in front of the residential section.

"We can't drive here," he said. "Why not go for a swim?"

Lorraine agreed, but the other girl balked.

"What the hell is wrong with you?" Sala demanded.

She gave him a stony look and said nothing. Lorraine and I got out of the car, leaving Sala with his problem. We walked several hundred yards down the beach and I was curious. "You really want to go in?" I said finally.

"Certainly," she replied, pulling her dress over her head. "I've wanted to do this all week. What an awful bore this place is—we've done nothing but sit, sit, sit."

I took off my clothes and watched her as she toyed with the idea of removing her underwear.

"Might as well keep it dry," I said.

She smiled, acknowledging my wisdom, then unhooked her bra and stepped out of her panties. We walked down to the water and waded in. It was warm and salty, but the breakers were so big that neither of us could stand up. For a moment I considered going out beyond them, but a look at that dark sea changed my mind. So we played in the surf for a while, letting ourselves be knocked around by the waves, and finally she struggled back to the beach, saying she was exhausted. I followed, offering her a cigarette as we sat down on the sand.

We talked for a while, drying off as best we could, and suddenly she reached over and pulled me down on top of her. "Make love to me," she said urgently.

I laughed and leaned down to bite her on the breast. She began to groan and jerk me around by the hair, and after a few minutes of this I lifted her onto the clothes so we wouldn't get full of sand. The smell of her body excited me tremendously and I got a savage grip on her buttocks, pounding her up and down. Suddenly she began to howl: at first I thought I was hurting her, then I realized she was having some sort of extreme orgasm. She had several of them, howling each time, before I felt the slow bursting of my own.

We lay there for several hours, going at it again when we felt rested. All in all I don't think we said fifty words. She seemed to want nothing but the clutch and howl of the orgasm, the rolling grip of two bodies in the sand.

I was stung at least a thousand times by *mimis*—tiny bugs with the jolt of a sweat bee. I was covered with horrible bumps when we finally dressed and limped back down the beach to where we had left Sala and his girl.

I was not surprised to find them gone. We walked out to the street and waited for a cab. I dropped her at the Caribé and promised to call the next day.

Three

WHEN I got to work I asked Sala what had happened with his girl.

"Don't mention that bitch," he muttered. "She got hysterical—I had to leave." He paused. "How was yours?"

"Fine," I said. "We went out about a mile, then raced back."

He eyed me curiously, then turned and went to the darkroom.

I spent the rest of the day doing rewrites. Just as I was leaving, Tyrrell called me over and said I had an early assignment at the airport the next morning. The mayor of Miami was coming in on the seven-thirty flight and I had to be there for an interview. Rather than take a cab, I decided to borrow Sala's car.

At the airport I saw the same sharp-faced little men, sitting by the window, waiting for the plane from Miami.

I bought a *Times* for forty cents and read about a blizzard in New York: "Merritt Parkway closed . . . BMT stalled four hours . . . snowplows in the streets . . . the Man in the News was a snowplow driver with a Staten Island background . . . Mayor Wagner was up in arms . . . everyone late to work . . ."

I looked out at the bright Caribbean morning, green and lazy and full of sun, then I put the *Times* away.

The plane from Miami arrived, but the mayor was not on it. After several inquiries I discovered that his visit had been canceled "for reasons of health."

I went to a phone booth and called the news room. Moberg answered. "No mayor," I said.

"What!" Moberg snapped.

"Claims to be ill. Not much to write about. What should I do?" I asked.

"Stay away from the office," he said. "There's a riot going on— two of our scabs got their arms broken last night." He laughed. "They're going to kill us all. Come on in after lunch—it should be safe by then."

I went back to the coffee shop and ate my breakfast: bacon, eggs, pineapple and four cups of coffee. Then, feeling relaxed and stuffed and not particularly caring if the mayor of Miami was dead or alive, I strolled out to the parking lot and decided to visit Yeamon. He had given me a map to his beach house, but I was not prepared for the sand road. It looked like something hacked out of a Philippine jungle. I went the whole way in low gear, the sea on my left, a huge swamp on my right—through miles of coconut palms, past wooden shacks full of silent, staring natives, swerving to avoid chickens and cows in the road, running over land crabs, creeping in first gear through deep stagnant puddles, bumping and jolting in ruts and chuckholes, and feeling for the first time since leaving New York that I had actually come to the Caribbean.

The early slant of the sun turned the palms a green-gold color. A white glare came off the dunes and made me squint as I picked my way through the ruts. A grey mist rose out of the swamp, and in front of the shacks were negro women, hanging washing on slatted fences. Suddenly I came on a red beer truck, making a delivery to a place called El Colmado de Jesús Lopo, a tiny thatched-roof store set off in a clearing beside the road. Finally, after forty-five minutes of hellish, primitive driving, I came in sight of what looked like a cluster of concrete pillboxes on the edge of the beach. According to Yeamon, this was it, so I turned off and drove about twenty yards through the palms until I came up beside the house.

I sat in the car and waited for him to appear. His scooter was parked on the patio in front of the house, so I knew he was there. When nothing happened after several minutes I got out and looked around. The door was open, but the house was empty. It was not a house at all, but more like a cell. Along one wall was a bed, covered by mosquito netting. The entire dwelling consisted of one twelve by twelve room, with tiny windows and a concrete floor. Inside it was damp and dark, and I hated to think what it was like with the door closed.

All this I saw at a glance; I was very conscious of my unannounced arrival and I didn't want to be caught nosing around like a spy. I crossed the patio and walked out to a sand bluff that dropped off sharply to the beach. To my right and left was nothing but white sand and palm trees, and in front was the ocean. About fifty yards out a barrier reef broke the surf.

Then I saw two figures clinging together near the reef. I recognized Yeamon and the girl who had come down with me on the plane. They were naked, standing in waist-deep water, with her legs locked around his hips and her arms around his neck. Her head was thrown back and her hair trailed out behind her, floating on the water like a blonde mane.

At first I thought I was having a vision. The scene was so idyllic that my mind refused to accept it. I just stood there and watched. He was holding her by the waist, swinging her around in slow circles. Then I heard a sound, a soft happy cry as she stretched out her arms like wings.

I left then, and drove back to Jesús Lopo's place. I bought a small bottle of beer for fifteen cents and sat on a bench in the clearing, feeling like an old man. The scene I had just witnessed brought back a lot of memories—not of things I had done but of things I failed to do, wasted hours and frustrated moments and opportunities forever lost because time had eaten so much of my life and I would never get it back. I envied Yeamon and felt sorry for myself at the same time, because I had seen him in a moment that made all my happiness seem dull.

It was lonely, sitting there on that bench with Señor Lopo staring out at me like a black wizard from behind his counter in a country where a white man in a cord coat had no business or even an excuse to hang around. I sat there for twenty minutes or so, enduring his stare, then I drove back out to Yeamon's, hoping they would be finished.

I approached the house cautiously, but Yeamon was yelling at me before I turned off the road. "Go back," he shouted. "Don't bring your working-class problems out here!"

I smiled sheepishly and pulled up beside the patio. "Only trouble could bring you out so early, Kemp," he said with a grin. "What happened—did the paper fold?"

I shook my head and got out. "I had an early assignment."

"Good," he said. "You're just in time for breakfast." He nodded toward the hut. "Chenault's whipping it up—we just finished our morning swim."

I walked out to the edge of the beach and looked around. Suddenly I felt an urge to get naked and run into the water. The sun was hot and I glanced enviously at Yeamon, wearing nothing but a pair of black trunks. I felt like a bill collector, standing there in a coat and tie, with my face dripping sweat and a damp shirt plastered to my back.

Then Chenault came out of the house. I could tell by her smile that she recognized me as the man who had run amok on the plane. I smiled nervously and said hello.

"I remember you," she said, and Yeamon laughed as I fumbled for something to say.

She was wearing a white bikini and her hair fell down to her waist. There was nothing of the secretary about her now; she looked like a wild and sensual child who had never worn anything but two strips of white cloth and a warm smile. She was tiny, but the shape of her body made her seem larger; not the thin, undeveloped build of most tiny girls, but a fleshy roundness that looked to be all hips and thighs and nipples and long-haired warmth.

"Goddamnit, I'm hungry," said Yeamon. "What about breakfast?"

"Almost ready," she said. "Do you want a grapefruit?"

"Damn right," he replied. "Sit down, Kemp. Stop looking so sick. You want a grapefruit?"

I shook my head.

"Don't be polite," he said. "I know you want one."

"Okay," I said. "Give me a grapefruit."

Chenault appeared with two plates. She gave one to Yeamon and put the other down in front of me. It was a big omelet with bacon laced over the top.

I shook my head, saying I'd already eaten.

She smiled. "Don't worry. We have plenty."

"I'm not kidding," I said. "I ate at the airport."

"Eat again," said Yeamon. "Then we'll get a few lobsters—you have all morning."

"Aren't you going in?" I said. "I thought that migrant story was due today."

He grinned and shook his head. "They put me on that sunken treasure thing. I'm going out with some divers this afternoon—they claim they've found the wreck of an old Spanish galleon just outside the harbor."

"Did they kill the migrant story?" I asked.

"No—I'll get on it again when I finish this one."

I shrugged and started to eat. Chenault came out with a plate of her own and sat down at the foot of Yeamon's chair.

"Sit here," I said, and started to get up.

She smiled and shook her head. "No, this is fine."

"Sit down," said Yeamon. "You're acting peculiar, Kemp—this getting up early doesn't agree with you."

I muttered something about decency and returned to my food. Over the top of my plate I could see Chenault's legs, small and firm and tan. She was so close to naked, and so apparently unaware of it, that I felt helpless.

After breakfast and a flagon of rum, Yeamon suggested that we take the speargun out to the reef and look for some lobster. I quickly agreed, feeling that almost anything would be preferable to sitting there and stewing in my own lust.

He had a set of skindiving gear, complete with a big, double-strand gun, and I used a mask and a snorkel that he'd bought for Chenault. We paddled out to the reef and I watched from the surface as he probed along the bottom for lobster. After a while he came up and gave me the gun, but I couldn't maneuver very well without flippers, so I gave it up and left the diving to him. I liked it better on the surface anyway, floating around in the gentle surf, looking back at the white beach and the palms behind it, and ducking every few moments to watch Yeamon below me in a different world, gliding along the bottom like some kind of monster fish.

We worked along the reef for about a hundred yards, then he said we should try the other side. "Got to be careful out there," he added, paddling toward a shallow opening in the reef, "might be sharks—you watch while I'm down."

Suddenly he doubled up and plunged straight down. Seconds later he came up with a huge green lobster, thrashing around on the end of his spear.

Soon he appeared with another one and we went in. Chenault was waiting for us on the patio.

"A fine lunch," Yeamon said, tossing them into a bucket beside the door.

"What now?" I asked.

"Just tear the legs off, and we'll boil them up," replied Yeamon.

"Damn," I said. "I wish I could stay."

"When do you have to be at work?" he asked.

"Pretty soon," I replied. "They're waiting for my report on the mayor of Miami."

"Fuck the mayor," he said. "Stay out here and we'll get drunk and kill a few chickens."

"Chickens?" I said.

"Yeah, my neighbors all have chickens. They run wild. I killed one last week when we didn't have any meat." He laughed. "It's fine sport—chasing them down with the spear."

"Jesus," I muttered. "These people will chase *you* down with a spear if they catch you shooting their chickens."

When I got back to the office I found Sala in the darkroom and told him his car was back.

"Good," he said. "We have to go out to the University. Lotterman wants you to meet the power mongers."

We talked a few minutes and then he asked me how much longer I intended to stay at the hotel.

"I have to move pretty soon," I said. "Lotterman told me I could stay there until I found a place of my own, but he said something about a week being plenty of time."

He nodded. "Yeah, he'll have you out pretty soon—or else he'll stop paying your bill." He looked up. "You can stay in my place if you want, at least until you find something you like."

I thought for a moment. He lived in a big vault of a room down in the Old City, a ground-floor apartment with a high ceiling and shuttered windows and nothing but a hotplate to cook on.

"I guess so," I said. "What's your rent?"

"Sixty."

"Not bad," I said. "You don't think I'll get on your nerves?"

"Hell," he replied. "I'm never there—it's too depressing."

I smiled. "Okay, when should we do it?"

He shrugged. "Whenever you want. Hell, stay at the hotel as long as you can. When he mentions it, tell him you're moving tomorrow."

He gathered his equipment and we went out the back door to avoid the mob in front. It was so hot that I began to sweat each time we stopped for a red light. Then, when we started moving again, the wind would cool me off. Sala weaved in and out of the traffic on Avenida Ponce de León, heading for the outskirts of town.

Somewhere in Santurce we stopped to let some schoolchildren cross the street and they all began laughing at us. "La cucaracha!" they yelled. "Cucaracha! cucaracha!"

Sala looked embarrassed.

"What's going on?" I asked.

"The little bastards are calling this car a cockroach," he muttered. "I should run a few of them down."

I grinned and leaned back in the seat as we drove on. There was a strange and unreal air about the whole world I'd come into. It was amusing and vaguely depressing at the same time. Here I was, living in a luxury hotel, racing around a half-Latin city in a toy car that looked like a cockroach and sounded like a jet fighter, sneaking down alleys and humping on the beach, scavenging for food in shark-infested waters, hounded by mobs yelling in a foreign tongue—and the whole thing was taking place in quaint old Spanish Puerto Rico, where everybody spent American dollars and drove American cars and sat around roulette wheels pretending they were in Casablanca. One part of the city looked like Tampa and the other part looked like a medieval asylum. Everybody I met acted as if they had just come back from a crucial screen test. And I was being paid a ridiculous salary to wander around and take it all in, to "find out what was going on."

I wanted to write all my friends and invite them down. I thought of Phil Rollins, breaking his ass in New York, chasing after stalled subways and gang-fights in Brooklyn; Duke Peterson, sitting in the White Horse and wondering what in hell to do next; Carl Browne in London, bitching about the climate and grubbing endlessly for assignments; Bill Minnish, drinking himself to death in Rome. I wanted to cable them all—"Come quick stop plenty of room in the rum barrel stop no work stop big money stop drink all day stop hump all night stop hurry it may not last."

I was considering this, watching the palms flash by me and feeling the sun on my face, when I was suddenly thrown against the windshield as we came to a screeching halt. At the same instant a pink taxicab streaked across the intersection, missing us by six feet.

Sala's eyes bulged and the veins stood out in his neck. "Mother of God!" he screamed. "Did you see that bastard? Right through the red light!"

He jerked the car into gear and we roared off. "Jesus!" he muttered. "These people are too much! I've got to get out of this place before they kill me."

He was trembling and I offered to drive. He ignored me. "Man, I'm serious," he said. "I've got to get away—my luck's running out."

He had said the same thing before and I think he believed it. He was forever talking about luck, but what he really meant was a very ordered kind of fate. He had a strong sense of it—a belief that large and uncontrollable things were working both for and against him, things that were moving and happening every minute all over the world. The rise of communism worried him because it meant that people were going blind to his sensitivity as a human being. The troubles of the Jews depressed him because it meant that people needed scapegoats and sooner or later he would be one of them. Other things bothered him constantly: the brutality of capitalism because his talents were being exploited, the moronic vulgarity of American tourists because it gave him a bad reputation, the careless stupidity of Puerto Ricans because they were forever making his life dangerous and difficult, and even, for some reason I never understood, the hundreds of stray dogs that he saw in San Juan.

Not much of what he said was original. What made him unique was the fact that he had no sense of detachment at all. He was like the fanatical football fan who runs onto the field and tackles a player. He saw life as the Big Game, and the whole of mankind was divided into two teams—Sala's Boys, and The Others. The stakes were fantastic and every play was vital—and although he watched with a nearly obsessive interest, he was very much the fan, shouting unheard advice in a crowd of unheard advisors and knowing all the while that nobody was paying any attention to him because he was not running the team and never would be. And like all fans he was frustrated by the knowledge that the best he could do, even in a pinch, would be to run onto the field and cause some kind of illegal trouble, then be hauled off by guards while the crowd laughed.

We never got to the university because Sala had an epileptic fit and we had to turn around. I was rattled, but he shook it off and refused to let me drive.

On the way back to the paper I asked him how he'd managed to keep his job as long as a year.

He laughed. "Who else can they get? I'm the only pro on the island."

We crept along in a huge traffic jam and finally he got so nervous that I had to drive. When we got to the paper the vicious bums had disappeared, but the newsroom was in turmoil. Tyrrell, the workhorse, had just quit, and Moberg had been beaten half to death by the union goons. They had seized him outside the building and avenged their loss to Yeamon.

Lotterman was sitting on a chair in the middle of the newsroom, groaning and jabbering while two cops tried to talk to him. A few feet away, Tyrrell sat calmly at his desk, going about his business. He had given a week's notice.

Four

A S I expected, my talk with Segarra turned out to be wasted
time. We sat at his desk for almost an hour, trading inanities
and chuckling at each other's jokes. Although he spoke perfect English there was still a language barrier, and I sensed immediately that no real meaning would ever pass between us. I got the
impression that he knew what was going on in Puerto Rico, but he
seemed to know nothing about journalism. When he talked like a
politician he made sense, but it was difficult to see him as the editor of a newspaper. He seemed to think that as long as he knew the
score, that was enough. The idea that he should pass on what he
knew to anyone else, especially to the public at large, would have
struck him as dangerous heresy. At one point he gave me a jolt
when he mentioned that he and Sanderson had been classmates at
Columbia.

It took me a long time to understand Segarra's function at the
News. They called him The Editor, but he was really a pimp and I
paid no attention to him.

Perhaps that's why I didn't make many friends in Puerto Rico—
at least not the kind of friends I might have made—because, as
Sanderson very gently explained to me one day, Segarra came from

one of the wealthiest and most influential families on the island and his father was a former attorney general. When Nick became editor of the *Daily News*, the paper made a lot of valuable friends.

I had not given Lotterman credit for this kind of devious thinking, but as time went by I saw that he used Segarra solely as a front man, a sleek, well-oiled figurehead to convince the literate public that the *News* was not a *yanqui* mouthpiece, but a fine local institution like rum and sugarballs.

After our first talk, Segarra and I exchanged an average of about thirty words a week. Once in a while he would leave a note in my typewriter, but he made a point of saying as little as possible. In the beginning this suited me well enough, even though Sanderson explained that as long as Segarra had the nix on me I was doomed to social oblivion.

But I had no social ambitions in those days. I had a license to wander. I was a working journalist and I had easy access to anything I needed, including the finest cotillions and the Governor's house and secret coves where debutantes swam naked at night.

After a while, however, Segarra began to bother me. I had a feeling that I was being cut out of things and that he was the reason for it. When I was not invited to parties that I would not have gone to in the first place, or when I called some government official on the phone and was brushed off by his secretary, I began to feel like a social leper. This wouldn't have bothered me at all had I felt it was my own doing, but the fact that Segarra was exercising some sinister control over me began to get on my nerves. Whatever he might have denied me was unimportant; it was the fact that he could deny me anything at all, even what I didn't want.

At first I was tempted to laugh it off, to give him as hard a time as I could and let him do his worst. But I didn't, because I was not quite ready to pack up and move on again. I was getting a little too old to make powerful enemies when I held no cards at all, and I had lost some of my old zeal that had led me, in the past, to do what I damn well felt like doing, with the certain knowledge that I could always flee the consequences. I was tired of fleeing, and tired of having no cards. It occurred to me one evening, as I sat by myself in Al's patio, that a man can live on his wits and his balls for only so long. I'd been doing it for ten years and I had a feeling that my reserve was running low.

Segarra and Sanderson were good friends, and, oddly enough, although Segarra considered me a boor, Sanderson went out of his way to be decent. A few weeks after I met him I had to call Adelante about a story I was doing, and I thought I might as well talk to Sanderson as anyone else.

He greeted me like an old buddy, and after giving me all the information I needed, he invited me out to his house for dinner that night. I was so surprised that I accepted without a thought. The tone of his voice made it seem so natural that I should eat dinner at his house that I had already hung up before I realized that it was not natural at all.

After work I took a cab out to his house. When I got there I found Sanderson on his porch with a man and a woman who had just come in from New York. They were on their way to St. Lucia to meet their yacht, which the crew had brought back from Lisbon. A mutual friend had told them to look up Sanderson when they stopped in San Juan and they had taken him completely by surprise.

"I've sent out for some lobster," he told us. "We have no choice but to drink until it arrives."

It turned out to be an excellent evening. The couple from New York reminded me of something I had not seen in a long time. We talked of yachts, which I knew because I had worked on them in Europe, and which they knew because they came from a world where everyone seemed to own one. We drank white rum, which Sanderson said was much better than gin, and by midnight we were all drunk enough to go down to the beach for a naked swim.

After that night I spent almost as much time at Sanderson's as I spent at Al's. His apartment looked like it had been designed in Hollywood for a Caribbean movie set. It was the bottom half of an old stucco house, right on the beach near the edge of town. The living room had a domed ceiling, with a fan hanging down and a wide door that opened on a screen porch. In front of the porch was a garden full of palms, with a gate leading down to the beach. The porch was higher than the garden, and at night you could sit there with a drink and see all the way into the city. Once in a while a cruise ship passed out at sea, brightly lit and heading for St. Thomas or the Bahamas.

When the night was too warm, or when you got too drunk, you could take a towel and go down to the beach for a swim. Afterward, there was good brandy, and if you were still drunk there was an extra bed.

Only three things bothered me at Sanderson's—one was Sanderson, who was such an excellent host that I wondered what was wrong with him; one was Segarra, who was very often there when I came by; and the other was a man named Zimburger, who lived in the top half of the house.

Zimburger was more beast than human—tall, paunchy and bald, with a face out of some fiendish comic strip. He claimed to be an investor and was forever talking about putting up hotels here and there, but as far as I could see the only thing he did was go to Marine Corps Reserve meetings on Wednesday nights. Zimburger had never got over the fact that he had been a captain in The Corps. Early on Wednesday afternoon he would put on his uniform and come down to Sanderson's porch to drink until it was time for the meeting. Sometimes he wore the uniform on Mondays, or Fridays— usually on some flimsy pretext.

"Extra training today," he would say. "Commander So-and-So wants me to help out with pistol instruction."

Then he would laugh and get another drink. He never took off his overseas cap, even after he had been indoors for five or six hours. He drank incessantly, and by the time it got dark he was steaming drunk and shouting. He would pace around the porch or the living room, snarling and denouncing the "cowards and the back-dusters in Washington" for not sending the Marines into Cuba.

"I'll go!" he would shout. "Goddamn right I'll go! Somebody has to stomp them bastards and it might as well be me!"

Often he wore his pistol belt and his holster—he had to leave his gun on the base—and from time to time he would slap leather and bark at some imaginary foe outside the door. It was embarrassing to see him go for his gun, because he seemed to think it was really there, riding large and loose on his flabby hip, "just like it was on Iwo Jima." It was a pitiful sight and I was always glad when he left.

I avoided Zimburger whenever I could, but sometimes he took us by surprise. I would go to Sanderson's with a girl I had met somewhere; we would have dinner and sit around talking afterward—and suddenly there would be a pounding on the screen door. In he would come, his face red, his khaki shirt stained with sweat, his overseas cap crushed down on his bullet-shaped head— and he would sit down with us for God knows how long, carrying on at the top of his lungs about some international disaster that could easily have been averted "if they'd just let the goddamn Marines do their job, instead of keeping us penned up like dogs."

For my money, Zimburger should not only have been penned up like a dog, but shot like a mad one. How Sanderson tolerated him I couldn't understand. He was never anything but gracious to Zimburger, even when it became obvious to everyone else that the man should be strapped up and rolled into the sea like a sack of waste. I guessed it was because Sanderson was too much a public relations man. I never once saw him lose his temper, and in his job he was saddled with more bores and bastards and phonies than any man on the island.

Sanderson's view of Puerto Rico was very different from any I'd heard at the *News*. He had never seen a place with more potential, he said. In ten years it would be a *paradise,* a new American gold coast. There was so much opportunity that it staggered his imagination.

He got very excited when he talked about all the things that were happening in Puerto Rico, but I was never sure how much of his talk he believed. I never contradicted him, but he knew I didn't take him quite seriously.

"Don't give me that crooked smile," he would say. "I worked for the paper—I know what those idiots say."

Then he'd get even more excited. "Where do you get this superior attitude?" he would say. "Nobody down here cares if you went to Yale or not. All you are to these people is a low-life reporter, just another bum from the *Daily News.*"

This business about Yale was a grisly joke. I had never been within fifty miles of New Haven, but in Europe I discovered that it was much easier to say I was a Yale graduate than to explain why I quit after two years at Vanderbilt and volunteered for the draft. I never told Sanderson I went to Yale; he must have got it from Segarra, who undoubtedly read my letter to Lotterman.

Sanderson had gone to the University of Kansas, then to Columbia's journalism school. He claimed to be proud of his farm-belt background, but he was so obviously ashamed of it that I felt sorry for him. Once when he was drunk he told me that the Hal Sanderson from Kansas was dead—he had died on the train to New York, and the Hal Sanderson I knew had been born the moment that train pulled into Penn Station.

He was lying, of course. For all his Caribbean clothes and his Madison Avenue manners, even with his surfside apartment and his Alfa Romeo roadster, there was so much Kansas in Sanderson that it was embarrassing to see him deny it. And Kansas was not all that was in him. There was a lot of New York, a little of Europe, and something else that has no country at all and was probably the largest single fact of his life. When he first told me that he owed twenty-five hundred dollars to a psychiatrist in New York and was spending fifty dollars a week on one in San Juan, I was dumbfounded. From that day on I saw him in a very different light.

Not that I thought he was crazy. He was a phony, of course, but for a long time I thought he was one of those phonies who can snap it on and off at will. He seemed honest enough with me, and in those rare moments when he relaxed I enjoyed him immensely. But it was not often that he dropped his guard, and usually it was rum that made him do it. He relaxed so seldom that his natural moments had an awkward, childish quality that was almost pathetic. He had come so far from himself that I don't think he knew who he was anymore.

For all his flaws, I respected Sanderson; he had come to San Juan as a reporter for a new paper that most people thought was a joke, and three years later he was vice president of the biggest public relations firm in the Caribbean. He had damn well worked at it—and if it was not the sort of thing I had much use for, I had to admit he had done it well.

Sanderson had good reason to be optimistic about Puerto Rico.

From his vantage point at Adelante, he was in on more deals and making more money than he knew what to do with. I had no doubt that, barring the possibility of a great upswing in analysts' fees, he was no more than ten years away from being a millionaire. He said five, but I doubled it because it seemed almost indecent that a man doing Sanderson's kind of work should make a million dollars before he was forty.

He was so much on top of things that I suspected that he had lost sight of the line between business and conspiracy. When somebody wanted land for a new hotel, when a top-level disagreement sent rumblings through the administration, or when anything of importance was on its way to happening, Sanderson usually knew more about it than the Governor.

This fascinated me, for I had always been an observer, one who arrived on the scene and got a small amount of money for writing what he saw and whatever he could find out by asking a few hurried questions. Now, listening to Sanderson, I felt on the verge of a massive breakthrough. Considering the confusion of The Boom and the grab-bag morality that was driving it along, I felt for the first time in my life that I might get a chance to affect the course of things instead of merely observing them. I might even get rich; God knows, it seemed easy enough. I gave it a lot of thought, and though I was careful never to mention it, I began to see a new dimension in everything that happened.

Five

SALA'S apartment on Calle Tetuán was about as homey as a cave, a dank grotto in the very bowels of the Old City. It was not an upscale neighborhood. Sanderson shunned it and Zimburger called it a sewer. It reminded me of a big handball court in some stench-ridden YMCA. The ceiling was twenty feet high, not a breath of clean air, no furniture except two metal cots and an improvised picnic table, and since it was on the ground floor we could never open the windows because thieves would come in off the street and sack the place. A week after Sala moved in he left one of the windows unlocked and everything he owned was stolen, even his shoes and his dirty socks.

We had no refrigerator and therefore no ice, so we drank hot rum out of dirty glasses and did our best to stay out of the place as much as possible. It was easy to understand why Sala didn't mind sharing; neither of us ever went there except to change clothes or sleep. Night after night I would sit uselessly at Al's, drinking myself into a stupor because I couldn't stand the idea of going back to the apartment.

After living there a week I'd established a fairly strict routine. I would sleep until ten or so, depending on the noise level in the street, then take a shower and walk up to Al's for breakfast. With a few exceptions, the normal workday at the paper was from noon until eight in the evening, give or take a few hours either way. Then we would come back to Al's for dinner. After that it was the casinos, an occasional party, or simply sitting at Al's and listening to each other's stories until we all got drunk and mumbled off to our beds. Sometimes I would go to Sanderson's and usually there were people there to drink with. Except for Segarra and the wretched greedhead Zimburger, almost everyone at Sanderson's was from New York or Miami or the Virgin Islands. They were buyers or builders or sellers in one way or another, and now that I look back on it I don't recall a single name or face out of the hundred or so that I met there. Not a distinctive soul in the lot, but it was a pleasant, social kind of atmosphere and a welcome break from those dreary nights at Al's.

One Monday morning I was awakened by what sounded like children being butchered outside the window. I looked through a crack in the shutter and saw about fifteen tiny Puerto Ricans, dancing on the sidewalk and tormenting a three-legged dog. I cursed them viciously and hurried up to Al's for breakfast.

Chenault was there, sitting alone in the patio and reading a secondhand copy of *Lady Chatterley's Lover*. She looked very young and pretty, wearing a white dress and sandals, with her hair falling loose down her back. She smiled as I went over to the table and sat down.

"What brings you in so early?" I asked.

She closed her book. "Oh, Fritz had to go somewhere and finish that story he's been working on. I have to cash some traveler's checks and I'm waiting for the bank to open."

"Who's Fritz?" I said.

She looked at me as if I were not quite awake.

"Yeamon?" I asked quickly.

She laughed. "I call him Fritz. That's his middle name—Addison Fritz Yeamon. Isn't that fine?"

I agreed that it was. I had never thought of him as anything but Yeamon. As a matter of fact I knew almost nothing about him at all. During the course of those evenings at Al's I had heard the life story of almost every man on the paper, but Yeamon invariably went straight home after work and I had come to regard him as a loner with no real past and a future so vague that there was no sense talking about it. Nonetheless, I felt that I knew him well enough so that we did not have to do much talking. From the very beginning I had felt a definite contact with Yeamon, a kind of tenuous understanding that talk is pretty cheap in this league and that a man who knew what he was after had damn little time to find it, much less to sit back and explain himself.

Nor did I know anything about Chenault, except that she had undergone a tremendous change since my first sight of her at the airport. She was tan and happy now, not nearly so tense with that nervous energy that had been so obvious when she wore her secretary suit. But not all of it was gone. Somewhere beneath that loose blonde hair and that friendly, little-girl smile I sensed a thing that was moving hard and fast toward some long-awaited opening. It made me a little nervous; and on top of that I remembered my initial lust for her and the sight of her locked with Yeamon that morning in the water. I also remembered those two immodest strips of white cloth around her ripe little body on the patio. All this was very much on my mind as I sat with her there at Al's and ate my breakfast.

It was hamburger with eggs. When I came to San Juan Al's menu consisted of beer, rum and hamburgers. It was a pretty volatile breakfast, and several times I was drunk by the time I got to work. One day I asked him to get some eggs and coffee. At first he refused, but when I asked him again he said he would. Now, for breakfast, you could have an egg on your hamburger, and coffee instead of rum.

"Are you here for good?" I said, looking up at Chenault.

She smiled. "I don't know. I quit my job in New York." She looked up at the sky. "I just want to be happy. I'm happy with Fritz—so I'm here."

I nodded thoughtfully. "Yeah, that seems reasonable."

She laughed. "It won't last. Nothing lasts. But I'm happy now."

"Happy," I muttered, trying to pin the word down. But it is one of those words, like Love, that I have never quite understood. Most people who deal in words don't have much faith in them and I am no exception—especially the big ones like Happy and Love and Honest and Strong. They are too elusive and far too relative when you compare them to sharp, mean little words like Punk and Cheap and Phony. I feel at home with these, because they're scrawny and easy to pin, but the big ones are tough and it takes either a priest or a fool to use them with any confidence.

I was not ready to put any labels on Chenault, so I tried to change the subject.

"What story is he working on?" I asked, offering her a cigarette.

She shook her head. "The same one," she replied. "He's had a terrible time with it—that thing about Puerto Ricans going to New York."

"Damn," I said. "I thought he finished that a long time ago."

"No," she said. "They kept giving him new assignments. But this one has to be in today—that's what he's doing now."

I shrugged. "Hell, he shouldn't worry about it. One story more or less on a sloppy paper like this doesn't make much difference."

About six hours later, I found out that it did make a difference, although not in the way I had meant. After breakfast I walked with Chenault to the bank, then I went to work. It was just about six when Yeamon came back from wherever he had been all afternoon. I nodded to him, then watched with mild curiosity as Lotterman called him over to the desk. "I want to talk to you about that emigration story," he said. "Just what in hell are you trying to put over on me?"

Yeamon looked surprised. "What do you mean?"

Lotterman suddenly began to shout. "I mean you're not getting away with it! You spent three weeks on that story and now Segarra tells me it's useless!"

Yeamon's face turned red and he leaned toward Lotterman as if he were going to grab his throat. "Useless?" he said quietly. "Why is it . . . useless?"

Lotterman was as angry as I'd ever seen him, but Yeamon looked so threatening that he quickly changed his tone—just slightly, but enough to notice. "Listen," he said. "I'm not paying your salary so you can write magazine articles—what the hell were you thinking about when you turned in twenty-six pages of copy?"

Yeamon leaned forward. "Break it up," he replied. "You don't have to run it all at once."

Lotterman laughed. "Oh—so that's it! You want me to run a serial—you're looking for a Pulitzer Prize, eh?" He stepped forward and raised his voice again. "Yeamon, when I want a serial I'll ask for a serial—are you too dense to understand that?"

Everyone was watching now and I half expected Yeamon to scatter Lotterman's teeth all over the newsroom. When he spoke I was surprised at his calm. "Look," he said sharply, "you asked for a story on why Puerto Ricans leave Puerto Rico—right?"

Lotterman stared at him.

"Okay, so I worked on the story for a week—not three, if you remember that other crap you gave me—and now you're yelling because it's twenty-six pages long! Well, goddamnit it should have been sixty pages long! If I'd written the story I wanted to write you'd be run out of town for publishing it!"

Lotterman seemed uncertain. "Well," he said after a pause, "if you want to do a sixty-page story that's your business—but if you want to work for me I'll have that story in a thousand words for tomorrow morning's paper."

Yeamon smiled faintly. "Segarra's good at that sort of thing—why don't you have *him* condense it?"

Lotterman swelled up like a toad. "What are you saying?" he shouted. "That you won't do it?"

Yeamon smiled again. "I was just wondering," he said, "if you've ever had your head twisted."

"What's that?" snapped Lotterman. "Did I hear you threaten to twist my head?"

Yeamon smiled. "A man never knows when his head might get twisted."

"Good God!" Lotterman exclaimed. "You sound like a nut, Yeamon—people get locked up for saying things like that!"

"Yes indeed," Yeamon replied. "Heads get TWISTED!" He said this in a loud voice and made a violent twisting gesture with his hands, never taking his eyes off Lotterman.

Now Lotterman seemed genuinely alarmed. "You *are* a nut," he said nervously. "Maybe you'd better resign, Yeamon—right now."

"Oh no," Yeamon said quickly. "No chance of that—I'm too busy."

Lotterman was getting shaky. I knew he didn't want to fire Yeamon, because he'd have to give him a month's severance pay. After a pause, he said again: "Yes, Yeamon, I think you'd better resign. You don't seem happy here—why don't you quit?"

Yeamon laughed. "I'm happy enough. Why don't you fire me?"

There was a tense silence. We all waited for Lotterman's next move, amused and a little bewildered by the whole scene. At first it had seemed like just another one of Lotterman's tirades, but Yeamon's maniacal replies had given it a weird and violent flavor.

Lotterman stared at him for a moment, looking more nervous than ever, then he turned and went into his office.

I sat back in my chair, grinning at Yeamon, then I heard Lotterman shouting my name. I spread my hands in a public shrug, then got up slowly and went to his office.

He was hunched over his desk, fumbling with a baseball that he used as a paperweight. "Take a look at this," he said. "Tell me if you think it's worth condensing." He handed me a sheaf of newsprint that I knew was Yeamon's story.

"Suppose it is," I said. "Then I condense it?"

"That's right," he replied. "Now don't give me any shit. Just read it and tell me what you can do with it."

I took it back to my desk and read it twice. After the first reading I knew why Segarra had called it useless. Most of it was dialogue, conversations with Puerto Ricans at the airport. They were telling why they were going to New York, what they were looking for and what they thought of the lives they were leaving behind.

At a glance, it was pretty dull stuff. Most of them seemed naive and ignorant—they hadn't read the travel brochures and the rum advertisements, they knew nothing of The Boom—all they wanted was to get to New York. It was a dreary document, but when I finished it there was no doubt in my mind as to why these people were leaving. Not that their reasons made sense, but they were reasons, nonetheless—simple statements, born in minds I could never understand because I had grown up in St. Louis in a house with two bathrooms and I had gone to football games and gin-jug parties and dancing school and I had done a lot of things, but I had never been a Puerto Rican.

It occurred to me that the real reason these people were leaving this island was basically the same reason I had left St. Louis and quit college and said to hell with all the things I was supposed to want—indeed, all the things I had a responsibility to want—to uphold, as it were—and I wondered how I might have sounded if someone had interviewed me at Lambert Airport on the day I left for New York with two suitcases and three hundred dollars and an envelope full of my clippings from an Army newspaper.

"Tell me, Mr. Kemp, just why are you leaving St. Louis, where your family has lived for generations and where you could, for the asking, have a niche carved out for yourself and your children so that you might live in peace and security for the rest of your well-fed days?"

"Well, you see, I . . . ah . . . well, I get a strange feeling. I . . . ah . . . I sit around here and I look at this place and I just want to get out, you know? I want to flee."

"Mr. Kemp, you seem like a reasonable man—just what is it about St. Louis that makes you want to flee? I'm not prying, you understand, I'm just a reporter and I'm from Tallahassee, myself, but they sent me out here to—"

"Certainly. I just wish I could . . . ah . . . you know, I'd like to be able to tell you that . . . ah . . . maybe I should say that I feel a rubber sack coming down on me . . . purely symbolic, you know . . . the venal ignorance of the fathers being visited on the sons . . . can you make something of that?"

"Well, ha-ha, I sort of know what you mean, Mr. Kemp. Back in Tallahassee it was a cotton sack, but I guess it was about the same size and—"

"Yeah, it's the goddamn sack—so I'm taking off and I guess I'll . . . ah . . ."

"Mr. Kemp, I wish I could say how much I sympathize, but you understand that if I go back with a story about a rubber sack they're going to tell me it's useless and probably fire me. Now I don't want to press you, but I wonder if you could give me something more concrete; you know—is there not enough opportunity here for aggressive young men? Is St. Louis meeting her responsibilities to youth? Is our society not flexible enough for young people with ideas? You can talk to me, Mr. Kemp—what is it?"

"Well, fella, I wish I could help you. God knows I don't want you to go back without a story and get fired. I know how it is—I'm a journalist myself, you know—but . . . well . . . I get The Fear . . . can you use that? St. Louis Gives Young Men The Fear—not a bad headline, eh?"

"Come on, Kemp, you know I can't use that; Rubber Sacks, The Fear."

"Goddamnit, man, I tell you it's fear of the sack! Tell them that this man Kemp is fleeing St. Louis because he suspects the sack is full of something ugly and he doesn't want to be put in with it. He senses this from afar. This man Kemp is not a model youth. He grew up with two toilets and a football, but somewhere along the line he got warped. Now all he wants is Out, Flee. He doesn't give a good shit for St. Louis or his friends or his family or anything else . . . he just wants to find some place where he can breathe . . . is that good enough for you?"

"Well, ah, Kemp, you sound a bit hysterical. I don't know if I can get the story on you or not."

"Well fuck you then. Get out of my way. They're calling my flight—hear that voice? Hear it?"

"You're deranged, Kemp! You'll come to no good end! I knew people like you back in Tallahassee and they all ended up—"

Yeah, they all ended up like Puerto Ricans. They fled and they couldn't say why, but they damn well wanted out and they didn't care if the newspapers understood or not. Somehow they got the idea that by getting the hell away from where they were they could find something better. They heard the word, the rotten devilish word that makes people incoherent with desire to move on—not everybody in the world lives in tin shacks with no toilets and no money at all and no food but rice and beans; not everybody cuts sugarcane for a dollar a day, or hauls a load of coconuts into town to sell for two cents each—the cheap, hot, hungry world of their fathers and their grandfathers and all their brothers and sisters was not the whole story, because if a man could muster the guts or even the desperation to move a few thousand miles there was a pretty good chance that he'd have money in his pocket and meat in his belly and one hell of a romping good time.

Yeamon had caught their mood perfectly. In twenty-six pages he had gone way beyond the story of why Puerto Ricans shove off for New York; in the end it was a story of why a man leaves home in the face of ugly odds, and when I finished it I felt small and silly for all the tripe I had written since I'd been in San Juan. Some of the conversations were amusing and others were pathetic—but through them all ran the main thread, the prime mover, the fact that these people thought they might have a chance in New York, and in Puerto Rico they had no chance at all.

When I finished reading it a second time I took it back to Lotterman and told him I thought he should run it as a five-part serial.

He slammed his baseball on the desk. "Goddamnit, you're as crazy as Yeamon! I can't run a serial nobody's going to read."

"They'll read it," I said, knowing they wouldn't.

"Don't give me that stuff!" he barked. "I read two pages and it bored me stiff—a goddamn mountain of griping. Where does he get that kind of nerve? He hasn't been here two months and he tries to con me into using a story that sounds like something out of *Pravda*—and he wants it run as a serial!"

"Well," I said. "You asked what I thought."

He glared up at me. "Is that your way of saying you won't do it?"

I wanted to flatly refuse—and I would have, I think, but I hesitated an instant too long. It was no more than an instant, but that was long enough for me to consider the consequences—fired, no salary, packing up again, fighting for a foothold somewhere else. So I said, "You're running the newspaper. I'm just telling you what I thought—since that's what you asked for."

He stared at me and I could see him mulling the thing over in his mind. Suddenly he whacked the ball off his desk and sent it bouncing into a corner. "Goddamnit!" he yelled. "Here I pay that guy a fat salary and what do I get out of him? A bunch of crap I can't use!" He fell back in the chair. "Well, he's finished. I knew he was trouble the minute I saw him. Now Segarra tells me he's running around the city on a motorcycle with no muffler, scaring the hell out of people. Did you hear him threaten to twist my head! Did you see his eyes? The guy's a nut—I should have him locked up!

"We don't need people like that," he said. "It's one thing if they're worth a damn, but he's not. He's just a big bum, trying to make trouble."

I shrugged and turned to go, feeling angry and confused and a little ashamed of myself.

Lotterman called after me. "Tell him to come in here. We'll pay him off and get him out of the building."

I crossed the room and told Yeamon that Lotterman wanted to see him. Just then I heard Lotterman call Segarra into his office. They were both in there when Yeamon went in.

Ten minutes later he reappeared and came over to my desk. "Well, no more salary," he said quietly. "Claims he doesn't owe me any severance pay either."

I shook my head sadly. "Man, what a rotten deal. I don't know what the hell is wrong with him."

Yeamon looked idly around the room. "Nothing unusual," he said. "I think I'll go up to Al's for a beer."

"I saw Chenault up there earlier," I said.

He nodded. "I took her home. She cashed in the last of her traveler's checks."

I shook my head again, trying to think of something quick and cheerful to say, but before I could think of anything he was halfway across the room.

"See you later," I called after him. "We'll get drunk."

He nodded without turning around. I watched him clean out his desk. Then he left, saying nothing to anyone.

I killed the rest of the day writing letters. At eight I found Sala in the darkroom and we drove up to Al's. Yeamon was alone in the patio, sitting at a corner table with his feet propped up on a chair and a distant expression on his face. He looked up as we approached. "Well," he said quietly. "The journalists."

We mumbled and sat down with the drinks we had brought from the bar. Sala leaned back and lit a cigarette. "So the son of a bitch fired you," he said.

Yeamon nodded. "Yep."

"Well, don't let him play games with that severance pay," Sala said. "If he gives you any trouble put the Labor Department on his ass—you'll get paid."

"I'd better," said Yeamon. "Otherwise I'll have to catch that bastard outside the building some night and beat it out of him."

Sala shook his head. "Don't worry. When he fired Art Glinnin he got socked for five bills. Glinnin finally took him to court."

"He paid me for three days," said Yeamon. "Figured it out to the last hour."

"Hell," said Sala, "report him tomorrow. Bust him. Let them serve a complaint—he'll pay."

Yeamon thought for a moment. "That should come to a little over four hundred. I could live for a while, anyway."

"This is a hell of a place to go broke," I said. "Four hundred's not much when you figure you need fifty just to get to New York."

He shook his head. "That's the last place I'll go. I don't get along with New York." He sipped his drink. "No, when I abandon this place I think I'll head south down the islands and look around for a cheap freighter to Europe." He nodded thoughtfully. "I don't know about Chenault."

We stayed at Al's all evening, talking about the places a man could go in Mexico and the Caribbean and South America. Sala was so bitter about Yeamon's being fired that he said several times that he was going to quit. "Who needs this place?" he shouted. "Blow it off the goddamn face of the earth—who needs it?"

I knew it was the rum talking, but after a while it began to talk for me too, and by the time we started back to the apartment I was ready to quit, myself. The more we talked about South America, the more I wanted to go there.

"It's a hell of a place," Sala kept saying. "Plenty of money floating around, English-language papers in all the big cities—by God, that may be the place!"

On the way down the hill we walked three abreast in the cobblestone street, drunk and laughing and talking like men who knew they would separate at dawn and travel to the far corners of the earth.

Six

NEEDLESS to say, Sala didn't quit and neither did I. The atmosphere at the paper was more tense than ever. On Wednesday, Lotterman got a summons from the Department of Labor, ordering him to a hearing on the question of Yeamon's severance pay. He cursed about it all afternoon, saying it would be a cold day in hell before he'd give that nut a dime. Sala began taking bets on the outcome, giving three-to-one odds that Yeamon would collect.

To make things worse, Tyrrell's departure had forced Lotterman to take over as city editor. This meant he did most of the work. It was only temporary, he said, but so far his ad in *Editor & Publisher* had drawn a blank.

I was not surprised. "Editor," it said. "San Juan daily. Begin immediately. Drifters and drinkers need not apply."

At one point he offered the job to me. I came in one day and found a note in my typewriter, saying Lotterman wanted to see me. When I opened the door to his office he was fumbling idly with his baseball. He smiled shrewdly and tossed it up in the air. "I've been thinking," he said. "You seem pretty sharp—ever handled a city desk?"

"No," I replied.

"Like to give it a whirl?" he asked, tossing the ball again.

I wanted no part of it. There would be a good raise, but there would also be a hell of a lot of extra work. "I haven't been here long enough," I said. "I don't know the city."

He tossed the baseball up in the air and let it thud on the floor. "I know," he said. "I was just thinking."

"What about Sala?" I said, knowing Sala would turn it down. He had so many freelance assignments that I wondered why he bothered to keep his job at all.

"Not a chance," he replied. "Sala doesn't give a damn about the paper—he doesn't give a damn about anything." He leaned forward and dropped the baseball on the desk. "Who else is there? Moberg's a drunk, Vanderwitz is a psycho, Noonan's a fool, Benetiz can't speak English . . . Christ! Where do I get these people?" He fell back in his chair with a groan. "I've got to have *somebody!*" he shouted. "I'll go crazy if I have to do the whole paper myself!"

"What about the ad?" I said. "No replies?"

He groaned again. "Sure—wineheads! One guy claimed to be the son of Oliver Wendell Holmes—as if I gave a goddamn!" He slammed the ball violently on the floor. "Who keeps sending these wineheads down here?" he shouted. "Where do they come from?"

He shook his fist at me and spoke as if he were uttering his last words: "Somebody has to fight it, Kemp—they're taking over. These wineheads are taking over the world. If the press goes under, we're sunk—you understand that?"

I nodded.

"By Jesus," he went on, "we have a responsibility! A free press is vital! If a pack of deadbeats get hold of this newspaper it's the beginning of the end. First they'll get this one, then they'll get a few more, and one day they'll get the *Times*—can you imagine it?"

I said I couldn't.

"They'll get us all!" he exclaimed. "They're dangerous—insidious! That guy claiming he was the son of Justice Holmes—I could pick him out of a crowd—he'd be the one with hair on his neck and a crazy look in his eye!"

Just then, as if on cue, Moberg came through the door, carrying a clipping from *El Diario*.

Lotterman's eyes became wild. "Moberg!" he screamed. "Oh Jesus—where do you get the nerve to come in here without knocking! By God I'll have you locked up! Get out!"

Moberg retreated quickly, rolling his eyes at me as he left.

Lotterman glared after him. "The nerve of that goddamn sot," he said. "Christ, a sot like that should be put to sleep."

Moberg had been in San Juan only a few months, but Lotterman seemed to loathe him with a passion that it would take most men years to cultivate. Moberg was a degenerate. He was small, with thin blond hair and a face that was pale and flabby. I have never seen a man so bent on self-destruction—not only self, but destruction of everything he could get his hands on. He was lewd and corrupt in every way. He hated the taste of rum, yet he would finish a bottle in ten minutes, then vomit and fall down. He ate nothing but sweet rolls and spaghetti, which he would heave the moment he got drunk. He spent all his money on whores and when that got dull he would take on an occasional queer, just for the strangeness of it. He would do anything for money, and this was the man we had on the police beat. Often he disappeared for days at a time. Then someone would have to track him down through the dirtiest bars in La Perla, a slum so foul that on maps of San Juan it appears as a blank space. La Perla was Moberg's headquarters; he felt at home there, he said, and in the rest of the city—except for a few horrible bars—he was a lost soul.

He told me that he'd spent the first twenty years of his life in Sweden, and often I tried to picture him against a crisp Scandinavian landscape. I tried to see him on skis, or living peacefully with his family in some cold mountain village. From the little he said of Sweden I gathered he'd lived in a small town and his parents had been comfortable people with enough money to send him to college in America.

He spent two years at NYU, living in the Village at one of those residence hotels that cater to foreigners. This apparently unhinged him. Once he was arrested on Sixth Avenue, he said, for pissing on a fireplug like a dog. It cost him ten days in the Tombs, and when he got out he left immediately for New Orleans. He floundered there for a while, then got a job on a freighter headed for the Orient. He worked on boats for several years before drifting into journalism. Now, thirty-three years old and looking fifty, his spirit broken and his body swollen with drink, he bounced from one country to another, hiring himself out as a reporter and hanging on until he was fired.

Disgusting as he usually was, on rare occasions he showed flashes of a stagnant intelligence. But his brain was so rotted with drink and dissolute living that whenever he put it to work it behaved like an old engine that had gone haywire from being dipped in lard.

"Lotterman thinks I'm a Demogorgon," he would say. "You know what that is? Look it up—no wonder he doesn't like me."

One night at Al's he told me he was writing a book, called *The Inevitability of a Strange World.* He took it very seriously. "It's the kind of book a Demogorgon would write," he said. "Full of shit and terror—I've selected the most horrible things I could imagine—the hero is a flesh eater disguised as a priest—cannibalism fascinates me—once down at the jail they beat a drunk until he almost died— I asked one of the cops if I could eat a chunk of his leg before they killed him . . ." He laughed. "The swine threw me out—hit me with a club." He laughed again. "I would have eaten it—why shouldn't I? There's nothing sacred about human flesh—it's meat like everything else—would you deny that?"

"No," I said. "Why should I deny it?"

It was one of the few times I talked to him that I could understand what he said. Most of the time he was incoherent. Lotterman was forever threatening to fire him, but we were so understaffed that he couldn't afford to let anyone go. When Moberg spent a few days in the hospital after his beating at the hands of the strikers, Lotterman had hopes that he might straighten out. But when he came back to work he was more erratic than before.

At times I wondered which would be the first to go—Moberg, or the *News.* The paper gave every appearance of being on its last legs. Circulation was falling off and we were losing advertising so steadily that I didn't see how Lotterman could hold out. He had borrowed heavily to get the paper going, and according to Sanderson, it had never made a nickel.

I kept hoping for an influx of new blood, but Lotterman had become so wary of "wineheads" that he rejected every reply to his ads. "I've got to be careful," he explained. "One more pervert and we're finished."

I feared he couldn't afford to pay any more salaries, but one day a man named Schwartz appeared in the office, saying he had just been thrown out of Venezuela, and Lotterman hired him immediately. To everyone's surprise he turned out to be competent. After a few weeks he was doing all the work that Tyrrell had done.

This took a lot of the strain off Lotterman, but it didn't do much for the paper. We went from twenty-four pages down to sixteen, and finally to twelve. The outlook was so bleak that people began saying *El Diario* had the *News*'s obituary set in type and ready to go.

I felt no loyalty to the paper, but it was good to have a salary while I fished for something larger. The idea that the *News* might fold began to worry me and I wondered why San Juan, with all its new prosperity, couldn't support such a small thing as an English-language newspaper. The *News* was no prize-winner, but it was at least readable.

A large part of the trouble was Lotterman. He was capable enough, in a purely mechanical way, but he had put himself in an untenable position. As an admitted ex-communist, he was under constant pressure to prove how much he'd reformed. At that time the U.S. State Department was calling Puerto Rico *"America's advertisement in the Caribbean—living proof that capitalism can work in Latin America."* The people who had come there to do the proving saw themselves as heroes and missionaries, bringing the holy message of Free Enterprise to the downtrodden jíbaros. They hated commies like they hated sin, and the fact that an ex-Red was publishing a paper in their town did not make them happy.

Lotterman simply couldn't cope with it. He went out of his way to attack anything that smelled even faintly of the political Left, because he knew he'd be crucified if he didn't. On the other hand, he was a slave to the freewheeling Commonwealth government, whose U.S. subsidies were not only supporting half the new industry on the island, but were paying for most of the *News* advertising as well. It was a nasty bind—not just for Lotterman, but for a good many others. In order to make money they had to deal with the government, but to deal with the government was to condone "creeping socialism"—which was not exactly compatible with their missionary work.

It was amusing to see how they handled it, because if they thought about it at all there was only one way out—to praise the ends and ignore the means, a time-honored custom that justifies almost anything except shrinking profits.

To go to a cocktail party in San Juan was to see all that was cheap and greedy in human nature. What passed for society was a loud, giddy whirl of thieves and pretentious hustlers, a dull sideshow full of quacks and clowns and philistines with gimp mentalities. It was a new wave of Okies, heading south instead of west, and in San Juan they were kingfish because they had literally taken over.

They formed clubs and staged huge social events, and finally one of them began publishing a merciless scandal sheet that terrified and intimidated everyone whose past was not politically pure. This took in half the gang, including poor Lotterman, who suffered some vicious libel almost every week.

There was no shortage of free liquor for the press, because all hustlers crave publicity. No occasion was too small for them to give what they called a "press party" in its honor. Each time Woolworth's or the Chase Manhattan Bank opened a new branch, they celebrated with an orgy of rum. Not a month went by without the opening of a new bowling alley; they were building them on every vacant lot, so many bowling alleys that it was horrible to ponder the meaning of it.

From the new San Juan Chamber of Commerce came a stream of statements and proclamations that made Jehovah's Witnesses seem pale and pessimistic—long breast-beating screeds, announcing one victory after another in the crusade for Big Money. And on top of all this, there was a never-ending round of private parties for visiting celebrities. Here again, no half-wit Kiwanian was too insignificant for a blow-out in his honor.

I usually went to these things with Sala. At the sight of his camera the guests would turn to jelly. Some of them would act like trained pigs and others would mill around like sheep, all waiting for "the man from the paper" to push his magic button and make their lavish hospitality pay off.

We tried to go early, and while Sala was herding them around for a series of meaningless photos that would probably never even be developed, I would steal as many bottles of rum as I could carry. If there was a bartender I would tell him I wanted a bit of drink for the press, and if he protested I would take them anyway. No matter what kind of outrage I committed, I knew they would never complain.

Then we would head for Al's, dropping the rum at the apartment on the way. We put all the bottles on an empty bookshelf and sometimes there were as many as twenty or thirty. In a good week we would hit three parties and average three or four bottles for each half hour of painful socializing. It was a good feeling to have a stock of rum that would never run out, but after a while I could no longer stand even a few minutes at each party, and I had to give it up.

Seven

ONE Saturday in late March, when the tourist season was almost over and the merchants were bracing themselves for the muggy low-profit summer, Sala had an assignment to go down to Fajardo, on the eastern tip of the island, and take some pictures of a new hotel that was going up on a hill overlooking the harbor. Lotterman thought the *News* could strike a cheerful note by pointing out that things were going to be even better next season.

I decided to go along for the ride. Ever since I'd come to San Juan I'd been meaning to get out on the island, but without a car it was impossible. My furthest penetration had been to Yeamon's, about twenty miles out, and Fajardo was twice as far in the same direction. We decided to get some rum and stop by his place on the way back, hoping to get there just as he paddled in from the reef with a bulging sack of lobsters. "He's probably damn good at it by now," I said. "God knows what he's living on—they must have a steady diet of lobster and chicken."

"Hell," Sala remarked, "chicken's expensive."

I laughed. "Not out there. He shoots them with a speargun."

"God almighty!" Sala exclaimed. "That's voodoo country—they'll murder him, sure as hell!"

I shrugged. I'd assumed from the very beginning that Yeamon would sooner or later be killed—by somebody or some faceless mob, for some reason or other, it seemed inevitable. There was a time I had been the same way. I wanted it all and I wanted it fast and no obstacle was big enough to put me off. Since then I had learned that some things were bigger than they looked from a distance, and now I was not so sure anymore just what I was going to get or even what I deserved. I was not proud of what I had learned but I never doubted it was worth knowing. Yeamon would either learn the same things, or he would certainly be croaked.

This is what I told myself on those hot afternoons in San Juan when I was thirty years old and my shirt stuck damply to my back and I felt myself on that big and lonely hump, with my hardnose years behind me and all the rest downhill. They were eerie days, and my fatalistic view of Yeamon was not so much conviction as necessity, because if I granted him even the slightest optimism I would have to admit a lot of unhappy things about myself.

W̲e came to Fajardo after an hour's drive in the hot sun and immediately stopped for a drink at the first bar. Then we drove up a hill on the outskirts of town, where Sala puttered around for almost an hour, setting up his camera angles. He was a grudging perfectionist, no matter how much contempt he had for his assignment. As "the only pro on the island," he felt he had a certain reputation to uphold.

When he finished we bought two bottles of rum and a bag of ice. Then we drove back to the turnoff that would take us to Yeamon's beach house. The road was paved all the way to the River at Loíza, where two natives operated a ferry. They charged us a dollar for the car, then poled us across to the other side, not saying a word the whole time. I felt like a pilgrim crossing the Ganges, standing there in the sun beside the car and staring down at the water while the ferrymen leaned on their poles and shoved us toward the palm grove on the other side. We bumped against the dock and they secured the barge to an upright log while Sala drove the car to solid ground.

We still had five miles of sand road before we got to Yeamon's place. Sala cursed the whole way, swearing he would turn back except that he'd be hit for another dollar to go back across the river. The little car thumped and bounced on the ruts and I thought it would come to pieces at any moment. Once we passed a pack of naked children stoning a dog beside the road. Sala stopped and took several pictures.

"Jesus," he muttered, "look at those vicious little bastards! We'll be lucky to get out of here alive."

When we finally got to Yeamon's we found him on the patio, wearing the same filthy black trunks and building a bookshelf out of driftwood. The place looked better now; part of the patio was covered with an awning made of palm fronds, and beneath it were two canvas deck chairs that looked like they belonged in one of the better beach clubs.

"Man," I said, "where did you get *those?*"

"Gypsies," he replied. "Five dollars apiece. I think they stole 'em in town."

"Where's Chenault?" Sala asked.

He pointed down at the beach. "Probably sunning herself down by that log. She puts on a show for the natives—they love her."

Sala brought the rum and the bag of ice from the car. Yeamon chuckled happily and poured the ice in a tub beside the door. "Thanks," he said. "This poverty is driving me nuts—we can't even afford ice."

"Man," I said. "You've bottomed out. You've got to get some work."

He laughed and filled three glasses with ice. "I'm still after Lotterman," he said. "It looks like I might get my money."

Just then Chenault came up from the beach, wearing the same white bikini and carrying a big beach towel. She smiled at Yeamon: "They came again. I heard them talking."

"Goddamnit," Yeamon snapped. "Why do you keep going down there? What the hell is wrong with you?"

She smiled and sat down on the towel. "It's my favorite place. Why should I leave just because of them?"

Yeamon turned to me. "She goes down to the beach and takes off her clothes—the natives hide back in the palms and watch her."

"Not always," Chenault said quickly. "Usually it's just on weekends."

Yeamon leaned forward and shouted at her. "Well goddamn you! Don't go down there anymore! From now on you stay up here if you want to lie around naked! I'll be goddamned if I'll spend all my time worrying about you getting raped." He shook his head with disgust. "One of these days they'll get you and if you keep on teasing the poor bastards I'll damn well let them have you!"

She stared down at the concrete. I felt sorry for her and stood up to make her a drink. When I handed it to her she looked up gratefully and took a long swallow.

"Drink up," said Yeamon. "We'll invite some of your friends and have a real party!" Then he fell back in the chair. "Ah, the good life," he muttered.

We sat there drinking for a while, Chenault saying nothing, Yeamon doing most of the talking, and finally he got up and picked a coconut off the sand beside the patio. "Come on," he said, "let's have a little football."

I was glad for anything that would clear the air, so I put down my drink and ran awkwardly out for a pass. He spiraled it perfectly, but it smacked my fingers like lead and I dropped it.

"Let's get down on the beach," he called. "Plenty of room to run."

I nodded and waved to Sala. He shook his head. "Go play," he muttered. "Me and Chenault have serious things to discuss."

Chenault smiled halfheartedly and waved us down to the beach. "Go on," she said.

I slid down the bluff to the hard-packed sand on the beach. Yeamon threw up his arm and ran at an angle toward the surf. I tossed the nut high and long, watching it fall just beyond him in the water and make a quick splash. He fell on it and went under, bringing it up in his hands.

I turned and sprinted away, watching it float down at me out of the hot blue sky. It hurt my hands again, but this time I hung on. It was a good feeling to snag a long pass, even if it was a coconut. My hands grew red and tender, but it was a good clean feeling and I didn't mind. We ran short, over-the-middle passes and long floaters down the sidelines, and after a while I couldn't help but think we were engaged in some kind of holy ritual, the reenactment of all our young Saturdays—expatriated now, lost and cut off from those games and those drunken stadiums, beyond the noise and blind to the false color of those happy spectacles—after years of jeering at football and all that football means, here I was on an empty Caribbean beach, running these silly pass patterns with all the zeal of a regular sandlot fanatic.

As we raced back and forth, falling and plunging in the surf, I recalled my Saturdays at Vanderbilt and the precision beauty of a Georgia Tech backfield, pushing us back and back with that awful belly series, a lean figure in a gold jersey, slashing over a hole that should never have been there, now loose on the crisp grass of our secondary and an unholy shout from the stands across the way; and finally to bring the bastard down, escape those blockers coming at you like cannonballs, then line up again and face that terrible machinery. It was a torturous thing, but beautiful in its way; here were men who would never again function or even understand how they were supposed to function as well as they did today. They were dolts and thugs for the most part, huge pieces of meat, trained to a fine edge—but somehow they mastered those complex plays and patterns, and in rare moments they were artists.

Finally I got too tired to run anymore and we went back up to the patio, where Sala and Chenault were still talking. They both seemed a little drunk, and after a few minutes of conversation I realized that Chenault was fairly out of her head. She kept chuckling to herself and mocking Yeamon's southern accent.

We drank for another hour or so, laughing indulgently at Chenault and watching the sun slant off toward Jamaica and the Gulf of Mexico. It's still light in Mexico City, I thought. I had never been there and suddenly I was overcome by a tremendous curiosity about the place. Several hours of rum, combined with my mounting distaste for Puerto Rico, had me right on the verge of going into town, packing my clothes, and leaving on the first westbound plane. Why not? I thought. I hadn't cashed this week's paycheck yet; a few hundred in the bank, nothing to tie me down—why not, indeed? It was bound to be better than this place, where my only foothold was a cheap job that looked ready to collapse.

I turned to Sala. "How much is it from here to Mexico City?"

He shrugged and sipped his drink. "Too much," he replied. "Why? Are you moving on?"

I nodded. "I'm pondering it."

Chenault looked up at me, her face serious for a change. "You'd love Mexico City, Paul."

"What the hell do you know about it?" Yeamon snapped.

She glared up at him, then took a long drink from her glass.

"That's it," he said. "Keep sucking it down—you're not drunk enough yet."

"Shut up!" she screamed, jumping to her feet. "Leave me alone, you goddamn pompous fool!"

His arm shot out so quickly that I barely saw the movement; there was the sound of a smack as the back of his hand hit her cheek. It was almost a casual gesture, no anger, no effort, and by the time I realized what had happened he was leaning back in the chair again, watching impassively as she staggered back a few feet and burst into tears. No one spoke for a moment, then Yeamon told her to go inside. "Go on," he snapped. "Go to bed."

She stopped crying and took her hand away from her cheek. "Damn you," she sobbed.

"Get in there," he said.

She glared at him a moment longer, then turned and went inside. We could hear the squeak of springs as she fell on the bed, then the sobbing continued.

Yeamon stood up. "Well," he said quietly, "sorry to subject you people to that sort of thing." He nodded thoughtfully, glancing at the hut. "I think I'll go into town with you—anything happening tonight?"

Sala shrugged. I could tell he was upset. "Nothing," he said. "All I want is food, anyway."

Yeamon turned toward the door. "Hang on," he said. "I'll get dressed."

After he went inside, Sala turned to me and shook his head

sadly. "He treats her like a slave," he whispered. "She'll crack up pretty soon."

I stared out to sea, watching the sun disappear.

We could hear him moving around inside, but there was no talk. When he came out he was dressed in his tan suit, with a tie flung loosely around his neck. He pulled the door shut and locked it from the outside. "Keep her from wandering around," he explained. "She'll probably pass out pretty soon, anyway."

There was a sudden burst of sobbing from inside the hut. Yeamon gave a hopeless shrug and tossed his coat in Sala's car. "I'll take the scooter," he said, "so I won't have to stay in town."

We backed out to the road and let him go ahead. His scooter looked like one of those things they used to parachute behind the lines in World War Two—a skeleton chassis, showing signs of a red paint job far gone with rust, and beneath the seat was a little engine that made a sound like a Gatling gun. There was no muffler and the tires were completely bald.

We followed him along the road, nearly hitting him several times when he slid in the sand. He set a fast pace and we were hard pressed to keep up without tearing the car to pieces. As we passed the native shacks little children came running out to the road to wave to us. Yeamon waved back, grinning broadly and giving a tall, straight-armed salute as he sped along, trailing a cloud of dust and noise.

We stopped where the paved road began, and Yeamon suggested we go to a place just a mile or so further on. "Pretty good food and cheap drink," he said, "and, besides, they'll give me credit."

We followed him down the road until we came to a sign that said CASA CABRONES. An arrow pointed to a dirt road that branched off toward the beach. It went through a grove of palms and ended in a small parking lot, next to a ratty restaurant with tables on the patio and a jukebox beside the bar. Except for the palms and the Puerto Rican clientele, it reminded me of a third-rate tavern in the American Midwest. A string of blue bulbs hung from two poles on either side of the patio, and every thirty seconds or so the sky above us was sliced by a yellow beam from the airport tower, no more than a mile away.

As we sat down and ordered our drinks I realized we were the only gringos in the place. The others were locals. They made a great deal of noise, singing and shouting with the jukebox, but they all seemed tired and depressed. It was not the rhythmic sadness of Mexican music, but the howling emptiness of a sound I have never heard anywhere but in Puerto Rico—a combination of groaning and whining, backed up by a dreary thumping and the sound of voices bogged down in despair.

It was terribly sad—not the music itself, but the fact that it was the best they could do. Most of the tunes were translated versions of American rock-and-roll, with all the energy gone. I recognized one as "Maybellene." The original version had been a hit when I was in high school. I recalled it as a wild and racy tune, but the Puerto Ricans had made it a repetitious dirge, as hollow and hopeless as the faces of the men who sang it now in this lonely wreck of a roadhouse. They were not hired musicians, but I had a feeling they were putting on a performance, and any moment I expected them to fall silent and pass the hat. Then they would finish their drinks and file quietly into the night, like a troupe of clowns at the end of a laughless day.

Suddenly the music stopped and several men rushed for the jukebox. A quarrel broke out, a flurry of insults—and then, from somewhere far in the distance, like a national anthem played to calm a frenzied crowd, came the slow tinkling of Brahms' Lullaby. The quarrel ceased, there was a moment of silence, several coins fell into the bowels of the jukebox, and then it broke into a whimpering yell. The men returned to the bar, laughing and slapping each other on the back.

We ordered three more rums and the waiter brought them over. We'd decided to drink a while, putting off dinner till later, and by the time we got around to ordering food the waiter told us the kitchen was closed.

"Never in hell!" Yeamon exclaimed. "That sign says midnight." He pointed to a sign above the bar.

The waiter shook his head.

Sala looked up at him. "Please," he said, "you're my friend. I can't stand this anymore. I'm hungry."

The waiter shook his head again, staring at the green order pad in his hand.

Suddenly Yeamon banged his fist on the table. The waiter looked fearful, then scurried behind the bar. Everyone in the place turned to look at us.

"Let's have some meat!" Yeamon shouted. "And more rum!"

A fat little man wearing a white short-sleeve shirt came running out of the kitchen. He patted Yeamon on the shoulder. "Good fellows," he said with a nervous smile. "Good customers—no trouble, okay?"

Yeamon looked at him. "All we want is meat," he said pleasantly, "and another round of drinks."

The little man shook his head. "No dinner after ten," he said. "See?" He jabbed his finger at the clock. It was ten-twenty.

"That sign says midnight," Yeamon replied.

The man shook his head.

"What's the problem?" Sala asked. "The steaks won't take five minutes. Hell, forget the potatoes."

Yeamon held up his glass. "Let's get three drinks," he said, waving three fingers at the bartender.

The bartender looked at our man, who seemed to be the manager. He nodded quickly, then walked away. I thought the crisis had passed.

In a moment he was back, bringing a little green check that said $11.50. He put it on the table in front of Yeamon.

"Don't worry about it," Yeamon told him.

The manager clapped his hands. "Okay," he said angrily. "You pay." He held out his hand.

Yeamon brushed the check off the table. "I said don't worry about it."

The manager snatched the check off the floor. "You pay!" he screamed. "Pay now!"

Yeamon's face turned red and he rose half out of his chair. "I'll pay it like I paid the others," he yelled. "Now get the hell away from here and bring us our goddamn meat."

The manager hesitated, then leaped forward and slapped the check on the table. "Pay now!" he shouted. "Pay now and get out— or I call police."

He had barely got the words out of his mouth when Yeamon grabbed him by the front of his shirt. "You cheap little bastard!" he snarled. "You keep yelling and you'll never get paid."

I watched the men at the bar. They were bug-eyed and tense as dogs. The bartender stood poised at the door, ready to either flee or run outside and get a machete—I wasn't sure.

The manager, out of control by this time, shook his fist at us and screeched, "Pay, you goddamn Yankees! Pay and get out!" He glared at us, then ran over to the bartender and whispered something in his ear.

Yeamon got up and put on his coat. "Let's go," he said. "I'll deal with this bastard later."

The manager seemed terrified at the prospect of welshers walking out on him. He followed us into the parking lot, cursing and pleading by turns. "Pay now!" he howled. "When will you pay? . . . you'll see, the police will come . . . no police, just pay!"

I thought the man was crazy and my only desire was to get him off our backs. "Christ," I said. "Let's pay it."

"Yeah," said Sala, bringing out his wallet. "This place is sick."

"Don't worry," said Yeamon. "He knows I'll pay." He tossed his coat in the car, then turned to the manager. "You rotten little creep, get a grip on yourself."

We got in the car. As soon as Yeamon started his scooter the manager ran back and began shouting to the men inside the bar. His screams filled the air as we pulled off, following Yeamon out the long driveway. He refused to hurry, idling along like a man intrigued with the scenery, and in a matter of seconds two carloads of screaming Puerto Ricans were right behind us. I thought they might run us down. They were driving big American cars and could have squashed the Fiat like a roach.

"Holy shit," Sala kept saying, "we're going to be killed."

When we came to the paved road, Yeamon pulled over and let us pass. We stopped a few yards ahead of him and I called back, "Come on, damnit! Let's get out of here."

The other cars came up beside him and I saw him throw up his hands as if he'd been hit. He jumped off the scooter, letting it fall, and grabbed a man whose head was outside the window. Almost at the same moment I saw the police drive up. Four of them leaped out of a little blue Volkswagen, waving their billy clubs. The Puerto Ricans cheered wildly and scrambled out of their cars. I was tempted to run, but we were instantly surrounded. One of the cops ran up to Yeamon and pushed him backward. "Thief!" he shouted. "You think gringos drink free in Puerto Rico?"

At the same time, both doors of the Fiat were jerked open and Sala and I were pulled out. I tried to break loose, but several people were holding my arms. Somewhere beside me I could hear Yeamon saying over and over: "Well, the man spit on me, the man spit on me . . ."

Suddenly everybody stopped shouting and the scene boiled down to an argument between Yeamon, the manager and a man who appeared to be the cop in charge. Nobody was holding me now, so I moved up to hear what was going on.

"Look," Yeamon was saying. "I paid the other bills—what makes him think I won't pay this one?"

The manager said something about drunk, arrogant Yankees.

Before Yeamon could reply, one of the cops stepped up behind him and slammed him on the shoulder with his billy. He shouted and lurched to one side, onto one of the men who had come after us in the cars. The man swung wildly with a beer bottle, hitting him in the ribs. The last thing I saw before I went down was Yeamon's savage rush on the man with the bottle. I heard several swacks of bone against bone, and then, out of the corner of my eye, I saw something come at my head. I ducked just in time to take the main force of the blow on my back. It buckled my spine and I fell to the ground.

Sala was screaming somewhere above me and I was thrashing around on my back, trying to avoid the feet that were pounding me like hammers. I covered my head with my arms and lashed out with my feet, but the awful hammering continued. There was not much pain, but even through the numbness I knew they were hurting me and I was suddenly sure I was going to die. I was still conscious, and the knowledge that I was being kicked to death in a Puerto Rican jungle for eleven dollars and fifty cents filled me with such terror that I began to scream like an animal. Finally, just as I thought I was passing out, I felt myself being shoved into a car.

Eight

I WAS half-unconscious during the ride, and when the car finally stopped I looked out and saw an angry mob howling on the sidewalk. I knew I couldn't stand another beating; when they tried to haul me out I clung desperately to the back of the seat until one of the cops hit me on the arm with his club.

To my surprise, the crowd made no move to attack us. We were pushed up the steps, past a group of sullen cops at the door, and led into a small, windowless room where they told us to sit on a bench. Then they closed the door and left us alone.

"Jesus Christ," said Yeamon. "This is incredible. We have to get hold of somebody."

"We're headed for La Princesa," Sala groaned. "The bastards have us now—this is the end."

"They have to let us use the phone," I said. "I'll call Lotterman."

Yeamon snorted. "He won't do a damn thing for *me*. Hell, he wants me locked up."

"He won't have any choice," I replied. "He can't afford to abandon me and Sala."

Yeamon looked doubtful. "Well . . . I can't think of anybody else to call."

Sala groaned again and rubbed his head. "Christ, we'll be lucky to get out of here alive."

"We got off easy," said Yeamon, gently feeling his teeth. "I thought we were done for when it started."

Sala shook his head. "These people are vicious," he muttered. "I was dodging that cop and somebody hit me from behind with a coconut—nearly broke my neck."

The door opened and the boss cop appeared, smiling as if nothing had happened. "Okay?" he said, watching us curiously.

Yeamon looked up at him. "We'd like to use the phone," he said.

The cop shook his head. "Your names?" he said, pulling out a small notebook.

"If you don't mind," said Yeamon. "I think we have a right to make a phone call."

The cop made a menacing gesture with his fist. "I said NO!" he shouted. "Give me your names!"

We gave our names.

"Where are you staying?" he asked.

"Goddamnit, we live here!" Sala snapped. "I work for the *Daily News* and I've lived on this stinking rock for more than a year!" He was trembling with rage and the cop looked startled. "My address is 409 Calle Tetuán," Sala continued, "and I want a lawyer immediately."

The cop thought for a moment. "You work for the *Daily News*?"

"You're damn right," Sala replied.

The cop looked down at us and smiled wickedly. "Tough guys," he said. "Tough Yankee journalists."

No one said anything for a moment, then Yeamon asked again to use the phone. "Look," he said. "Nobody's trying to be tough. You just beat the hell out of us and now we want a lawyer—is that too much to ask?"

The cop smiled again. "Okay, tough guys."

"What the hell is this 'tough guy' business?" Sala exclaimed. "Where the Christ is a phone?"

He started to get up and he was still in a crouch, halfway off the bench, when the cop stepped forward and gave him a savage rabbit punch on the neck. Sala dropped to his knees and the cop kicked him in the ribs. Three more cops burst into the room as if they'd been waiting for the signal. Two of them grabbed Yeamon, twisting his arms behind his back, and the other one knocked me off the bench and stood over me with his stick. I knew he wanted to hit me and I didn't move, trying not to give him an excuse. After a long moment, the boss cop yelled, "Okay, tough guys, let's go." I was jerked off the floor and we were forced down the hall at a half-trot, our arms twisted painfully behind our backs.

At the end of the hall we came into a big room full of people and cops and a lot of desks—and there, sitting on a table in the middle of the room, was Moberg. He was writing in a notebook.

"Moberg!" I yelled, not caring if I was hit as long as I attracted his attention. "Call Lotterman! Get a lawyer!"

At the sound of Moberg's name, Sala looked up and screamed with rage and pain: "Swede! For Christ's sake call somebody! We're being killed!"

We were pushed through the room at high speed and I had no more than a glimpse of Moberg before we were in another hallway. The cops paid no attention to our shouts; apparently they were used to people screaming desperately as they were led away to wherever we were being taken. My only hope was that Moberg had not been too drunk to recognize us.

We spent the next six hours in a tiny concrete cell with about twenty Puerto Ricans. We couldn't sit down because they had pissed all over the floor, so we stood in the middle of the room, giving out cigarettes like representatives of the Red Cross. They were a dangerous-looking lot. Some were drunk and others seemed crazy. I felt safe as long as we could supply them with cigarettes, but I wondered what would happen when we ran out.

The guard solved this problem for us, at a nickel a cigarette. Each time we wanted one for ourselves we had to buy twenty—one for every man in the cell. After two rounds, the guard sent out for a new carton. We figured out later that our stay in the cell cost us more than fifteen dollars, which Sala and I paid, since Yeamon had no money.

It seemed like we had been there for six years when the guard finally opened the door and beckoned us out. Sala could hardly walk and Yeamon and I were so tired that we had trouble supporting him. I had no idea where we were going. Probably to the dungeon, I thought. This is the way people disappear.

We went back through the building, along several hallways, and finally into a large courtroom. As we were shoved through the door, looking as dirty and disheveled as the most horrible bums in the cell we had just left, I looked around anxiously for some familiar face.

The courtroom was jammed and I looked for several minutes before I saw Moberg and Sanderson standing solemnly in one corner. I nodded to them and Moberg held up his fingers in a circle.

"Thank God," said Sala. "We've made contact."

"Is that Sanderson?" Yeamon asked.

"Looks like it," I said, not having the faintest idea what it meant.

"What's that prick doing here?" Sala mumbled.

"We could do a hell of a lot worse," I said. "We're damn lucky anybody's here."

It was almost an hour before they called our case. The boss cop was the first to speak and his testimony was delivered in Spanish. Sala, who understood parts of what he was saying, kept muttering: "That lying bastard . . . claims we threatened to tear the place up . . . attacked the manager . . . ran out on our bill . . . hit a cop . . . Christ Jesus! . . . started a fight when we got to headquarters . . . God, this is too much! We're done for!"

When the boss cop had finished, Yeamon asked for a translation of the testimony, but the judge ignored him.

The manager testified next, sweating and gesturing with excitement, his voice rising to an hysterical pitch as he swung his arms and shook his fists and pointed at us as if we had killed his entire family.

We understood nothing of what he said, but it was obvious that things were going against us. When it finally came our turn to speak, Yeamon got up and demanded a translation of all the testimony against us.

"You heard it," said the judge in perfect English.

Yeamon explained that none of us spoke Spanish well enough to understand what had been said. "These people spoke English before," he said, pointing at the cop and the manager. "Why can't they speak it now?"

The judge smiled contemptuously. "You forget where you are," he said. "What right do you have to come here and cause trouble, and then tell us to speak your language?"

I could see that Yeamon was losing his temper and I motioned to Sanderson to do something. Just then I heard Yeamon say he "would expect fairer treatment under Batista."

A dead silence fell on the courtroom. The judge stared at Yeamon, his eyes bright with anger. I could almost feel the axe descending.

Sanderson called from the back of the room: "Your Honor, could I have a word?"

The judge looked up. "Who are you?"

"My name is Sanderson. I'm with Adelante."

A man I had never seen stepped quickly up to the judge and whispered in his ear. The judge nodded, then looked back at Sanderson. "Go ahead," he said.

Sanderson's voice seemed out of place after the wild denunciations of the cop and the manager. "These men are American journalists," he said. "Mr. Kemp is with the *New York Times,* Mr. Yeamon represents the American Travel Writers' Association, and Mr. Sala works for *Life* magazine." He paused, and I wondered just how much good this kind of thing was going to do. Our earlier identification as Yankee journalists had been disastrous.

"Perhaps I'm wrong," Sanderson continued, "but I think this testimony has been a little confusing, and I'd hate to see it result in any unnecessary embarrassment." He glanced at the boss cop, then back to the judge.

"Jesus," Yeamon whispered. "I hope he knows what he's doing."

I nodded, watching the judge's face. Sanderson's last comment had been delivered in a tone of definite warning, and it crossed my mind that he might be drunk. For all I knew, he had come straight from some party where he'd been drinking steadily since early afternoon.

"Well, Mr. Sanderson," said the judge in an even voice. "What do you suggest?"

Sanderson smiled politely. "I think it might be wise to continue this hearing when the atmosphere is a little less strained."

The same man who had spoken to the judge earlier was back at the bench. There was a quick exchange of words, then the judge spoke to Sanderson.

"You have a point," he said, "but these men have behaved in an arrogant way—they have no respect for our laws."

Sanderson's face darkened. "Well, Your Honor, if the case is going to be tried tonight, I'll have to ask for a recess until I can contact Adolfo Quinones." He nodded. "I'll have to wake him up, of course, get Señor Quinones out of bed, but I don't feel qualified to act any further as an attorney."

There was another hurried conference at the bench. I could see that the name Quinones had given the court some pause. He was the *News'* attorney, an ex-senator, and one of the most prominent men on the island.

We all watched nervously as the conference continued. Finally the judge looked over and told us to stand. "You will be released on bail," he said. "Or you may wait in jail—as you like." He jotted something down on a piece of paper.

"Robert Sala," he said. Sala looked up. "You are charged with public drunkenness, disorderly conduct and resisting arrest. Bail is set at one thousand dollars."

Sala grumbled and looked away.

"Addison Yeamon," said the judge. "You are charged with public drunkenness, disorderly conduct and resisting arrest. Bail is set at one thousand dollars."

Yeamon said nothing.

"Paul Kemp," said the judge. "You are charged with public drunkenness, disorderly conduct and resisting arrest. Bail is set at three hundred dollars."

This was almost as much of a shock as anything that had happened all night. I felt as if I'd committed a treachery of some kind. It seemed to me that I'd resisted well enough—had it been my screaming? Was the judge taking pity on me because he knew I'd been stomped? I was still pondering it as we were led out of the courtroom and into the hall.

"What now?" said Yeamon. "Can Sanderson afford that kind of bail?"

"Don't worry," I said. "He'll handle it." As I said it I felt like a fool. If worst came to worst, I could cover my bail out of my own pocket.

And I knew somebody would post Sala's, but Yeamon was a different matter. Nobody was going to make sure he came to work on Monday. The more I thought about it, the more certain I was that in a few minutes we were going to go free and he would go back to that cell, because there wasn't a soul on the island with a thousand dollars who had even the slightest interest in keeping Yeamon out of jail.

Suddenly Moberg appeared, followed by Sanderson and the man who'd been huddling with the judge. Moberg laughed drunkenly as he approached us. "I thought they were going to kill you," he said.

"They almost did," I replied. "What about this bail? Can we get that much money?"

He laughed again. "It's paid. Segarra told me to sign a check." He lowered his voice. "He said to pay the fines if they weren't more than a hundred dollars. He's lucky—there weren't any fines."

"You mean we're out?" said Sala.

Moberg grinned. "Of course. I signed for it."

"Me too?" said Yeamon.

"Certainly," Moberg replied. "The deed is done—you're all free."

As we started for the door, Sanderson shook hands with the man he'd been talking with, and hurried after us. It was almost dawn and the sky was a light grey. Except for a few people around the police station, the streets were calm and empty. A few big freighters stood at anchor in the bay, waiting for morning and the tugboats that would bring them in.

By the time we got to the street, I could see the first rays of the sun, a cool pink glow in the eastern sky. The fact that I'd spent all night in a cell and a courtroom made that morning one of the most beautiful I've ever seen. There was a peace and a brightness about it, a chilly Caribbean dawn after a night in a filthy jail. I looked out at the ships and the sea beyond them, and I felt crazy to be free with a whole day ahead of me.

Then I realized I would sleep most of the day, and my excitement disappeared. Sanderson agreed to drop us at the apartment and we said good night to Moberg, who was going off to look for his car. He'd forgotten where he'd left it, but he assured us it was no problem. "I'll find it by the smell," he said. "I can smell it for blocks." And he shuffled off down the street, a small figure in a dirty grey suit, sniffing for his car.

Sanderson later explained that Moberg had first called Lotterman, who was not home, then Quinones, who was in Miami. Then he had called Segarra, who told him to sign a check for what he assumed would be small fines. Sanderson had been at Segarra's house, just ready to leave when Moberg called, and he had stopped by the court on his way home.

"Damn good you did," I said. "We'd be back in that goddamn dungeon if you hadn't come."

Yeamon and Sala mumbled agreement.

"Enjoy it while you can," Sanderson replied. "You won't be out for long."

We rode the rest of the way in silence. As we passed the Plaza Colón I heard the first sounds of morning—a bus beginning its run, the shouts of early fruit peddlers—and from somewhere up on the hill came the wail of a police siren.

Nine

AFTER only a few hours of sleep, I was awakened by a great shout. It was Sala, sprung up as if from a nightmare. "Mother of balls!" he yelled. "The car! The vultures!"

After a moment of confusion I remembered that we had left his car on the road near Casa Cabrones. The Puerto Ricans take a real interest in abandoned cars—they set upon them like hungry animals and tear them apart. First go the hubcaps, then the wheels, then the bumpers and doors, and finally they haul away the carcass—twenty or thirty of them, like ants dragging a dead beetle, hauling it off to some junk dealer for ten *yanqui* dollars, then fighting with knives and broken bottles for shares of the money.

Yeamon woke up slowly, groaning with pain. Around his mouth was a crust of dried blood. He sat up on the mattress and stared at us.

"Wake up," I said. "Your scooter's out there too."

Sala swung his legs over the edge of the cot. "It's too late. They've had twelve hours—Christ, they can strip a car in twelve minutes. We'll be lucky to find an oil spot."

"Gone?" said Yeamon. He was still staring at us, not quite awake.

I nodded. "Probably."

"Well by God let's get out there!" he exclaimed, leaping off the mattress. "Catch 'em and smash a few teeth!"

"No hurry," said Sala. "It's all over by now." He stood up and flexed his back. "Jesus, it feels like I've been stabbed." He came over to me. "What's wrong with my shoulder—is that a knife hole back there?"

"No," I told him. "Just a scrape—maybe a fingernail."

He cursed and went into the bathroom for a shower.

Yeamon had already washed his face and was hurriedly getting dressed. "Let's hustle," he said. "We'll take a cab." He opened one of the windows and let in some light.

Reluctantly, I began to dress. There were bruises all over my body and it was painful to move. I wanted to go back to bed and sleep all day, but I could see there was no hope for it.

We walked several blocks down to the Plaza Colón and got a cab. Yeamon told the driver where to go.

I had never seen the city on a Sunday morning. Usually I got up about noon and went to Al's for a long breakfast. Now the streets were almost empty. There was no sign of the weekday chaos, the screech and roar of an army of salesmen careening through town in uninsured cars. The waterfront was nearly deserted, the stores were closed, and only the churches seemed to be doing any business. We passed several of them, and in front of each one was a colorful knot of people—tan-skinned men and boys in freshly pressed suits, flowery women with veils, little girls in white dresses, and here and there a priest in a black robe and a tall black hat.

Then we sped across the long causeway to Condado. Things were different here. I saw no churches and the sidewalks were full of tourists in sandals and bright bermuda shorts. They streamed in and out of the big hotels, chattering, reading papers, carrying satchels, all wearing sunglasses and looking very busy.

Yeamon mopped his face with a handkerchief. "Man," he said, "I don't think I can stand to lose that scooter. Jesus—fired, beaten, arrested . . ."

I nodded and Sala said nothing. He was leaning over the driver's shoulder, as if he expected at any moment to catch sight of a mob dismantling his car.

After what seemed like hours we turned off the airport road and onto the narrow lane to Casa Cabrones. We were still several hundred yards away when I saw Sala's car. "There it is," I said, pointing up the road.

"Christ," he muttered. "A miracle."

As we pulled up to it I realized it was sitting on two coconut logs, instead of its wheels. They were gone, and so was Yeamon's scooter.

Sala took it calmly. "Well—better than I thought." He got into the car and checked around. "Nothing gone but the wheels—damn lucky."

Yeamon was in a rage. "I'll recognize that thing!" he shouted. "One of these days I'll catch somebody riding it."

I was sure we were due for more trouble if we hung around Casa Cabrones. The thought of another beating made me nervous. I walked a few hundred feet toward the bar, looking to see if anyone was coming. It was closed and the parking lot was empty.

On the way back to the car, I saw something red in the bushes beside the driveway. It was Yeamon's scooter, covered with a layer of palm fronds. Someone had hidden it, intending to pick it up later.

I called him and he dragged it out. Nothing was missing. He kicked it over and it started perfectly. "Damn," he said. "I should sit here and wait for that punk to come back for it—give him a little surprise."

"Sure," I said. "Then spend the summer in La Princesa. Come on—let's get out of here."

Back at the car, Sala was figuring up the cost of four new tires and wheels. He looked very depressed.

"Let's get some breakfast," said Yeamon. "I've got to have food."

"Are you nuts?" Sala replied. "I can't leave this car—they'll finish it off." He reached into his wallet. "Here," he said to Yeamon. "Go down to that gas station and call the Fiat dealer and tell him to send four wheels. Here's his home phone—tell him it's for Mr. Lotterman."

Yeamon took the card and clattered off down the road. In a few minutes we heard him coming back. Then we sat for an hour until the wrecker arrived. To my surprise, the man had sent four wheels. We put them on, Sala signed Lotterman's name to a ticket, and then we drove in to the Long Beach Hotel for breakfast. Yeamon followed on his scooter.

The patio was crowded, so we sat inside at the snack bar. All around us were people I had spent ten years avoiding—shapeless women in wool bathing suits, dull-eyed men with hairless legs and self-conscious laughs, all Americans, all fearsomely alike. These people should be kept at home, I thought; lock them in the basement of some goddamn Elks Club and keep them pacified with erotic movies; if they want a vacation, show them a foreign art film; and if they still aren't satisfied, send them into the wilderness and run them with vicious dogs.

I glared at them, trying to eat the rotten breakfast the waitress had put in front of me—slimy eggs, fat bacon and weak American coffee.

"Goddamnit," I said. "This isn't Nedick's—don't you have Puerto Rican coffee?"

She shook her head.

Sala went out and bought a *Miami Herald.* "I like this place," he said with a grin. "I like to sit up here and look down at the beach and think of all the good things I could do with a Luger."

I put two dollars on the table and got up.

"Where are you going?" Yeamon asked, looking up from a part of the paper he had taken from Sala.

"I don't know," I said. "Probably Sanderson's. Anyplace where I can get away from these people."

Sala looked up. "You and Sanderson are pretty good buddies," he said with a smile.

I was too intent on leaving to pay any attention to him, but after I got out in the street I realized that he'd meant to be insulting. I guessed he was bitter because my bail was so much smaller than his. Hell with him, I thought. Sanderson had nothing to do with it.

Several blocks up the street I stopped at an outdoor restaurant for some Puerto Rican coffee. I bought a *New York Times* for seventy cents. It made me feel better, reminding me that a big familiar world was going about its business just over the horizon. I had another cup of coffee and took the *Times* with me when I left, lugging it along the street like a precious bundle of wisdom, a weighty assurance that I was not yet cut off from that part of the world that was real.

It took me a half hour to get to Sanderson's, but the walk was along the beach and I enjoyed it. When I got there I found him stretched out in his garden on a plastic sun pad. He looked thinner than he did when he was dressed.

"Hello, slugger," he said. "How was jail?"

"Horrible," I said.

"Well," he replied, "next time it will be worse. You will be a marked man."

I stared at him, wondering what sort of twisted humor he was practicing on me.

Sanderson propped himself up on his elbows and lit a cigarette. "What started it?" he asked.

I told him, deleting a few minor points here and there, categorically denying what little I knew of the official version.

I leaned back in the chair, looking out at the white beach and the sea and the palms all around us, and thinking how strange it was to be worried about jail in a place like this. It seemed almost impossible that a man could go to the Caribbean and be put in jail for some silly misdemeanor. Puerto Rican jails were for Puerto Ricans—not Americans who wore paisley ties and button-down shirts.

"Why was your bail so much lower," he asked, "did They start the trouble?"

Here it was again. I was beginning to wish they had charged me with something brutal, like "violent assault," or "mauling an officer."

"Hell, I don't know," I said.

"You're lucky," he said. "You can get a year in jail for resisting arrest."

"Well," I said, trying to change the subject, "I think your speech saved the day—they didn't seem very impressed when we said we worked for the *News*."

He lit another cigarette. "No, that wouldn't impress anybody." He looked up again. "But don't think I lied for you. The *Times* is looking for a travel stringer down here and they asked me to find somebody. As of tomorrow, you're it."

I shrugged. "Fine."

I went inside for another drink. While I was in the kitchen I heard a car drive up. It was Segarra, dressed like some gigolo on the Italian Riviera. He nodded stiffly as he came through the door. "Good afternoon, Paul. What was all the trouble last night?"

"I don't remember," I said, pouring my drink down the sink. "Get Hal to tell you. I have to go."

He gave me a disapproving glance, then went through the house to the garden. I went to the door to tell Sanderson I was leaving.

"Come by the office tomorrow," he said. "We'll talk about your new job."

Segarra looked puzzled.

Sanderson smiled at him. "Stealing another one of your boys," he said.

Segarra frowned and sat down. "Fine. Take all of them."

I left and walked out to Calle Modesto, wondering how to kill the rest of the day. It was always a problem. Sunday was my day off and usually I had Saturday too. But I was getting tired of riding around with Sala or sitting at Al's, and there was nothing else to do. I wanted to get out on the island, look at some of the other towns, but for that I needed a car.

Not just a car, I thought, I need an apartment too. It was a hot afternoon and I was tired and sore. I wanted to sleep, or at least rest, but there was no place to go. I walked for several blocks, ambling along in the shade of the big flamboyan trees, thinking of all the things I might be doing in New York or London, cursing the warped impulse that had brought me to this dull and steaming rock, and finally I stopped at a native bar to get a beer. I paid for the bottle and took it with me, sipping it as I walked along the street. I wondered where I could sleep. Sala's apartment was out of the question. It was hot and noisy and depressing as a tomb. Maybe Yeamon's, I thought, but it was too far out and there was no way to get there. When I finally faced the fact that I had no choice but to walk the streets, I decided to start looking for my own apartment—a place where I could relax by myself and have my own refrigerator and make my own drinks and maybe even take a girl once in a while. The idea of having my own bed in my own apartment cheered me so much that I felt anxious to be rid of this day and get on to the next, so I could begin looking.

I realized that to tie myself down with an apartment and perhaps a car was more of a commitment than I wanted to make right now—especially since I might be hauled off to jail at any moment, or the paper might fold, or I might get a letter from some old friend about a job in Buenos Aires. Just yesterday, for that matter, I'd been ready to go to Mexico City.

But I knew I was coming to a point where I would have to make up my mind about Puerto Rico. I had been here three months and it seemed like three weeks. So far, there was nothing to get hold of, none of the real pros and cons I had found in other places. All the while I had been in San Juan I'd condemned it without really disliking it. I felt that sooner or later I would see that third dimension, that depth that makes a city real and that you never see until you've been there awhile. But the longer I stayed, the more I came to suspect that for the first time in my life I had come to a place where this vital dimension didn't exist, or was too nebulous to make any difference. Maybe, God forbid, the place was what it appeared to be—a melange of Okies and thieves and bewildered jíbaros.

I walked for more than a mile, thinking, smoking, sweating, peering over tall hedges and into low windows on the street, listening to the roar of the buses and the constant barking of stray dogs, seeing almost no one but the people who passed me in crowded autos, heading for God knows where—whole families jammed in cars, just driving around the city, honking, yelling, stopping now and then to buy pastillos and a shot of coco frío, then getting back in the car and moving on, forever looking, wondering, marveling at all the fine things the *yanquis* were doing to the city: Here was an office building going up, ten stories tall—here was a new highway, leading nowhere—and of course there were always the new hotels to look at, or you could watch the *yanqui* women on the beach—and at night, if you arrived early enough to get a good seat, there was *televisión* in the public squares.

I kept walking, more frustrated with every step. Finally, in desperation, I hailed a cab and went to the Caribé Hilton, where they were staging an international tennis tournament. I used my press card to get in and sat in the stands the rest of the afternoon.

The sun didn't bother me here. It seemed to belong with the clay courts and the gin and the white ball zipping back and forth. I remembered other tennis courts and long-gone days full of sun and gin and people I would never see again because we could no longer talk to each other without sounding dull and disappointed. I sat there in the grandstand, hearing the swack of the furry ball and knowing it would never sound like it did on those days when I knew who was playing, and cared.

The match was over at dusk and I took a cab up to Al's. Sala was there, sitting alone at a corner table. I saw Sweep on the way to the patio and told him to bring two rums and three hamburgers. Sala looked up as I approached.

"You have that fugitive look," he said. "A man on the run."

"I talked to Sanderson," I said. "He thinks it may not come to court—or if it does it might take three years."

The moment I said this I regretted it. Now we would get into the subject of my bail again. Before he could reply I held up my hands. "Forget it," I said. "Let's talk about something else."

He shrugged. "Christ, I can't think of anything that isn't depressing or threatening. I feel hemmed in by disaster."

"Where's Yeamon?" I asked.

"He went home," he replied. "Right after you left he remembered Chenault was still locked in the hut."

Sweep arrived with our drinks and food and I took them off the tray.

"I think he's crazy as a loon," Sala exclaimed.

"You're right," I replied. "God knows how he'll end up. You can't just go through life like that—never giving an inch, anytime, anywhere."

Just then Bill Donovan, the sports editor, came howling up to the table.

"Here they are!" he shouted. "The gentlemen of the press—sneak drinkers!" He laughed happily. "You fuckers really tied one on last night, eh? Man, you're lucky Lotterman went to Ponce!" He sat down at the table. "What happened? I hear you had it out with the cops."

"Yeah," I said. "Beat the piss out of 'em—real laughs."

"Goddamnit," he said, "Sorry I missed it. I love a good fight—especially with cops."

We talked for a while. I liked Donovan, but he was forever talking about getting back to San Francisco, "where things are happening." He made it sound so good on the Coast that I knew he had to be lying, but I could never tell just where the truth ended and the lies began. If even half of what he said was true, then I wanted to go there immediately; but with Donovan I couldn't even count on that necessary half, and listening to him was always frustrating.

We left about midnight and walked down the hill in silence. The night was muggy, and all around me I felt the same pressure, a sense of time rushing by while it seemed to be standing still. Whenever I thought of time in Puerto Rico, I was reminded of those old magnetic clocks that hung on the walls of my classrooms in high school. Every now and then a hand would not move for several minutes—and if I watched it long enough, wondering if it had finally broken down, the sudden click of the hand jumping three or four notches would startle me when it came.

Ten

SANDERSON'S office was on the top floor of the tallest building in the Old City. I sat in a leather lounge chair, and below me I could see the entire waterfront, the Caribé Hilton and most of Condado. There was a definite feeling of being in a control tower.

Sanderson had his feet on the window sill. "Two things," he was saying. "This business with the *Times* won't amount to much—a few articles a year—but Zimburger's project is a big one."

"Zimburger?" I said.

He nodded. "I didn't want to mention it yesterday because he might have dropped in."

"Wait a minute," I said. "Are we talking about the same Zimburger—the General?"

He looked annoyed. "That's right, he's one of our clients."

"Damn," I said. "Business must be falling off. The man's a jackass."

He rolled a pencil in his fingers. "Kemp," he said slowly, "Mister Zimburger is building a marina—a damn big one." He paused. "He's also going to build one of the finest hotels on the island."

I laughed and fell back in the chair.

"Look," he said sharply, "you've been here long enough to begin learning a few things, and one of the first things you should learn is that money comes in odd packages." He tapped his pencil on the desk. "Zimburger—known to you as 'the jackass'—could buy and sell you thirty times. If you insist on going by appearances you'd be better off in some place like Texas."

I laughed again. "You may be right. Now why don't you tell me what you have in mind. I'm in a hurry."

"One of these days," he said, "this silly arrogance of yours is going to cost you a lot of money."

"Goddamnit," I replied, "I didn't come here to be analyzed."

He smiled stiffly. "All right. The *Times* wants a general article for their spring travel section. Mrs. Ludwig will get some material together for you—I'll tell her what you need."

"What do they want?" I said. "A thousand happy words?"

"More or less," he replied. "We'll handle the photos."

"Okay," I said. "That's a back-breaker—now what about Zimburger?"

"Well," he said. "Mister Zimburger wants a brochure. He's building a marina on Vieques island, between here and St. Thomas. We'll get the photos and do the layout—you write the text, about fifteen hundred words."

"What will he pay?" I asked.

"He won't," Sanderson replied. "He'll pay us a flat fee—we'll pay you twenty-five dollars a day, plus expenses. You'll have to make a trip to Vieques, probably with Zimburger."

"Jesus," I said.

He smiled. "No real hurry. Let's say next Friday."

"The brochure will be aimed at investors," he added. "This is one hell of a big marina—two hotels, a hundred cottages, the whole works."

"Where did Zimburger get his money?" I asked.

He shook his head. "It's not just Zimburger. He has several people with him on this—as a matter of fact, he asked me in on it."

"What stopped you?"

He swung around to face the window again. "I'm not ready to retire yet. This is a pretty interesting place to work."

"I'll bet it is," I said. "What's your cut here—ten percent of every dollar invested on the island?"

He grinned. "You think like a mercenary, Paul. We're here to help, to keep the wheels turning."

I got up to go. "I'll come by tomorrow and pick up the stuff."

"How about lunch?" he said, looking at his watch. "It's about that time."

"Sorry," I said. "I have to run."

He smiled. "Late for work?"

"That's right," I said. "I have to get back and work on an exposé."

"Don't let your boy scout ethics run away with you," he said, still smiling. "Oh yes—while we're on the subject of scouts, tell your friend Yeamon to stop by when he gets a chance. I have something for him."

I nodded. "Put him to work with Zimburger. They'd get along fine."

When I got back to the office Sala called me over to his desk and showed me a copy of *El Diario*. On the front page was a picture of the three of us. I hardly recognized myself—slit-eyed, sneaky-looking, hunched on the bench like a hardened criminal. Sala looked drunk and Yeamon looked like a maniac.

"When did they get this?" I said.

"I don't remember," he replied. "But they damn well got it."

Underneath the photo was a small story. "What's it say?" I asked.

"Same thing the cop said," he replied. "We'll be lucky if we aren't lynched."

"Has Lotterman said anything?"

"He's still in Ponce."

I was beginning to get the fear. "You better carry a gun," Moberg advised me. "They'll be after you now. I know those swine—they'll try to kill you." By six o'clock I was so depressed that I gave up trying to work, and went to Al's.

Just as I turned onto Calle O'Leary I heard Yeamon's scooter approaching from the opposite direction. It made a hellish sound in those narrow streets and you could hear it six blocks away. We arrived in front of Al's at the same time. Chenault was riding on the back, and she hopped off while he cut the engine. They both seemed drunk. On the way back to the patio we ordered hamburgers and rum.

"Things are getting worse," I said, pulling up a chair for Chenault.

Yeamon scowled. "That bastard Lotterman dodged the hearing today. It was a hell of a thing—those people at the Labor Department saw our picture in *El Diario*. I'm sort of glad Lotterman didn't show. He might have won today."

"No wonder," I said. "That was a very ugly photograph." I shook my head. "Lotterman's in Ponce—we're lucky."

"Damnit," he said. "I need that money this weekend. We're going over to St. Thomas for the carnival."

"Oh yeah," I said. "I've heard about that—it's supposed to be pretty wild."

"I've heard it's wonderful!" Chenault exclaimed. "It's supposed to be as good as the one in Trinidad."

"Why don't you come with us?" Yeamon suggested. "Tell Lotterman you want to do the story."

"I'd like to," I said. "San Juan is driving me nuts."

Yeamon started to say something, but Chenault cut him off. "What time is it?" she said anxiously.

I looked at my watch. "Almost seven."

She quickly stood up. "I have to go—it starts at seven." She picked up her purse and started toward the door. "I'll be back in an hour," she called. "Don't get too drunk."

I looked at Yeamon.

"There's some kind of a ceremony going on at the big cathedral," he said wearily. "God only knows what it is, but she has to see it."

I smiled and shook my head.

He nodded. "Yeah, it's hell. I'm damned if I know what to do with her."

"Do with her?" I said.

"Yeah, I've about decided this place is rotten to the core and I should get out."

"Oh," I said. "That reminds me. Sanderson has some kind of

work for you—writing travel articles. His integrity demands that he justify what he said about us the other night."

He groaned. "Christ, travel articles. How low can a man fall?"

"Figure that out with Sanderson," I said. "He wants you to call him."

He leaned back and stared at the wall, saying nothing for several moments. "His integrity," he said finally, as if he'd been dissecting the word. "It seems to me that a guy like Sanderson has about as much integrity as a Judas Goat."

I sipped my drink.

"What makes you deal with a guy like that?" he asked. "You're always going over there—is there something to him that I can't see?"

"I don't know," I said. "What do you see?"

"Not much," he replied. "I know what Sala says—he claims he's queer—and of course he's a phony and a prick and God knows what else." He paused. "But Sala just tosses words around: Phony, Prick, Queer—so what? I'm curious as to what the hell you see in the guy."

Now I understood Sala's crack at breakfast the other day. And I felt that whatever I said about Sanderson now would be crucial—not for Sanderson, but for me. Because I knew why I dealt with him and most of my reasons were pretty small—he was in and I was out, and he looked like a pretty good pipeline to a lot of things I wanted. On the other hand, there was something about him that I liked. Perhaps it was Sanderson's struggle with himself that fascinated me—the hardnose man of the world, gradually blotting out the boy from Kansas. I remembered him telling me that the Hal Sanderson from Kansas had died when his train got to New York—and any man who can say a thing like that, and attempt to say it with pride, is worth listening to unless you have something a hell of a lot better to do with your time.

Yeamon's voice snapped me out of my pondering. "Okay," he said with a wave of his hand, "if you give it that much thought there's bound to be something to it, but I still think he's rotten."

"You think too much," I said.

"Got to think all the time," he muttered. "That's my trouble—I take vacations from thinking." He nodded. "It works out the same way as all the other vacations—you relax for two weeks, then spend fifty weeks making up for it."

"I don't quite follow you," I said.

He smiled. "You interrupted me. We were talking about Chenault—and all of a sudden you brought up the Judas Goat."

"Okay," I said. "What about her? Is this your way of saying you're going to leave her with me?"

He tapped the table with his fingers. "Kemp, I'd rather you wouldn't say things like that. I'm pretty square when it comes to trading girls around, especially a girl I like." He said it calmly, but I could hear the edge in his voice.

I shook my head. "You're an inconsistent bastard—that's the last thing I'd expect to hear from you."

"I'm not much on consistency," he said, talking easily again. "No, I was just thinking out loud—I don't do that very often."

"I know," I said.

He sipped his drink. "I spent all day yesterday thinking," he said. "I should leave this place, and I don't know what to do about Chenault."

"Where do you figure on going?" I asked.

He shrugged. "I don't know—maybe down the islands, maybe Europe."

"Europe's not bad," I said. "If you have a job."

"I won't," he said.

"No," I agreed. "You probably won't."

"That's what I was thinking about," he said. "And I wondered why the hell I wanted to go to Europe, anyway—why should I?"

I shrugged. "Why not?"

"You know," said Yeamon, "I haven't been home in three years, but the last time I was there, I spent a lot of time in the woods."

"You're losing me again," I said. "I don't even know where you're from."

"A place called London, Kentucky," he said. "Laurel County—a fine place to disappear."

"You planning on disappearing?" I asked.

He nodded. "Could be. Not in Laurel County, though." He paused. "My father decided to play games with his money, and we lost the farm."

I lit a cigarette.

"It was a fine place," he said. "A man could go out there and shoot all day and run his dogs and raise all manner of hell, and not a soul in the world would bother him."

"Yeah," I said. "I did some hunting around St. Louis."

He leaned back and stared into his drink. "I got to thinking about that yesterday, and it gave me the idea that I might be on the wrong track."

"How's that?" I said.

"I'm not sure," he replied. "But I have a feeling that I'm following a course that somebody laid out a long time ago—and I have one hell of a lot of company."

I looked up at the plantain tree and let him go on.

"You're the same way," he said. "We're all going to the same damn places, doing the same damn things people have been doing for fifty years, and we keep waiting for something to happen." He looked up. "You know—I'm a rebel, I took off—now where's my reward?"

"You fool," I said. "There is no reward and there never was."

"Jesus," he said. "That's horrible." He raised the bottle to his lips and finished it off. "We're just drunkards," he said, "helpless drunkards. To hell with it—I'll go back to some Godforsaken little town and be a fireman."

I laughed, and just then Chenault came back. We sat in the patio and drank for several hours until Yeamon stood up and said they were going home. "Think about that St. Thomas thing," he said. "We might as well play the game while we can."

"Why not?" I muttered. "I'll probably go. Might be the last fun I'll have."

Chenault waved goodbye and followed Yeamon out to the street.

I sat there for a while, but it was too depressing. Between Yeamon's talk and my picture in *El Diario,* I was beginning to feel suicidal. My skin felt creepy and I began to wonder if maybe all this drinking was getting the best of me. Then I remembered a story the *News* had run last week about an epidemic of parasites in the local water supply, little worms that destroy the intestines. Jesus, I thought, I better get out of here. I paid my tab and bolted out to the street and looked up and down, wondering where I could go. I was afraid to walk, for fear of being recognized and beaten by an angry mob—but the thought of going home to the nest of fleas and poison crab lice I had been sleeping in for three months filled me with terror. Finally, I took a cab to the Caribé Hilton. I sat at the bar for an hour or so, hoping to meet a girl who'd invite me up to her room, but the only person I met was a football coach from Atlanta who wanted me to walk on the beach. I told him I would, but first I had to borrow a meat-whip from the kitchen.

"What for?" he asked.

I stared at him. "Don't you want to be flogged?"

He laughed nervously.

"You wait here," I said. "I'll get the whip." I got up and went to the restroom, and when I returned he was gone.

There were no girls in the bar—only middle-aged women and bald men in dinner jackets. I was shaking. Jesus, I thought, maybe I'm getting the DTs. I drank as fast as I could, trying to get drunk. More and more people seemed to be staring at me. But I couldn't speak. I felt lonely and exposed. I stumbled out to the street and flagged a cab. I was too crazed to check into a hotel. There was no place to go but that filthy roach-infested apartment. It was the only home I had.

I turned on the lights and opened the windows, then I made a large drink and stretched out on the cot to read my magazine. There was a faint breeze, but the noise from the street was so terrible that I gave up trying to read and turned out the lights. People kept passing on the sidewalk and looking in, and now that they couldn't see me I expected looters to come crawling through the window at any moment. I lay back on the cot with a bottle of rum resting on my navel and plotted how to defend myself.

If I had a Luger, I thought, I could drill the bastards. I leaned on one elbow and pointed a finger at the window, seeing what kind of a shot I would get. Perfect. There was just enough light in the street for a good silhouette. I knew it would happen quickly, I'd have no choice: just pull the trigger and go deaf from the terrible noise, a frenzy of screaming and scratching followed by the ghastly thump of a body knocked back and down to the sidewalk. There would be a mob, of course, and I'd probably have to shoot a few in self-defense. Then the cops would arrive and that would be it. They'd recognize me and probably kill me right there in the apartment.

Jesus, I thought, I'm doomed. I'll never get out of here alive.

I thought I saw things moving on the ceiling and voices in the alley were calling my name. I began to tremble and sweat, and then I fell into a twisted delirium.

Eleven

T HAT night finished me with Sala's tomb. The next morning
I got up early and went out to Condado to seek an apartment. I wanted sunlight and clean sheets and a refrigerator where I could keep beer and orange juice, food in the pantry
and books on the shelves so I could stay home once in a while, a
breeze coming in through the window and a peaceful street outside, an address that sounded human—instead of c/o or Gen. Del. or
Please Forward or Hold for Arrival.

A ten-year accumulation of these vagrant addresses can weigh
on a man like a hex. He begins to feel like the Wandering Jew.
That's the way I felt. After one night too many sleeping on some
stinking cot in a foul grotto where I didn't want to be anyway and
had no reason to be except that it was foreign and cheap, I decided
to hell with it. If that was absolute freedom then I'd had a bellyful
of it, and from here on in I would try something a little less pure
and one hell of a lot more comfortable. I was not only going to have
an address, but I was going to have a car, and if there was anything
else to be had in the way of large and stabilizing influences, I would
have those too.

There were several apartments advertised in the paper, but the
first few I looked at were too expensive. Finally I found one over

somebody's garage. It was just what I wanted—plenty of air, a big flamboyan tree for shade, bamboo furniture and a new refrigerator.

The woman wanted a hundred, but when I said seventy-five she quickly agreed. I had seen a big "51" sticker on a car in front of her house and she told me that she and her husband were going all out for statehood. They owned La Bomba Café in San Juan. Did I know it? Indeed I did—knew it well, ate there often, incomparable food for the price. I told her I worked for the *New York Times* and would be in San Juan for a year, writing a series of stories about statehood for Puerto Rico. For this, I would need absolute privacy.

We grinned at each other and I gave her a month's rent in advance. When she asked for another seventy-five on deposit I told her I'd get my expense check next week and would pay her then. She smiled graciously and I left before she could dun me for anything else.

Knowing I had a place of my own cheered me immensely. Even if I was fired I had enough in the bank to rest for a while, and with Sanderson shelling out twenty-five bills a day I would have no worries at all.

I walked out to Avenida Ashford and took a bus to the office. Halfway there, I remembered that this was my day off, but I wanted to check my mail so I went in. As I crossed the newsroom toward the mail slots, Sala called me from the darkroom.

"Man," he said, "you should have been here earlier. Lotterman found out about Moberg signing that check for our bail—tried to croak him with a pair of scissors, chased him all the way down to the street." He nodded. "It was hell. I thought Moberg was a goner."

"Good God," I muttered. "What about the check—is it still good?"

"I guess so," he replied. "He'll lose face if it bounces."

I nodded doubtfully. This screwed my plan to get a car. I was going to borrow money from Lotterman and pay it back out of my salary at ten or fifteen a week. I was standing there by the darkroom, racking my brain for alternatives, when Lotterman popped out of his office and called me.

"I want to see you," he barked. "You too, Sala—don't try to duck back in there."

Sala ignored him and went into the darkroom. Seconds later he appeared with a pack of cigarettes. "Duck, hell!" he snorted, loud enough for Lotterman and everybody else to hear. "The day I have to duck a punk like that I'll toss in the towel."

As it happened, Lotterman heard nothing. I had never seen him in such a state. He tried to sound angry, but he seemed more confused than anything else, and after listening to him for a few moments I had the impression that he was on the verge of dissolving into some kind of apoplexy.

He started off by telling us what a terrible thing it was for "that goddamn crazy Yeamon" to get us into trouble. "And then Moberg," he said with a groan. "Moberg, that crazy worthless sot, he's been stealing from me." He whacked the desk with his fist. "That sleazy drunken cockroach of a man who goes out and puts the slam on me for twenty-three hundred dollars!" He stared up at us. "Can you boys understand what that does to my bank balance? Do you have any idea what it costs to keep this paper going?" He fell back in the chair. "Good Lord, I've put my life savings on the line for the simple reason that I believe in journalism—and here this odious, pus-filled roach goes out and tries to destroy me with one blow.

"And Yeamon!" he shouted. "I knew it the minute I saw him! I said to myself, Christ, get rid of this guy quick—he's pure trouble." He shook a warning finger at us. "I want you to stay away from him, understand? What the hell is he doing here anyway? Why doesn't he go back where he came from? What's he living on?"

We both shrugged. "I think he has a trust fund," I said. "He's been talking about investing some money."

"God almighty!" Lotterman exclaimed. "That's just the kind we don't want here!" He shook his head. "And he had the nerve to tell me he was broke—borrowed a hundred dollars and threw it away on a motorcycle—can you beat that?"

I couldn't beat it and neither could Sala.

"Now he's hounding me for blood money," Lotterman went on. "By God, we'll see." He slumped back in the chair again. "It's almost too horrible to believe," he said. "I've just paid a thousand dollars to get him out of jail—a dangerous nut who threatened to twist my head. And Moberg," he muttered. "Where did he come from?" He shook his head and waved us out of the office. "Go on," he said. "Tell Moberg I'm going to have him locked up."

As we started to go he remembered something else. "Wait a minute," he called. "I don't want you boys to think I *wouldn't* have got you out of jail. Of course I would—you know that, don't you?"

We assured him that we did, and left him mumbling at his desk. I went back to the library and sat down to think. I was going to have a car, regardless of what I had to do to get it. I'd seen a Volkswagen convertible for five hundred and it seemed in pretty good shape. Considering the fantastic price of cars in San Juan, it would be a real bargain if I could get it for four hundred.

I called Sanderson. "Say," I said casually, "what's the least I'll get out of this Zimburger deal?"

"Why?" he asked.

"I want an advance. I need a car."

He laughed. "You don't need a car—you want a car. How much do you need?"

"About a thousand," I said. "I'm not greedy."

"You must be out of your mind," he replied. "The best I could do under any circumstances would be two fifty."

"Okay," I said. "It's a drop in the bucket, but it might help. When can I get it?"

"Tomorrow morning," he said. "Zimburger's coming in and I think we should get together and set this thing up. I don't want to do it at home." He paused. "Can you come in around ten?"

"Okay," I said. "See you then."

When I put down the phone I realized I was preparing to make the plunge. I would move into my own apartment at the end of the week, and now I was about to buy a car. San Juan was getting a grip on me. I hadn't had a car in five years—not since the old Citroën I bought in Paris for twenty-five dollars, and sold a year later for ten, after driving it all over Europe. Now I was ready to shoot four hundred on a Volkswagen. If nothing else, it gave me a sense of moving up in the world, for good or ill.

On my way to Sanderson's the next day I stopped at the lot where I'd seen the car. The office was empty, and on a wall above one of the desks was a sign saying "SELL—NOTHING HAPPENS UNTIL SOMEBODY SELLS SOMETHING."

I found the dealer outside. "Get this one ready to go," I said, pointing to the convertible. "I'll give you four hundred for it at noon."

He shook his head. "Five hundred dollars," he said, lifting the sign on the windshield as if I'd overlooked it.

"Nonsense," I replied. "You know the rules—nothing happens until somebody sells something."

He looked surprised, but the slogan had registered.

"The fat is in the fire," I said, turning to go. "I'll be back at noon to pick it up."

He stared after me as I hurried out to the street.

Zimburger was already there when I got to Sanderson's office. He was wearing a bright blue suit and a red shirt with no tie. At a glance, he looked like a wax dummy in the window of some moldy PX. After twenty years in The Corps, Zimburger felt uneasy in civilian clothes. "Too damn baggy," he explained. "Cheap workmanship, flimsy material."

He nodded emphatically. "Nobody keeps an eye on things anymore. It's the law of the tooth and the fang."

Sanderson came in from the outer office. He was dressed, as usual, like the resident governor of Pago Pago. This time he was wearing a black silk suit with a bow tie.

Zimburger looked like an off-duty prison guard, a sweating potbellied vet who had somehow scraped up a wad of money.

"All right," he said. "Let's get down to business. Is this guy the writer?" He pointed at me.

"This is Paul Kemp," said Sanderson. "You've seen him at the house."

Zimburger nodded. "Yeah, I know."

"Mr. Kemp writes for the *New York times*," said Sanderson. "We're lucky to have him with us on this."

Zimburger looked at me with renewed interest. "A real writer, eh? I guess that means trouble." He laughed. "I knew writers in the Marines—they were all trouble. Hell, I used to be one myself. They had me writing training manuals for six months—dullest damn work I ever did."

Sanderson leaned back in his chair and put his feet on the desk.

"Kemp will go over to Vieques with you whenever it's convenient," he said. "He wants to look at the site."

"Hell yes!" Zimburger replied. "It'll knock his eyes out—not a better beach in the Caribbean." He turned to me. "You'll get some real material out of this place. Nobody's ever done a story on Vieques—especially the *New York Times*."

"Sounds good," I said. "When do you want to go?"

"How about tomorrow?" he said quickly.

"Too soon," Sanderson told him. "Kemp is doing a job for the *News* right now. Why not make it this weekend?"

"Fine with me," Zimburger replied. "I'll line up a plane for Thursday." He looked at his watch and stood up. "I'm off," he said. "Hell, it's almost noon and I haven't made any money—wasted half the day." He looked at me and gave me a snappy salute, grinning as he hurried out the door.

I took a crowded elevator down to the street and hailed a cab. At the car lot the salesman was waiting for me. I greeted him cordially and paid him in cash for the car and quickly drove it away. It was yellow, with a black top and good tires and an AM/FM radio.

It was almost one, so I went straight to the paper instead of stopping at Al's for lunch.

I spent all afternoon at police headquarters, talking to a man who had killed his daughter.

"Why?" I asked him, as several cops looked on and Sala snapped his picture.

He yelled something in Spanish and the cops told me he thought his daughter was "no good." She wanted to go to New York. She was only thirteen, but he claimed she'd been whoring for the price of a plane ticket.

"Okay," I said. "Muchas gracias." I had enough for a story and the cops took him away. I wondered how long he would stay in jail before the trial. Probably two or three years, considering he'd already confessed. Hell, what was the sense of a trial; the docket was crowded enough.

And a damn good thing it is, I thought. All afternoon I had a feeling that cops were giving us the eye, but I couldn't be sure.

We went up to Al's for dinner. Yeamon was there in the patio and I told him about Lotterman's outburst.

"Yeah," he said. "I thought about that on the way in to see the lawyer." He shook his head. "Hell, I didn't even go. He has me now—did he say anything about canceling my bail?"

"He won't," said Sala. "It would make him look bad—unless he figures you're about to skip out."

"I am," said Yeamon. "We're going to South America."

"Both of you?" I said.

He nodded. "We may have to wait awhile now," he said. "I was counting on that severance money."

"Did you call Sanderson?" I asked.

He shook his head.

"Call him," I said. "He has green money. I bought a new car today."

He laughed. "I'll be damned. Is it here?"

"Hell yes," I said. We went out to the street to look at the car. Yeamon agreed that it had a fine, sporting appearance.

"But you know what it means," he said with a grin. "You're hooked. First a job, then a car—pretty soon you'll get married and settle in for good." He laughed. "You'll get like old Robert—always going to take off mañana."

"Don't worry," Sala replied. "I'll know when to take off. When you get to be a working pro, then come back and tell me how to manage my life."

We started back inside. "What's a working pro, Robert?" Yeamon asked. "Somebody who has a job?"

"Somebody who can get a job," Sala replied. "Because he knows what he's doing."

Yeamon thought for a minute. "You mean because he knows what somebody else wants done?"

Sala shrugged. "Say it however you want."

"I did," said Yeamon. "And I don't mean to knock your talents. But if you're as good as you say you are, and if you hate San Juan as much as you claim to, it seems to me like you'd put two and two together, and be a working pro in a place you liked."

"Mind your own fucking business!" Sala snapped. "I don't see that kind of logic in the way you live—you get straight with yourself, then I'll pay you for professional counsel, okay?"

"For God's sake," I said. "Let's forget this crap."

"Suits me," said Sala. "We're all fuck-ups anyway—except that I'm a pro."

Sweep brought a tray of hamburgers.

"When are you taking off?" I asked Yeamon.

"Depends on the money," he replied. "I thought I'd check out St. Thomas this weekend, see if we can get a hop on one of those boats going south." He looked up. "You still coming with us?"

"Ah, Christ," I exclaimed. I told him about Zimburger and Vieques. "I could have put it off," I said, "but all I could think about was getting that money and the car."

"Hell," he said. "Vieques is halfway between here and St. Thomas. There's a ferry every day."

We finally agreed that I'd meet them there on Friday. They were flying over in the morning and planned to come back sometime Sunday night.

"Stay away from St. Thomas," said Sala. "Bad things happen to people in St. Thomas. I can tell you some incredibly horrible stories."

"So what?" said Yeamon. "It's a good drunk. You should come with us."

"No thanks," Sala replied. "We had our good drunk, remember? I can do without those beatings."

We finished our food and ordered more drinks. Yeamon started talking about South America and I felt a reluctant excitement flicker somewhere inside me. Even Sala got excited. "Christ, I'd like to go there," he kept saying. "No reason why I can't. Hell, I can make a living anywhere."

I listened and didn't say much, because I remembered how I'd felt that morning. And besides, I had a car in the street and an apartment in Condado and a golden tap on Zimburger. I thought about that. The car and the apartment didn't bother me at all, but the fact that I was working for Zimburger gave me the creeps. Yeamon's talk made it seem even worse. They were going to South America, and I was going to Zimburger. It gave me a strange feeling, and the rest of that night I didn't say much, but merely sat there and drank, trying to decide if I was getting older and wiser, or just plain old.

The thing that disturbed me most was that I really didn't want to go to South America. I didn't want to go anywhere. Yet, when Yeamon talked about moving on, I felt the excitement anyway. I could see myself getting off a boat in Martinique and ambling into town to look for a cheap hotel. I could see myself in Caracas and Bogotá and Rio, wheeling and dealing through a world I had never seen but knew I could handle because I was a champ.

But it was pure masturbation, because down in my gut I wanted nothing more than a clean bed and a bright room and something solid to call my own at least until I got tired of it. There was an awful suspicion in my mind that I'd finally gone over the hump, and the worst thing about it was that I didn't feel tragic at all, but only weary, and sort of comfortably detached.

Twelve

THE next morning I drove down to Fajardo at top speed. I was covering a real estate deal, but it turned into an ugly experience and I was forced to abandon it. On the way back I stopped at a roadside stand and bought a pineapple, which the man cut up into little cubes for me. I ate them as I labored through traffic, driving slowly now, with one hand, reveling in the luxury of being master of my own movements for a change. Next weekend, I decided, I would drive over to Ponce on the south coast.

When I got to the *News* building, Moberg was just getting out of his car.

"I trust you're armed," I said. "Old daddio may run off his nut when he sees you."

He laughed. "We compromised. He made me sign a note, saying I'd give him my car if anybody skipped."

"Jesus," I said. "Yeamon's already talking about leaving."

He laughed again. "I don't care. Fuck him. I'll sign anything. It's the right thing to do."

"Ah, Moberg," I said, "you're a nutty bastard."

"Yes," he said. "I'm about as nutty as they come."

Lotterman didn't show up all afternoon. Sala claimed he was making the rounds of the banks, trying to float a loan to keep the paper going. It was only a rumor, but everyone in the office was talking as if the end had come.

About three, Yeamon called to say he'd been to see Sanderson. "He gave me a few shitty articles to do," he said. "Says he'll get me about thirty bucks apiece for them—wouldn't give me an advance, though."

"That's not bad," I said. "Do a good job on those and demand something bigger—he has more money than God."

"Yeah," he muttered. "I guess so. If I could get one thing worth about five hundred, I'd have enough to take off."

Sanderson called an hour or so later. "Can you be at the airport by seven on Thursday morning?" he asked.

"Good God," I said. "I suppose so."

"You'll have to be," he said. "Figure on staying most of the day. Zimburger wants to get back before dark."

"I'm not coming back," I said. "I'm going over to St. Thomas for the carnival."

He laughed. "I should have known you'd be attracted to something like that. I'd stay out of town if I were you. The locals get a little wild. The best parties are on the boats—the yachting set has a carnival of their own."

"I'm not making any plans," I replied. "I'm just going over there and plunge into it—a good relaxing drunk."

After work I stopped by Sala's place and picked up my clothes, then drove out to my new apartment. I had no gear to speak of, so all I had to do was hang a few things in the closet and put some beer in the refrigerator. Everything else was furnished—sheets, towels, kitchen tools, everything but food.

It was *my* place, and I liked it. I slept for a while, then I drove down to a little colmado and bought some eggs and bacon for breakfast.

I had already cooked the bacon the next morning when I realized I'd forgotten to buy coffee. So I drove down to the Condado Beach Hotel and had breakfast there. I bought a *Times* and ate by myself at a small table on the lawn. It was a fairly expensive place and no one from the *News* was likely to be there. The hacks who weren't at Al's would be at The Holiday, a crowded outdoor restaurant on the beach near the edge of town.

I spent all afternoon on the waterfront, trying to find out if the paper was going to be shut down by a strike. Just before I got off I told Schwartz I wouldn't be in the next day; I felt a sickness coming on.

"Jesus Christ," he muttered. "You guys are getting like rats on a sinking ship. Sala tied up the darkroom all afternoon with his own work, and I caught Vanderwitz making a long-distance call to Washington." He shook his head. "We can't have a panic here; why don't you guys calm down?"

"I'm calm," I replied. "I just need a day to straighten out my affairs."

"Okay," he said wearily. "It's none of my business. Do whatever you want."

I drove up to Al's and ate dinner by myself, then I went home and wrote the article that Sanderson wanted to send to the *Times*. It was a simple thing and I wrote it mostly from the material he'd given me—prices going down for the summer, more young people on vacations, various outlying spots to visit. It took me about two hours and when I finished I decided to take it on over to him and have a few drinks before going to bed. I had to get up at six the next morning, but it was still early and I wasn't sleepy.

There was nobody there when I arrived, so I went in and made a drink, then went out to the porch and sat down in one of the long chairs. I turned on the fan and put an album of show tunes on the phonograph.

I decided that when I got a little more money I would look for a place like this for myself. The one I had now was good for a start, but it didn't have a porch or a garden or a beach, and I saw no reason why I shouldn't have those things.

Sanderson came in after I'd been there about an hour. With him was a man who claimed to be the brother of a famous trumpet player. We made fresh drinks and Sanderson read my article and said it was excellent. "I hope you don't need the money right now," he said. "It might take a week or so." He shrugged. "It won't be much anyway—say fifty dollars."

"Fine with me," I said, settling back in the chair.

"I'll see what else I can shove off on you," he said. "We're overloaded right now. Stop in when you get back from St. Thomas."

"Good deal," I said. "Things are looking pretty bleak at the paper—I may have to depend on this stuff pretty soon."

He nodded. "Bleak is right. You'll find out on Monday just how bad it is."

"What's going to happen on Monday?" I asked.

"I can't say," he replied. Then he smiled. "It wouldn't help if you knew, anyway. Just relax—you won't starve."

The man with the famous brother had been staring out at the beach, saying nothing. His name was Ted. Now he turned to Sanderson and asked in a bored voice: "How's the diving out there?"

"Not much," Sanderson replied. "Pretty well fished out."

We talked for a while about diving. Sanderson spoke with authority about "rapture of the deep" and diving on Palancar Reef. Ted had been living in southern France for two years, and had once worked for Jacques Cousteau.

Sometime after midnight I realized I was getting drunk, so I got up to go. "Well," I said. "I have a date with Zimburger at the crack of dawn, I better get some sleep."

I got up late the next morning. There was no time for breakfast, so I dressed hurriedly and grabbed an orange to eat on the way to the airport. Zimburger was waiting outside a small hangar at the far end of the runway. He nodded as I got out of the car and I walked over to where he was standing with two other men. "This is Kemp," he told them. "He's our writer—works for the *New York Times*." He grinned and watched us shake hands.

One of them was a restaurant man and the other was an architect. We'd be back by mid-afternoon, Zimburger told me, because Mr. Robbis, the restaurant man, had to go to a cocktail party.

We flew over in a small Apache, with a pilot who looked like a refugee from the Flying Tigers. He said nothing the whole time and seemed totally unaware of our presence. After a dull, thirty-minute ride above the clouds, we nosed down toward Vieques and went hurtling into a small cow pasture that served as an airport. I gripped my seat, certain we were going to flip, but after several violent bounces we came to a stop.

We climbed out and Zimburger introduced us to a huge man named Martin, who looked like a professional shark-hunter. He wore a crisp khaki outfit and motorcycle sunglasses, and his hair was bleached almost white from the sun. Zimburger referred to him as "my man here on the island."

The general plan was to pick up some beer and sandwiches at Martin's bar, then drive to the other side of the island to see the property. Martin drove us into town in his Volkswagen bus, but the native who was supposed to make the sandwiches had disappeared. Martin had to make them himself; he left us on the empty dance floor and went back to the kitchen in a rage.

It took about an hour. Zimburger was talking earnestly to the restaurant man, so I decided to go out and look for some coffee. The architect said he knew of a drugstore up the street.

He'd been drinking steadily since five A.M., when Zimburger had unaccountably roused him out of bed. His name was Lazard and he sounded bitter.

"This Zimburger's a real screwball," he told me. "He's had me running in circles for six months."

"What the hell," I said. "As long as he pays."

He looked over at me. "Is this the first time you've worked with him?"

"Yeah," I said. "Why? Does he welsh?"

Lazard looked unhappy. "I'm not sure. He's a fine one for free drinks and all that, but sometimes I wonder."

I shrugged. "Well, Adelante's paying me. I don't have to deal with him—probably a good thing."

He nodded and we went into the drugstore. The menu was a strip of Coca-Cola signs on the wall. There were red leatherette stools, a Formica-top counter, and thick tan mugs for the coffee. The woman who ran it was sloppy white, with a heavy southern accent.

"Come right on in," she said. "What'll it be, fellas?"

Great mother of God, I thought. What town are we in?

Lazard bought a copy of the *News* for twenty cents and immediately noticed my byline on the front page. "I thought you worked for the *New York Times,*" he said, pointing to my name above the article on the waterfront strike.

"Just gave 'em a hand," I said. "They're short-staffed right now—asked me to help out until they can hire some more people."

He nodded and smiled. "Man, that's the life, you know. What do you have—a roving assignment?"

"More or less," I said.

"That's a terrific deal," he replied. "Go anywhere you want . . . steady salary . . . no worries . . ."

"Hell," I said, "you've got a pretty good thing yourself." I smiled. "Here we're both sitting on this godforsaken island, and being paid for it."

"Not me," he replied. "Oh, I'm getting my expenses, but if this thing falls through it could set me back two years." He nodded gravely. "I'm not that well established. I can't afford to have my name associated with any botched jobs—even if they're not my fault." He finished his coffee and set the mug on the counter. "That's where you're in the clear," he said. "All you have to do is write your story. With me, it's sink or swim on every job."

I felt sorry for Lazard. He obviously didn't like the smell of what he'd got into, but he couldn't afford to be cautious. He was not much older than I was, and a thing like this would be a fine break for him if it came through. And if it didn't, it would be a bad break—but even then he'd be in no worse shape than I'd been in for the past five years. I was tempted to tell him so, but I knew it wouldn't make him feel any better. Then he'd start feeling sorry for me too, and I didn't need that.

"Yeah," I said. "A man wants many chestnuts in the fire."

"Right," he replied, getting up to go. "That's why I envy you—you've got all kinds of things going."

I was beginning to believe him. The more he talked, the better I felt. On the way back to Martin's bar I looked at the town. It was almost deserted. The streets were wide and the buildings were low; most of them were built of concrete blocks and painted light pastel colors, but they all seemed empty.

We turned the corner toward Martin's place and started down a hill toward the waterfront. There were scraggy palms on both sides of the street, and at the bottom of the hill a long pier poked into the harbor. At the end of it were four fishing boats, rolling lazily in the groundswell that came in from Vieques Sound.

The bar was called The Kingfish. It had a tin roof and a bamboo fence around the entrance. The Volkswagen bus was parked outside the door. Inside, Zimburger and Robbis were still talking. Martin was packing the beer and the sandwiches in a big cooler.

I asked him why the town looked so deserted.

"No maneuvers this month," he replied. "You ought to see this place when five thousand U.S. Marines come in—it's a madhouse."

I shook my head, remembering that Sanderson had told me how two-thirds of the island was a Marine target range. A strange place to build a luxury resort, unless you wanted to fill it with retired Marines for cannon fodder.

It was after ten when we finally started for the other side of the island. It was only four miles wide, a good drive through tall fields of sugar cane and along narrow roads lined with flamboyan trees. Finally we came over a rise and looked down on the Caribbean. The minute I saw it I felt that here was the place I'd been looking for. We drove across another cane field and then through a grove of palms. Martin parked the bus, and we walked out to look at the beach.

My first feeling was a wild desire to drive a stake in the sand and claim the place for myself. The beach was white as salt, and cut off from the world by a ring of steep hills that faced the sea. We were on the edge of a large bay and the water was that clear, turquoise color that you get with a white sand bottom. I had never seen such a place. I wanted to take off all my clothes and never wear them again.

Then I heard Zimburger's voice, an ugly chattering that brought me back to reality. I had not come here to admire this place, but to write a thing that would sell it. Zimburger called me over and pointed up at a hill where he planned to put the hotel. Then he pointed to other hills where the houses would be. This went on for almost an hour—walking up and down the beach, staring at swamps that would blossom into shopping centers, lonely green hills that would soon be laced with sewer pipes, a clean white beach where cabana lots were already cleared and staked off. I took notes until I could stand no more of it, then I went back to the bus and found Martin drinking a beer.

"Progress marches on," I muttered, plunging my hand into the cooler.

He smiled. "Yeah, this is gonna be some place."

I opened the beer and swilled it down, then reached for another. We talked for a while, and Martin told me he'd first come to Vieques as a Marine. He knew a good thing when he saw one, he said, so instead of staying for twenty, as he'd planned, he got out after ten and came back to Vieques to set up a bar. Now, in addition to The Kingfish, he owned a laundry, five houses in Isabel Segunda, the only newspaper concession, and he was setting up a car rental agency to handle Zimburger's influx. On top of everything else, he was "general overseer" for Zimburger's property, which put him in on the ground floor. He smiled and sipped his beer. "You might say this place has been good to me. If I'd stayed in the States I'd be just another ex-jarhead."

"Where you from?" I asked.

"Norfolk," he said. "But I'm not too homesick. San Juan's as far as I've been from this place in six years." He paused, looking around at the little green island that had been so good to him. "Yeah, I grew up in Norfolk, but I don't remember it much—seems too long ago."

We had another beer, then Zimburger and Robbis and Lazard came back from the beach. Lazard was sweating and Robbis looked very impatient.

Zimburger gave me a friendly slap on the shoulder. "Well," he said with a grin, "you ready to write that article? Didn't I tell you this site was a beaut?"

"Sure," I said. "I'm all set."

He shook his head with mock disappointment. "Ah, you writers—never a good word for anything." He laughed nervously. "Goddamn writers—no telling what they'll do."

All the way back to town Zimburger talked incessantly about his plans for Vieques. Finally Martin broke in to say that we were all going to eat lunch at his club—he'd sent the boys out for some fresh lobster.

"You mean *langosta*," said Zimburger.

Martin shrugged. "Hell, every time I say that I have to go through a long explanation—so I just call it lobster."

"It's the Caribbean lobster," Zimburger said to Robbis. "Bigger and better than the other kind, and it doesn't have claws." He grinned. "Old God sure was in a good mood when he made this place."

Robbis stared out the window, then turned and spoke to Martin. "I'll have to take a raincheck on that," he said stiffly. "I have an appointment in San Juan, it's getting late."

"Hell's bells," said Zimburger. "We got time to kill. It's only about one."

"I'm not in the habit of killing time," said Robbis, turning again to stare out the window.

I could tell by his tone that something had gone wrong out there on the beach. From the morning conversation, I'd gathered that Robbis represented some chain of restaurants whose name I was supposed to recognize. Apparently Zimburger was counting on adding a Vieques branch to that chain.

Out of the corner of my eye I looked at Lazard. He seemed in a worse mood than Robbis. It gave me a definite pleasure, which bordered on euphoria when Zimburger announced, in a surly tone, that we would fly back to San Juan immediately.

"I think I'll stay overnight," I said. "I have to be in St. Thomas tomorrow to cover that carnival." I looked at Martin: "What time does the ferry leave?"

We were coming into town now, and Martin shifted quickly into second to climb a steep hill. "The ferry was yesterday," he said. "But we got a boat going over. Hell, I may take you myself."

"Good enough," I said. "No sense in me going back to San Juan. You can drop me at the hotel."

"Later," he replied with a grin. "We'll eat first—can't let all that . . . ah . . . langosta go to waste."

We drove Zimburger and Robbis and Lazard out to the airport, where the pilot was sleeping peacefully in the shadow of the plane. Zimburger yelled at him and he slowly got up, never changing his weary expression. Obviously, this man gave a damn for nothing at all; I felt like nudging Lazard and telling him that we had both missed the boat.

But Lazard was brooding and all I said to him was, "See you around." He nodded and climbed into the plane. Robbis followed, and then Zimburger, who sat next to the stony-faced pilot. They were all staring straight ahead when the plane bucked off down the runway and skimmed over the trees toward Puerto Rico.

I spent the next few hours at Martin's bar. A friend of his ate lunch with us; he was another ex-Marine, who owned a bar on a hill outside of town. "Drink up," Martin kept telling me. "It's all on the house." He grinned maliciously. "Or maybe I should say it's all on Mister Zimburger—you're his guest, right?"

"Right," I replied, and accepted another glass of rum.

Finally we had the lobster. I could tell it had been thawing all day, but Martin proudly said his boys had just brought it in. I had a vision of Martin ordering his lobsters from Maine, then tearing the claws off and sticking them in the freezer until he could palm them off on Zimburger's guests—and then etching it very carefully on the expense sheet. One journalist—forty dollars a day, labor and entertainment.

After I'd eaten two langostas, swilled countless drinks, and grown extremely weary of their babbling, I got up to go. "Which way is the hotel?" I asked, stooping to pick up my leather bag.

"Come on," said Martin, heading for the door. "I'll take you up to the Carmen."

I followed him out to the bus. We drove up the hill about three blocks to a low pink building, with a sign that said Hotel Carmen. The place was empty, and Martin told the woman to give me the best room in the house; it was on him.

Before leaving, he said he'd take me over to St. Thomas tomorrow in the launch. "We'll have to take off about ten," he said. "I have to be there at noon to meet a friend."

I knew he was lying, but it didn't matter. Martin was like an auto mechanic who'd just discovered the insurance company, or a punk gone mad on his first expense account. I looked forward to the day when he and Zimburger would find each other out.

The best room in the Carmen cost three dollars, and had a balcony overlooking the town and the harbor. I was very full and half drunk, and when I got in the room I went to sleep immediately.

Two hours later I was awakened by someone tapping on the door. "Señor," the voice said. "You have dinner with Señor Kingfish, no?"

"I'm not hungry," I said. "I just ate lunch."

"Sí," the voice replied, and I heard quick footsteps on the stairs going down to the street. It was still light and I couldn't get back to sleep, so I went out to get a bottle of rum and some ice. In the same building with the hotel was what appeared to be a storage bin full of liquor. A grinning Puerto Rican sold me a bottle of rum for a dollar, and a bag of ice for two dollars. I paid and went back upstairs to my room.

I mixed a drink and went out on the balcony to sit down. The town still looked deserted. Far out on the horizon I could see the neighboring island of Culebra, and from somewhere in that direction came the shuddering thump of explosions. I recalled Sanderson telling me that Culebra was an aerial bombing range for the U.S. Navy. Once it had been a magic place, but no longer.

I had been there about twenty minutes when a Negro came down the street on a small grey horse. The hoofbeats rang through the town like pistol shots. I watched him clatter up the street and disappear over a small rise. The hoofbeats carried back to me long after he was out of sight.

Then I heard another sound, the muted rhythm of a steel band. It was getting dark now, and I couldn't tell what direction the music was coming from. It was a soft, compelling sound, and I sat there and drank and listened to it, feeling at peace with myself and the world, as the hills behind me turned a red-gold color in the last slanting rays of the sun.

Then it was night. A few lights came on in the town. The music came in long bursts, as if someone was explaining something between choruses, and then it would start again. I heard voices below me on the street, and now and then the hoofbeats of another horse.

Isabel Segunda seemed more active at night than it had been during the long, hot day.

It was the kind of town that made you feel like Humphrey Bogart: you came in on a bumpy little plane, and, for some mysterious reason, got a private room with a balcony overlooking the town and the harbor; then you sat there and drank until something happened. I felt a tremendous distance between me and everything real. Here I was on Vieques island, a place so insignificant that I had never heard of it until I'd been told to come here—delivered by one nut, and waiting to be taken off by another.

It was almost May. I knew that New York was getting warm now, that London was wet, that Rome was hot—and I was on Vieques, where it was always hot and where New York and London and Rome were just names on a map.

Then I remembered the Marines—no maneuvers this month—and I remembered why I was here. Zimburger wants a brochure . . . aimed at investors . . . your job is to sell the place . . . don't be late or he'll . . .

I was being paid twenty-five dollars a day to ruin the only place I'd seen in ten years where I'd felt a sense of peace. Paid to piss in my own bed, as it were, and I was only here because I'd got drunk and been arrested and had thereby become a pawn in some high-level face-saving bullshit.

I sat there a long time, and thought about a lot of things. Foremost among them was the suspicion that my strange and ungovernable instincts might do me in before I had a chance to get rich. No matter how much I wanted all those things that I needed money to buy, there was some devilish current pushing me off in another direction—toward anarchy and poverty and craziness. That maddening delusion that a man can lead a decent life without hiring himself out as a Judas Goat.

Finally I got drunk and went to bed. Martin woke me up the next day and we had breakfast in the drugstore before taking off for St. Thomas. The day was bright and blue, and we had a good crossing. By the time we came into the harbor of Charlotte Amalie I'd forgotten Vieques and Zimburger and everything else.

Thirteen

WE were still in open water when I heard the noise. The island loomed up like a big mound of grass in the ocean, and from it came the melodious pounding of steel drums, a steady roar of engines, and much shouting. It grew louder as we entered the harbor, and there was still a half mile of blue water between us and the town when I heard the first explosion. Then several more in rapid succession. I could hear people screaming, the wail of a trumpet, and the steady rhythm of drums.

There were thirty or forty yachts in the harbor; Martin eased his launch among them, heading for an empty spot at the pier. I grabbed my bag and hopped out, telling Martin I was in a hurry to meet some people. He nodded and said he was in a hurry too; he had to go over to St. John to see a man about a boat.

I was glad to be rid of him. He was one of those people who could go to New York and be "fascinating," but here in his own world he was just a cheap functionary, and a dull one at that.

As I walked toward the center of town the noise became deafening. The street reverberated with the sound of roaring engines, and

I pressed forward to see what it meant. When I got to the corner the crowd was so thick I could barely move. Down the middle of the street ran a bar, more than three blocks long, a series of wooden booths full of rum and whiskey. In each one of them, several bartenders worked feverishly to supply the mob with drink. I stopped in front of one that said "Rum 25¢." They served the drinks in paper flagons, a chunk of ice and a violent slug of rum to each one.

Further down the street I came to the center of the crowd. I kept inching forward until I found myself in an open space, ringed by thousands of people. It was a Go-Kart race, little engines mounted on wooden chassis, driven by wild-eyed drunkards, screeching and sliding around a course laid out in what appeared to be the town plaza.

At close range the noise was unbearable. People were shoving me from side to side and my drink kept spilling down my shirt, but there was nothing I could do. Most of the faces around me were black, but all through the crowd I could see American tourists, white and sweating and most of them wearing carnival hats.

Across the square was a large building with a balcony that looked down on the race. I decided to go there. It was only a hundred yards away, but it took me thirty minutes to fight and slither through the mob, and by the time I sat down on the balcony I was weak and soaked with sweat.

My drink had been knocked out of my hands somewhere below, so I went to the bar for another. For fifty cents I got a dash of rum and a lot of water—but it came in a glass, with normal ice cubes, and I felt a confidence that I could drink it at my leisure. I was in the Grand Hotel, an ancient grey structure with white pillars and ceiling fans and a balcony that ran the length of the block.

I wondered how I was going to locate Yeamon. We'd arranged to meet at the post office at noon, but I was already more than an hour late, and the post office was closed. I could see it from the balcony, so I decided to stay there until I caught sight of him, then try to get his attention. In the meantime, I would drink, rest, and ponder the meaning of this mob.

. . .

The Go-Kart races were over now, and the crowd turned to the band for amusement. Another band appeared, and then others at different corners of the square, each leading a train of dancers. Four steel bands, playing the same wild tune, came together in the middle of the square. The sound was incredible; people were singing and stomping and screaming. Here and there I saw tourists trying to get out of it, but most of them were carried along in the mob. The bands moved off together, heading down the main street. Behind them the crowd linked arms, thirty abreast, blocking the street and both sidewalks—chanting the music as they jerked and staggered along.

I had been there a while when a man came up and stood by the railing in front of me. I nodded hello, and he smiled. "My name's Ford," he said, extending his hand. "I live here. You down for the carnival?"

"I guess so," I replied.

He looked over the railing again and shook his head. "A violent thing," he said solemnly. "Be careful, you never know what might happen."

I nodded. "By the way, maybe you can tell me some other hotels in town. The bartender says this one's full."

He laughed. "Nope, not an empty room on the island."

"Damn," I said.

"Why worry?" he replied. "Sleep on the beach. Lots of people do—better than most hotels."

"Where?" I said. "Are there any close to town?"

"Sure," he replied, "but they'll all be full. Your best bet is Lind-bergh Beach, out by the airport. It's the nicest."

I shrugged. "Well, it may come to that."

He laughed. "Good luck." Then he reached into his shirt pocket. "Come out and have dinner if you have time. It's not expensive—it only sounds that way." He laughed and waved goodbye. I looked at his card; it was an advertisement for a hotel called Pirate's Castle—Owen Ford, prop.

"Thanks," I muttered, tossing the card over the railing. I was tempted to go out there and eat a huge meal, then hand him a card saying, "Worldwide Congress of Non-Paying Journalists—Paul Kemp, prop."

I felt a tap on my shoulder. It was Yeamon, looking wild-eyed and carrying two bottles of rum. "I thought you'd be up here," he said with a grin. "We've been checking the post office all day—then I realized that any professional journalist would seek the highest and safest spot in town." He fell down in a wicker chair. "What else but the balcony of the Grand Hotel?"

I nodded. "It's nice, but don't get comfortable. This place is sold out like all the others." Then I looked around. "Where's Chenault?"

"I left her downstairs in the gift shop," he said. "She'll be up— can we get ice here?"

"I guess so," I said. "I've been getting drinks."

"For God's sake," he replied. "Don't buy rum here. I found a place where you can get it for seventy-five cents a gallon—all we really need is ice."

"Fine," I said. "Go ask."

As he started for the bar, Chenault appeared. "Over here," he called, and she came over to the rail. Yeamon went to the bar and Chenault sat down.

She fell back in the chair and groaned. "My lord!" she said. "We've been dancing all day. I'm nearly dead."

She looked happy. She also looked as pretty as I'd ever seen her. She was wearing sandals and a madras skirt and a white sleeveless blouse, but the difference was in her face. It was red and healthy and damp with sweat. Her hair hung loose and free on her shoulders and her eyes glittered with excitement. There was something especially sexual about her now. Her small body, still wrapped very tastefully in plaids and white silk, seemed ready to explode with energy.

Yeamon came back with three glasses of ice, cursing because the bartender had charged him thirty cents for each one. He put them on the floor and filled them with rum. "These bastards," he mumbled. "They'll get rich selling ice—look how the rotten stuff melts."

Chenault laughed and kicked him playfully in the back. "Stop that silly complaining," she said. "You'll spoil the fun."

"Balls," he replied.

Chenault smiled and sipped her drink. "If you'd let yourself go, you'd enjoy it."

He finished pouring the drinks and stood up. "Don't give me that crap," he said. "I don't need a mob to enjoy myself."

She didn't seem to hear him. "It's too bad," she said. "Fritz just can't enjoy himself because he can't let go." She looked at me. "Don't you agree?"

"Leave me out of it," I said. "I came here to drink."

She giggled and held up her glass. "That's right," she said. "We came here to drink—just have a good time and let go!"

Yeamon frowned and turned his back on us, leaning on the railing and staring down at the plaza. It was almost empty now, but far down the street we could hear the drums and the howl of the crowd.

Chenault finished her drink and stood up. "Come on," she said. "I feel like dancing."

Yeamon shook his head wearily. "I don't know if I can stand any more of it."

She pulled at his arm. "Come on, it'll do you good. You too, Paul." She reached out with her other hand and tugged at my shirt.

"Why not?" I said. "We might as well try it."

Yeamon straightened up and reached for the glasses. "Wait a minute," he said. "I can't face it again without rum—I'll get some more ice."

We waited for him at the top of the stairs that led down to the street. Chenault turned to me with a big smile. "We have to sleep on the beach," she said. "Did Fritz tell you?"

"No," I said. "But I found out anyway. I know one that comes highly recommended."

She grabbed my arm and squeezed it. "Good. I *want* to sleep on the beach."

I nodded, seeing Yeamon approach with the drinks. I enjoyed Chenault in this wild condition, but it made me nervous. I recalled the last time I'd seen her full of drink, and the idea that anything like that might happen again, especially in a place like this, was not a happy prospect.

We went down the stairs and walked along the streets, sipping our drinks. Then we caught up with the mob. Chenault grabbed hold of somebody's waist in the last row of dancers and Yeamon got in beside her. I stuffed the bottle I'd been carrying into my pants pocket and fell in next to Yeamon. In a moment we were sealed in by more people behind us. I felt hands on my waist and heard a shrill voice screaming, "Take it off! Take it off!"

I looked over my shoulder and saw a white man who looked like a used car salesman. Then the mob surged left and I saw the man stumble and fall. The dancers trampled him without missing a beat.

The bands kept circling the town and the mob kept growing larger. I was dripping with sweat and ready to collapse from the constant dancing, but there was no way out of it. I looked to my left and saw Yeamon, smiling grimly as he executed the jerky shuffle-step that carried us along. Chenault was laughing happily and swinging her hips to the constant thump of the drums.

Finally my legs threatened to give out. I tried to catch Yeamon's attention, but the noise was deafening. In desperation, I lunged across the chain of dancers, knocking people off balance, and grabbed Yeamon's arm. "Out!" I yelled. "I can't stand it."

He nodded and pointed toward a side street a few hundred yards ahead. Then he grabbed Chenault by the arm and began edging toward the sidelines. I whooped distractedly as we bulled through the crowd.

When we got clear of the mob we stood there and let it pass, then we started off toward a restaurant that Yeamon had seen earlier in the day. "It looks decent, anyway," he said. "I hope to God it's cheap."

The place was called Olivers. It was a makeshift, thatched-roof affair on top of a concrete building with boarded-up windows. We struggled up the stairs and found an empty table. The place was crowded, and I pushed to the bar. Singapore slings were fifty cents each, but it was worth that much just to sit down.

From our table we could look up and down the waterfront. It was jammed with all kinds of boats—sleek power cruisers and scraggy, native sloops full of bananas, tied up alongside sleek eight-meter racing hulls from Newport and Bermuda. Beyond the channel buoys stood a few big motor yachts that people said were gambling ships. The sun went down slowly behind a hill across the harbor and lights began to flicker in buildings on the wharf. Somewhere across town we could still hear the frenzied beat of the dance as it moved through the streets.

A waiter appeared, wearing an Old Spice yachting cap. We all ordered the seafood platter. "And three glasses of ice," Yeamon told him. "Right away, if you don't mind."

The waiter nodded and disappeared. After a ten-minute wait Yeamon went to the bar and got three glasses of ice. We poured our drinks under the table and set the bottle on the floor.

"What we need is a gallon jug," said Yeamon. "And some kind of a knapsack to carry ice."

"Why the gallon jug?" I asked.

"For that seventy-five-cent rum," he replied.

"Hell with it," I said. "It's probably worthless." I nodded toward the bottle on the floor. "This is cheap enough—you can't beat good rum at a dollar a bottle."

He shook his head. "Nothing worse than traveling with a rich journalist—throw dollars around like beans."

I laughed. "I'm not the only one working for Sanderson these days," I said. "The big money is just around the corner—never lose faith."

"Not for me," he replied. "I'm supposed to be doing an article on this carnival—checking with the tourist bureau and all that." He shrugged. "No dice. I can't sneak around digging up facts while everybody else is drunk."

"Nobody's drunk," said Chenault. "We're just letting go."

He smiled lazily. "That's right, we're kicking off the traces, really raising hell—why don't you write a good stiff note to the Smith College alumni letter and tell 'em where they missed the boat?"

She laughed. "Fritz is jealous of my background. I have so much more to rebel against."

"Balls," said Yeamon. "You don't have anything to rebel *with*."

The waiter arrived with the food and we stopped talking. It was dark when we finished, and Chenault was anxious to get into the streets again. I was in no hurry. This place was peaceful, now that the crowd had thinned out, but it was close enough to the chaos that we could join it anytime we wanted.

Finally she dragged us down to the street, but the dance had petered out. We wandered around the town, stopping at the liquor store to buy two more bottles of rum, then returning to the Grand Hotel to see what was happening there.

A party was going on at one end of the balcony. Most of these people appeared to be expatriates—not tourists, but the type who looked like they might live here on the island, or at least somewhere in the Caribbean. They were all very tan. A few had beards, but most of them were freshly shaven. The ones with beards wore shorts and old polo shirts, the boating set. The others wore linen suits and leather shoes that sparkled in the dim light of the balcony chandeliers.

We barged in and sat down at a table. I was fairly drunk by now and I didn't care if we were thrown out or not. The party broke up just a few minutes after we arrived. Nobody said anything to us and I felt a little foolish when we were left on the balcony by ourselves. We sat there for a while, then wandered down to the street. A few blocks away we could hear a band warming up. Soon the street was jammed once again with people, all clinging to each other and dancing the strange dinga that we'd learned earlier in the day.

We humored Chenault for a few hours, hoping she'd get tired of the dancing, but finally Yeamon had to drag her out of the mob. She pouted until we found ourselves in a club full of drunken Americans. A calypso band was hammering and the floor was full of dancers. By this time I was drunk. I fell into a chair and watched as Yeamon and Chenault tried to dance. The bouncer came over to me and said I owed fifteen dollars for the cover charge, and I gave it to him, rather than argue.

Yeamon came back to the table alone. He had left Chenault to dance with an American who looked like a nazi. "You rotten butcher!" I yelled, shaking my fist at him. But he didn't see me, and the music was so loud that he couldn't hear. Finally Chenault left him and came back to the table.

Yeamon led me through the crowd. People were screaming and grabbing at me and I didn't know where I was being taken. My only thought was to lie down and sleep. When we got outside I slumped in a doorway while Yeamon and Chenault argued about what to do next.

Yeamon wanted to go to the beach, but Chenault was for more dancing. "Don't order me around, you goddamn puritan!" she screamed. "I'm having a good time and all you do is sulk!"

He knocked her down with a quick whack to the head, and I heard her groaning somewhere near my feet as he shouted for a cab. I helped him lift her into the back seat and we explained to the driver that we wanted to go to Lindbergh Beach. He grinned widely and started off. I was tempted to reach over the seat and give him a rabbit punch. He thinks we're going to rape her, I thought. He thinks we grabbed her off the street and now we're taking her out to the beach to hump her like dogs. And the bastard was grinning about it; a criminal degenerate with no morals.

Lindbergh Beach was across the road from the airport. It was surrounded by a tall cyclone fence, but the driver took us to a place where we could climb over it by using a tree. Chenault refused to make any effort, so we shoved her over and let her fall in the sand. Then we found a good spot that was partly surrounded by trees. There was no moon, but I could hear the surf a few yards in front of us. I spread my filthy cord coat on the sand for a pillow, then fell down and went to sleep.

The sun woke me up the next morning. I sat up and groaned. My clothes were full of sand. Ten feet to my left Yeamon and Chenault were sleeping on their clothes. They were both naked and her arm was thrown over his back. I stared at her, thinking that no one could blame me if I lost my wits and pounced on her, after first crippling Yeamon with a blow on the back of his skull.

I considered trying to cover them with her raincoat, but I was afraid they'd wake up as I hovered over them. I didn't want that, so I decided to go swimming and wake them up by shouting from the water.

I took off my clothes and tried to shake the sand out, then shuffled naked into the bay. The water was cool, and I rolled around

like a porpoise, trying to get clean. Then I swam to a wooden raft
about a hundred yards out. Yeamon and Chenault were still asleep.
At the other end of the beach was a long white building that looked
like a dance hall. An outrigger canoe was pulled up on the sand in
front of it, and under the nearby trees I could see chairs and tables
with thatched umbrellas. It was somewhere around nine o'clock,
but there was no one in sight. I lay there for a long time, trying not
to think.

Fourteen

CHENAULT came awake with a shriek, snatching the raincoat around her as she peered up and down the beach.

"Out here," I yelled. "Come on in."

She looked out at me and smiled, holding the raincoat between us like a veil. Then Yeamon woke up, looking puzzled and angry at whatever had broken his sleep.

"Let's go!" I yelled. "Up for the morning dip."

He stood up and ambled toward the water. Chenault called after him, waving his shorts. "Here!" she said sternly. "Put these on!"

I waited for them on the raft. Yeamon came first, thrashing across the bay like a crocodile. Then I saw Chenault swimming toward us, wearing her panties and bra. I began to feel uncomfortable. I waited until she got to the raft, then I slid off. "I'm hungry as hell," I said, treading water. "I'm going over to the airport for breakfast."

When I got to the beach I looked around for my bag. I remembered putting it in a tree the night before, but I couldn't remember which one. Finally I found it, jammed into the crotch of two branches just above where I'd been sleeping. I put on some clean pants and a rumpled silk shirt.

Just before I left I glanced out at the raft and saw Yeamon jump naked into the water. Chenault laughed and tore off her bra and panties, then leaped in on top of him. I watched for a moment, then tossed my bag over the fence and climbed over after it.

I walked along a road that paralleled the runway, and after a half mile or so I came to the main hangar, a huge Quonset hut that bustled with activity. Planes landed every few minutes. Most of them were small Cessnas and Pipers, but every ten minutes or so a DC-3 would come in, bringing a fresh pack of revelers from San Juan.

I shaved in the men's room, then pushed through the crowd to the restaurant. The people just off the planes were getting their free drinks, and in one corner of the hangar was a group of drunken Puerto Ricans, beating on their luggage to the tune of some chant I couldn't understand. It sounded like a football cheer: "Busha boomba, balla wa! Busha boomba, balla wa!" I suspected they would never make it into town.

I bought a *Miami Herald* and had a big breakfast of pancakes and bacon. Yeamon arrived an hour or so later. "Christ, I'm hungry," he said. "I need a massive breakfast."

"Is Chenault still with us?" I asked.

He nodded. "She's downstairs shaving her legs."

It was almost noon when we got a bus to town. It let us off at a public market and we started walking in the general direction of the Grand Hotel, stopping now and then to look in the few store windows that were not boarded up.

As we neared the middle of town the noise increased. But this was a different sound—not the roar of happy voices or the musical thump of drums, but the wild screams of a small group of people. It sounded like a gang war, punctuated by guttural cries and breaking glass.

We hurried toward it, cutting down a side street that led to the shopping district. When we turned the corner I saw a frenzied mob, jamming the street and blocking both sidewalks. We slowed down and approached cautiously.

About two hundred people had looted one of the big liquor stores. Most of them were Puerto Ricans. Cases of champagne and scotch lay broken in the street, and everyone I saw had a bottle.

They were screaming and dancing, and in the middle of the crowd a giant Swede wearing a blue jockstrap was blowing long blasts on a trumpet.

As we watched, a fat American woman raised two magnums of champagne above her head and smashed them together, laughing wildly as the glass and the booze rained down on her bare shoulders. A percussion corps of drunkards was beating with beer cans on empty scotch crates. It was the same chant I'd heard at the airport: "Busha boomba, balla wa! Busha boomba, balla wa!" All over the street people danced feverishly by themselves, jerking and yelling to the rhythm of the chant.

The liquor store was nothing but a shell, a bare room with broken windows in the front. People kept running in and out of it, grabbing stray bottles and drinking them as fast as they could before somebody else jerked them away. Empty bottles were tossed casually into the street, making it a sea of broken glass, studded with thousands of beer cans.

We stayed on the edge of it. I wanted to get my hands on some of that stolen booze, but I was afraid of the police. Yeamon wandered into the store and came out moments later with a magnum of champagne. He smiled sheepishly and tucked it into his bag, saying nothing. Finally my lust for drink overcame my fear of jail and I made a run for a case of scotch that was lying in the gutter near the front of the store. It was empty and I looked around for another. In the forest of dancing feet I saw several unbroken bottles of whiskey. I rushed toward them, shoving people out of the way. The noise was deafening and I expected at any moment to be smashed on the head with a bottle. I managed to rescue three quarts of Old Crow, all that was left of a case. The other bottles were broken and hot whiskey oozed through the streets. I got a firm grip on my loot and leaned into the mob, aiming for the spot where I'd left Yeamon and Chenault.

We hurried off down a side street, passing a blue jeep marked "Poleece." In it, a gendarme in a pith helmet sat half asleep, idly scratching his crotch.

We stopped at the place where we'd eaten the night before. I put the whiskey in my satchel and ordered three drinks while we pondered the next move. The program said a pageant of some kind was

scheduled at the ballpark in a few hours. It sounded harmless
enough, but then nothing at all had been officially scheduled for
that hour when the mob looted the liquor store. That was supposed
to be a "Rest Period." There was another "Rest Period" between the
ballpark festivities and the "All Out Tramp," officially scheduled for
eight o'clock sharp.

It had an ominous sound. All the other Tramps were listed as beginning and ending at certain times. The "Birds and Bees Tramp,"
on Thursday, began at eight and ended at ten. The "High Com-
bustible Tramp," which seemed to be the one we'd been caught in
the night before, ran from eight until midnight. But the program
said only that the "All Out Tramp" would begin at eight, and in small
brackets on the same line was a note saying "climax of carnival."

"This thing tonight could get out of control," I said, tossing the
program on the table. "At least I hope so."

Chenault laughed and winked at me. "We'll have to get Fritz
drunk, so he can enjoy it."

"Balls," Yeamon muttered, not looking up from the program.
"You get drunk again tonight and I'll abandon your ass."

She laughed again. "Don't try to say I was drunk—I remember
who hit me."

He shrugged. "It's good for you—clears your head."

"No sense arguing about it," I said. "We're bound to get drunk—
look at all this whiskey." I patted my satchel.

"And this," said Chenault, pointing to the magnum of champagne under Yeamon's chair.

"Christ help us," Yeamon muttered.

We finished our drinks and wandered over to the Grand Hotel.
From the balcony we could see people heading for the ballpark.

Yeamon wanted to go out to Yacht Haven and find a boat leaving
soon for South America. I wasn't particularly anxious to join the
mob at the ballpark and I remembered Sanderson saying most of
the good parties were on the boats, so we decided to go there.

It was a long walk in the sun, and by the time we got there I was
sorry I hadn't offered to pay for a cab. I was sweating horribly and
my bag seemed to weigh forty pounds. The entrance was a palm-
lined driveway that led to a swimming pool, and beyond the pool
was a hill that led down to the piers. There were more than a hun-

dred boats, everything from tiny harbor sloops to huge schooners, and their naked spars swayed lazily against a background of green hills and a blue Caribbean sky. I stopped on the pier and looked down at a forty-foot racing sloop. My first thought was that I had to have one. It had a dark blue hull and a gleaming teakwood deck, and I would not have been surprised to see on the bow a sign, saying: "For Sale—One Soul, no less."

I nodded thoughtfully. Hell, anybody could have a car and an apartment, but a boat like this was the nuts. I wanted it, and considering the value I placed on my soul in those days, I might have struck a bargain if that sign had been there on the bow.

We spent all afternoon at Yacht Haven, desperately scouring the docks for an outgoing boat where Yeamon and Chenault could sign on with no questions asked. One man offered to take them as far as Antigua in a week or so, another was going to Bermuda, and finally we located a big yawl that was headed for Los Angeles, via the Panama Canal.

"Great," said Yeamon. "How much would you charge us to ride that far?"

"Nothing," said the owner of the yawl, a poker-faced little man wearing white trunks and a baggy shirt. "I won't take you."

Yeamon looked stunned.

"I pay my crew," said the man. "And besides that I have my wife and three kids—no room for you." He shrugged and turned away.

Most of the boat people were gracious, but a few were openly rude. One captain—or maybe a mate—laughed at Yeamon and said: "Sorry, pal. I don't carry scum on my boat."

Far out at the end of the pier we noticed a gleaming white hull flying the French flag and rocking leisurely in deep water.

"That's the finest craft in the harbor," said a man standing next to us. "A world cruiser, seventy-five feet long, eighteen knots, radar dome, electric winches and a walkaround bed."

We continued along the pier and came to a boat called the *Blue Peter*, where a man who later introduced himself as Willis told us to come aboard for a drink. Several other people were there and we stayed for hours. Yeamon went off after a while to check the other boats, but Chenault and I stayed and drank. Several times I noticed Willis staring at Chenault, and when I mentioned that we were sleeping on the beach he said we could leave our bags on the boat, instead of lugging them around. "Sorry I can't offer you bunks," he added. "But I only got two." He grinned. "One of 'em's double, of course, but that still makes it crowded."

"Yeah," I said.

We left our bags there, and by the time we started for town we were all drunk. Willis rode with us in a cab as far as the Grand Hotel, and said he'd probably see us later in one of the bars.

Fifteen

SOMETIME after midnight we found ourselves in front of a place called the Blue Grotto, a crowded waterfront dance hall with a two dollar cover charge. I tried to pay, but people laughed and a squatty woman grabbed my arm. "Oh, no," she said. "You come with us. We go to the real party."

I recognized our friends from the street dance. A bully was slapping Yeamon on the back and babbling about a "whip fight" and some spics with a case of gin. "I know these people," said Chenault, "let's go with them."

We ran down the street to where they had a car, and about six more people piled in with us. At the end of the main street we turned up toward the hills above town, climbing and twisting on a dark little road through what appeared to be the residential section. The houses at the bottom of the hill were wooden, with peeling paint, but as we went higher, more and more houses were made of concrete blocks. Finally they became almost elaborate, with screen porches and lawns.

We stopped at a house full of lights and music. The street in front of it was jammed with cars and there was no place to park. The driver let us out and said he'd join us when he found a place for the car. The squatty girl gave a loud whoop and ran up the steps to the front door. I followed reluctantly and saw her talking to a fat woman in a bright green dress. Then she pointed back at me. Yeamon and Chenault and the others caught up as I stopped at the door.

"Six dollars, please," said the woman, holding out her hand.

"Christ!" I said. "How many does that pay for?"

"Two," she said. "You and the young lady." She nodded at the girl who had ridden out from town on my lap.

I cursed silently and gave up six dollars. My date repaid me with a coy smile, and took my hand as we entered the house. My God, I thought, this pig is after me.

Yeamon was right behind us, muttering about the six dollar fee. "This better be good," he told Chenault. "You might as well figure on getting a job when we get back to San Juan."

She laughed, a happy little shriek that had nothing to do with Yeamon's remark. I glanced at her, and saw the excitement in her eyes. That dip in the harbor had sobered me up a bit, and Yeamon seemed pretty steady, but Chenault had the look of a hophead, ready to turn on.

We went down a dark hall and into a room full of music and noise. It was jammed from wall to wall, and over in one corner a band was playing. Not the steel band I expected to see, but three horns and a drum. The sound was familiar, but I couldn't place it. Then, looking up at the ceiling where the light bulbs were wrapped in blue gelatin, I knew the sound. It was the music of a Midwestern high school dance in some rented club. And not just the music; the crowded, low-ceilinged room, the makeshift bar, doors opening onto a brick terrace, people giggling and shouting and drinking booze out of paper cups—it was all exactly the same, except that every head in the room was black.

Seeing this made me a bit self-conscious and I began looking around for a dark corner where I could drink without being seen. My date still had me by the arm, but I shook her off and moved toward one corner of the room. No one paid any attention to me as I eased through the mob, bumping dancers here and there, keeping my head lowered and moving cautiously toward what looked like a vacant spot.

A few feet to my left was a door and I edged toward it, bumping more dancers. When I finally got outside I felt like I'd escaped from a jail. The air was cool and the terrace was almost empty. I walked out to the edge and looked down on Charlotte Amalie at the bottom of the hill. I could hear music floating up from the bars along Queen Street. Off to my right and left I could see Land Rovers and open taxis full of people moving along the waterfront, heading for other parties, other yachts and dim-lit hotels where red and blue lights glittered mysteriously. I tried to remember which other places we'd been told to go for the "real fun," and I wondered if they were any better than this one.

I thought of Vieques, and for a moment I wanted to be there. I remembered sitting on the hotel balcony and hearing the hoofbeats in the street below. Then I remembered Zimburger, and Martin, and the Marines—the empire builders, setting up frozen food stores and aerial bombing ranges, spreading out like a piss puddle to every corner of the world.

I turned to watch the dancers, thinking that since I'd paid six dollars to get into this place, I might as well try to enjoy it.

The dancing was getting wilder now. No more swaying fox-trot business. There was a driving rhythm to the music; the movements on the floor were jerky and full of lust, a swinging and thrusting of hips, accompanied by sudden cries and groans. I felt a temptation to join in, if only for laughs. But first I would have to get drunker.

On the other side of the room I found Yeamon, standing by the entrance to the hall. "I'm ready to do the dinga," I said with a laugh. "Let's cut loose and go crazy."

He glared at me, taking a long slug of his drink.

I shrugged and moved on toward the hall closet, where the button-down bartender was laboring over the drinks. "Rum and ice," I shouted, holding my cup aloft. "Heavy on the ice."

He seized it mechanically, dropped in a few lumps of ice, a flash of rum, then he handed it back. I stabbed a quarter into his palm and went back to the doorway. Yeamon was staring at the dancers, looking very morose.

I stopped beside him and he nodded toward the floor. "Look at that bitch," he said.

I looked and saw Chenault, dancing with the small, spade-

bearded man we had met earlier. He was a good dancer, and whatever step he was doing was pretty involved. Chenault was holding
her arms out like a hula charmer, a look of tense concentration on
her face. Now and then she would spin, swirling her madras skirt
around her like a fan.

"Yeah," I said. "She's hell on this dancing."

"She's part nigger," he replied, in a tone that was not soft.

"Careful," I said quickly. "Watch what you say in this place."

"Balls," he said loudly.

Great Jesus, I thought. Here we go. "Take it easy," I said. "Why
don't we head back to town?"

"Fine with me," he replied. "Try talking to her." He nodded at
Chenault, dancing feverishly just a few feet away.

"Hell," I said. "Just grab her. Let's go."

He shook his head. "I did. She screamed like I was killing her."

There was something in his voice that I'd never heard before, an
odd wavering that suddenly made me nervous. "Jesus," I muttered,
looking around at the crowd.

"I'll just have to bat her in the head," he said.

Just then I felt a hand on my arm. It was my pig, my squatty date.
"Let's go, big boy!" she whooped, dragging me onto the floor. "Let's
do it!" She squealed and began to stomp her feet.

Good God, I thought. What now? I watched her, holding my
drink in one hand and a cigarette in the other. "Come on!" she
shouted. "Give me some business!" She hunched toward me,
pulling her skirt up around her thighs as she wiggled back and
forth. I began to stomp and weave; my dancing was shaky at first,
then I leveled out to a sort of distracted abandon. Somebody
bumped me and I dropped my drink on the floor. It made no difference to the frenzied couples that hemmed us in.

Suddenly I was next to Chenault. I shrugged helplessly and kept
up the stomp. She laughed and bumped me with her hips. Then
she danced back to her partner, leaving me with my pig.

Finally I shook my head and quit, making gestures to indicate I
was too tired to go on. I went back to the bar for a fresh drink. Yeamon was nowhere in sight and I presumed he'd been sucked into
the dance. I made my way through the bodies and out to the terrace, hoping for a place to sit down. Yeamon was sitting on the rail-

ing, talking to a teenage girl. He looked up with a smile. "This is Ginny," he said. "She's going to teach me the dance."

I nodded and said hello. Behind us the music was growing wilder, and at times it was almost drowned out by the screaming of the crowd. I tried to ignore it, looking out over the town, seeing the peace below us and wanting to be down there.

But the music from the house was getting crazier. There was a new urgency about it, and the shouts of the mob took on a different tone. Yeamon and Ginny went in to see what was happening. The crowd was moving back to make room for something, and I walked over to see what it was.

They had made a big circle, and in the middle of it Chenault and the small, spade-bearded man were doing the dance. Chenault had dropped her skirt and was dancing in her panties and her white sleeveless blouse. Her partner had taken off his shirt exposing his glistening black chest. He wore nothing but a pair of tight, red tore- ador pants. Both of them were barefoot.

I looked at Yeamon. His face was tense as he stood on tiptoe to watch. Suddenly he called her name. "Chenault!" But the crowd was making so much noise that I could barely hear him three feet away. She seemed oblivious to everything but the music and the freak who led her around the floor. Yeamon called again, but no- body heard.

Now, as if in some kind of trance, Chenault began to unbutton her blouse. She popped the buttons slowly, like a practiced strip- per, then flung the blouse aside and pranced there in nothing but her bra and panties. I thought the crowd would go crazy. They howled and pounded on furniture, shoving and climbing on each other to get a better view. The whole house shook and I thought the floor might cave in. Somewhere across the room I heard glass breaking.

I looked again at Yeamon. He was waving his hands in the air now, trying to get Chenault's attention. But he looked like just an- other witness, carried away with the spectacle.

Now they were close together and I saw the brute reach around Chenault and unhook the strap of her bra. He undid it quickly, ex- pertly, and she seemed unaware that now she wore nothing but her thin silk panties. The bra slid down her arms and fell to the floor. Her breasts bounced violently with the jerk and thrust of the dance. Full, pink-nippled balls of flesh, suddenly cut loose from the cotton modesty of a New York bra.

I watched, fascinated and terrified, and then I heard Yeamon beside me as he lunged toward the dance floor. There was a commotion and then I saw the big bartender move up behind him and grab his arms. Several others pushed him back, treating him like a harmless drunk as they made room for the dance to go on.

Yeamon was screaming hysterically, struggling to keep his balance. "Chenault!" he shouted. "What the hell are you doing?" He sounded desperate, but I felt paralyzed.

They were coming together again, weaving slowly toward the middle of the circle. The noise was an overpowering roar from two hundred wild throats. Chenault still wore that dazed, ecstatic expression as the man reached out and eased her panties over her hips and down to her knees. She let them drop silently on the floor, then stepped away, breaking into the dance again, moving against him, freezing there for a moment—even the music paused—then dancing away, opening her eyes and flinging her hair from side to side.

Suddenly Yeamon broke loose. He leaped into the circle and they were on him immediately, but this time he was harder to pin. I saw him smack the bartender in the face, using his arms and elbows to keep them off, screaming with such a fury that the sound of it sent chills up my spine, and finally going down under a wave of bodies.

The melee stopped the dance. For an instant I saw Chenault standing alone; she looked surprised and bewildered, with that little muff of brown hair standing out against the white skin, and her blonde hair falling around her shoulders. She looked small and naked and helpless, and then I saw the man grab her arm and start pulling her toward the door.

I staggered through the crowd, cursing, shoving, trying to get to the hall before they disappeared. Behind me I could hear Yeamon, still yelling, but I knew they had him now and my only thought was to find Chenault. Several people whacked me before I got to the door, but I paid no attention. Once I thought I heard her scream, but it could have been anyone.

When I finally got outside I saw a crowd at the bottom of the stairs. I hurried down and found Yeamon lying there on the ground bleeding from the mouth and groaning. Apparently they had dragged him out a back door. The bartender was leaning over him and wiping his mouth with a handkerchief.

I forgot about Chenault and shoved through the ring of people, mumbling apologies as I made my way to where Yeamon was stretched out. When I got there the bartender looked up and said, "Is this your friend?"

I nodded, bending down to see if he was hurt.

"He's okay," somebody said. "We tried to be easy with him, but he kept swinging."

"Yeah," I said.

Yeamon was sitting up now, holding his head in his hands. "Chenault," he mumbled. "What the hell are you doing?"

I put my hand on his shoulder. "Okay," I said. "Take it easy."

"That filthy sonofabitch," he said loudly.

The bartender tapped me on the arm. "You better get him out of here," he said. "He's not hurt now, but he will be if he stays around."

"Can we get a cab?" I asked.

He nodded. "I'll get you a car." He stepped back and yelled across the crowd. Somebody answered and he pointed at me.

"Chenault!" Yeamon shouted, trying to get up off the ground.

I shoved him back down, knowing that the moment he got up we'd have another fight. I looked up at the bartender. "Where's the girl?" I said. "What happened to her?"

He smiled faintly. "She enjoyed herself."

I realized then that we were going to be sent off without Chenault. "Where is she?" I said too loudly, trying to keep the panic out of my voice.

A stranger stepped up to me and snarled, "Man, you better get out."

I shuffled nervously in the dirt, looking back at the bartender, who seemed to be in charge. He smiled maliciously, pointing behind me. I turned and saw a car coming slowly through the crowd. "Here's your cab," he said. "I'll get your friend." He stepped over to

Yeamon and jerked him to his feet. "Big man go to town," he said with a grin. "Leave little girl here."

Yeamon stiffened and began to shout. "You bastards!" He swung savagely at the bartender, who dodged easily and laughed while four men shoved Yeamon into the car. They shoved me in after him, and I leaned out the window to yell at the bartender: "I'll be back with the police—that girl better be all right." Suddenly I felt an awful jolt on the side of my face, and I drew back just in time to let the second punch go flying past my nose. Without quite knowing what I was doing, I rolled up the window and fell back on the seat. I heard them all laughing as we started down the hill.

Sixteen

ALL I could think about was getting the police, but the driver of the car refused to take us to the station or even tell us where it was. "Better forget it," he said quietly. "Everybody mind his own business." He let us out in the middle of town and said it would be all right if we gave him two dollars to pay for the gas. I grumbled bitterly and gave it to him, but Yeamon refused to get out of the car. He kept insisting that we were going back up the hill to get Chenault.

"Come on," I said, tugging at his arm. "We'll get the cops. They'll take us up." Finally I got him out and the car pulled away.

We found the police station, but there was nobody in it. The lights were on and we went in to wait. Yeamon passed out on a bench and I was so groggy that I could barely keep my eyes open. After about an hour I decided we'd be better off looking for a cop in the streets. I woke Yeamon up and we started down toward the bars. The carnival was dissipating now and the streets were full of drunks, mostly tourists and Puerto Ricans. Little knots of people wandered from bar to bar, passing bodies in doorways, and a few just sprawled on the sidewalk. It was almost four, but the bars were still full of people. It looked like the town had been bombed.

There was no sign of a cop anywhere, and by this time we were both ready to fall down from exhaustion. Finally we gave up and took a cab out to Lindbergh Beach, where we dragged ourselves over the fence and fell down in the sand to sleep.

Sometime during the night it started raining and when I woke up I was soaking wet. I thought it was dawn, but when I looked at my watch it said nine o'clock. My head felt swollen to twice its normal size and there was a big, painful bump in front of my right ear. I took off my clothes and went into the bay for a swim, but it made me feel worse instead of better. The morning was cold and dreary, and a light rain peppered the water. I sat on the raft for a while and thought about the night before. The more I remembered, the more depressed I became, and I dreaded the idea of going back into town to look for Chenault. At that point I didn't really care if she lived or died. All I wanted was to walk across the road and get on a plane for San Juan, leaving Yeamon asleep on the beach and hoping I'd never see either one of them again.

After a while I swam in and woke him up. He looked sick. We went to the airport for breakfast, then got a bus to town. After getting our clothes off the boat at Yacht Haven, we went to the police station, where the gendarme on duty was playing solitaire with a deck of cards that showed naked women in various lustful poses.

He grinned and looked up when Yeamon finished talking. "Man," he said slowly, "what can I do about your girl if she likes somebody else?"

"Likes, hell!" Yeamon shouted. "She was dragged off!"

"Okay," he said, still smiling. "I live here all my life an' I know how girls get dragged off at carnivals." He laughed softly. "You tell me she had all her clothes off, dancin' for all those people—and then you say she was raped?"

The cop made several more remarks of the same kind, and finally Yeamon's eyes got wild and he began to shout in a voice that was angry and desperate. "Listen!" he yelled. "If you don't do something about this I'm going up to that house with a goddamn butcher knife and kill everybody I see!"

The cop looked startled. "Take it easy, mon. You heading for real trouble if you keep runnin' your mouth."

"Look," I said. "All we want you to do is go up there with us and find the girl—is that too much to ask?"

He looked down at his cards for a moment, as if by consulting them he could divine the meaning of our appearance, and what to do about it. Finally he shook his head sadly and looked up. "Ah, you troublesome people," he said quietly. "You jus' can't learn."

Before we could say anything, he stood up and put on his pith helmet. "Okay," he said. "Let's go take a look."

We followed him into the street. His attitude made me nervous, almost embarrassed for the trouble we were causing.

By the time we pulled up in front of the house I wanted to jump out and run away. Whatever we found was going to be bad. Maybe they had taken her somewhere else, to some other party, and staked her out on a bed, a white, pink-nippled nightcap to wind up the carnival. I shuddered as we went up the stairs, then I glanced over at Yeamon. He looked like a man on his way to the guillotine.

The cop rang the bell and it was answered by a meek-looking black woman who stuttered nervously and swore she had seen nothing of a white girl and knew nothing about a party the night before.

"Balls!" Yeamon snapped. "You had a hell of a party here last night and I paid six dollars to get into it."

The woman denied having knowledge of any party. She said there were people sleeping inside, but no white girl.

The cop asked if he could come in and take a look. She shrugged and let him in, but when Yeamon tried to follow she got excited and shut the door in his face.

In a few minutes the cop reappeared. "No sign of a white girl," he said, looking Yeamon straight in the eye.

I didn't want to believe him because I didn't want to face the other possibilities. This should have been simple—find her, wake her up, and take her away. But now nothing was simple. She might be anywhere, behind any door on the island. I looked at Yeamon, expecting him to run amok and start swinging at any moment. But he was slumped against the porch railing and he looked ready to cry. "Oh jesus lord," he muttered, staring down at his shoes. It was such a genuine despair that the cop put his hand on Yeamon's shoulder.

"Sorry, mon," he said quietly. "Come on now. Let's go."

We drove back down the hill to the station and the cop promised to look for a girl of Chenault's description. "I'll tell the others," he said. "She'll turn up." He smiled kindly at Yeamon. "You got no business lettin' a woman run you 'round in circles like this anyhow."

"Yeah," Yeamon replied. Then he put Chenault's raincoat and her small suitcase on the desk. "Give this to her when she turns up," he said. "I don't feel like lugging it around."

The cop nodded and put her clothes on a shelf in the back of the room. Then he wrote down my address in San Juan so he could send a message if they found her. We said goodbye and walked down the street to the Grand Hotel for breakfast.

We ordered rum and ice with hamburgers and ate them in silence while we read the newspapers. Finally, Yeamon looked up and said casually, "She's just a whore. I don't know why this should bother me."

"Don't worry about it," I said. "She went crazy—totally crazy."

"You're right," he said. "She's a whore. I knew it the first time I saw her." He leaned back in the booth. "I met her at a party on Staten Island about a week before I came down here; the minute I saw her I said to myself, now this girl is a rattling fine whore—not the money type, but the type that just wants to hump." He nodded. "She came back to my place with me and I fell on her like a bull. She stayed there all week, didn't even go to work. At the time I was staying with a friend of my brother's and I made him sleep on a cot in the kitchen—pretty much ran him out of his own place." He smiled sadly. "Then when I left for San Juan she wanted to come with me—it was all I could do to make her wait a few weeks."

I had several Chenaults on my mind right then: a chic little girl in New York with a secret lust and a Lord & Taylor wardrobe; a tan little girl with long blonde hair, walking on the beach in a white bikini; a yelling, drunken hellion in a loud St. Thomas bar; and then the girl I had seen last night—dancing in those flimsy panties and bouncing those pink-nippled breasts, weaving her hips while a crazy thug pulled the panties down her legs . . . and then that last glimpse, standing in the middle of the room, alone for just an instant, that little muff of brown hair standing out like a beacon against the white flesh of her belly and thighs . . . that sacred little muff, carefully nurtured by parents who knew all too well its power and its value, sent off to Smith College for cultivation and slight exposure to the wind and weather of life, tended for twenty years by a legion of parents and teachers and friends and advisers, then farmed out to New York on a wing and a prayer.

We finished breakfast and took a bus to the airport. The lobby was jammed with pitiful drunkards: men dragging each other into bathrooms, women sick on the floor in front of benches, tourists babbling with fear. I took one look at the scene and knew that we might wait all day and all night before we got a seat on a plane. Without tickets, we might be here for three days. It looked hopeless.

Then we had a wild piece of luck. We had gone to the coffee shop and were looking around for a seat when I saw the pilot who had flown me over to Vieques on Thursday. He seemed to recognize me as I approached. "Ho," I said. "Remember me? Kemp—*New York Times.*"

He smiled and held out his hand. "That's right," he said. "You were with Zimburger."

"Pure coincidence," I said with a grin. "Say, can I hire you to take us back to San Juan? We're desperate."

"Sure," he said. "I'm going back at four. I have two passengers and two empty seats." He nodded. "You're lucky you found me this early—I wouldn't have had them long."

"Christ," I said. "You've saved our lives. Charge me anything you want—I'll bill it to Zimburger."

He grinned broadly. "Well, glad to hear that. I can't think of anybody I'd rather ram it to." He finished his coffee and put the cup on the counter. "Got to run now," he said. "Be on the runway at four—it's the same red Apache."

"Don't worry," I said. "We'll be there."

The mob was piling up now. A plane left for San Juan every half hour, but all the seats were reserved. The people waiting for vacancies were beginning to get drunk again, hauling out bottles of scotch and passing them around.

It was impossible to think. I wanted peace, the privacy of my own apartment, a glass instead of a paper cup, four walls between me and this stinking mob of drunks that pressed on us from all sides.

At four we went out to the runway and found the Apache warming up. The flight back took about thirty minutes. With us was a young couple from Atlanta; they had come over from San Juan earlier in the day and now they couldn't get back soon enough. They were absolutely appalled by the wild and uppity nigras.

I was tempted to tell them about Chenault, giving them all the details and finishing up with a hideous vision of where she was now, and what she was doing. Instead, I sat quietly and stared down at the white clouds. I felt like I'd survived a long and perilous binge, and now I was going home.

My car was in the airport lot where I'd left it, and Yeamon's scooter was chained to a railing by the attendant's shack. He unlocked it and said he was going on out to his house, despite my advice that he stay at my place so he could pick her up if she came in sometime during the night.

"Hell," I said. "She might already be back for that matter. For all we know, she thought we abandoned her last night, so she went to the airport."

"Yeah," he said, jerking the scooter off its stand. "That must be what happened, Kemp. Maybe she'll have dinner ready when I get back to the house."

I followed him out the long driveway and waved goodbye as I turned off on the highway toward San Juan. When I got back to the apartment I went to sleep immediately and didn't wake up until noon the next day.

On my way down to the office I wondered if I should say anything about Chenault, but the moment I walked into the newsroom I forgot all about her. Sala called me over to his desk, where he was talking excitedly with Schwartz and Moberg. "It's all over," he yelled. "You should have stayed in St. Thomas." Segarra had quit and Lotterman had left the night before for Miami, presumably in a last-ditch effort to get new financing. Sala was convinced the paper was going under, but Moberg thought it was a false alarm. "Lotterman has plenty," he assured us. "He went to see his daughter—he told me right before he left."

Sala laughed bitterly. "Wake up, Moberg—do you think Greasy Nick would have dumped a soft job like this if he didn't have to? Face it, we're unemployed."

"Goddamnit," Schwartz exclaimed. "I was just getting settled here—this is the first job I've had in ten years that I wanted to keep."

Schwartz was about forty and although I didn't see much of him except at work, I liked him. He did a good job on the desk, never bothered anybody, and spent his free time drinking in the most expensive bars he could find. He hated Al's, he said; it was too clubby, and dirty besides. He liked the Marlin Club and the Caribé Lounge and the other hotel bars where a man could wear a tie and drink in peace and occasionally see a good floor show. He worked hard, and when he finished working he drank. After that he slept, and then he went back to work. Journalism to Schwartz was a jigsaw puzzle a simple process of putting a paper together so that everything fit. Nothing more. He considered it an honorable trade and he'd learned it well; he had it down to a formula and he was damn well going to keep it that way. Nothing annoyed him more than a screwball or a crank. They made his life difficult and caused him to brood endlessly.

Sala grinned at him. "Don't worry, Schwartz—you'll get a pension—probably forty acres and a mule, too."

I remembered Schwartz's first appearance at the *News*. He wandered into the newsroom and asked for a job the same way he'd walk into a barbershop and ask for a haircut, and with no more idea of being turned down. Now, if there was another English-language paper in town, the collapse of the *News* would mean no more to Schwartz than the death of his favorite barber. It wasn't the loss of a job that upset him, but the fact that his pattern was being threatened. If the paper folded, he'd be forced into some strange and irregular action. And Schwartz was not that way. He was perfectly capable of doing a strange and irregular thing, but only if he'd planned it. Anything done on the spur of the moment was not only stupid, but immoral. Like going to the Caribé without a tie. He viewed Moberg's way of life as a criminal shame and called him "that job-hopping degenerate." I knew it was Schwartz who had put into Lotterman's head the idea that Moberg was a thief.

Sala looked up at me. "Schwartz is afraid they'll cut off his credit at the Marlin and he'll lose that special seat at the end of the bar—the one they save for the dean of the white journalists."

Schwartz shook his head sadly. "You cynical fool. We'll see how you feel when you start looking for a job."

Sala got up and started for the darkroom. "No more jobs in this place," he said. "When Greasy Nick jumps ship, you can bet the word is out."

A few hours later we went across the street for a drink. I told Sala about Chenault and he twisted nervously in his seat as I talked.

"Man, that's awful!" he exclaimed when I finished. "Christ, it makes me sick!" He whacked the table with his fist. "Goddamnit, I knew something like that would happen—didn't I tell you?"

I nodded, staring down at my ice.

"Why the hell didn't you do something?" he demanded. "Yeamon's pretty good at slapping people around—where was *he* all that time?"

"It happened too fast," I said. "He tried to stop it, but they stomped him."

He thought for a moment. "Why did you take her to that place?"

"Come on," I said. "I didn't go over there to play chaperon to some lunatic girl." I looked across the table at him. "Why didn't *you* stay home and read a good book the night you got whipped by the cops?"

He shook his head and fell back in the booth. After two or three minutes of silence, he looked up. "What the hell are we heading for, Kemp? I'm really beginning to think we're all doomed." He scratched his face nervously and lowered his voice. "I'm serious," he said. "We keep getting drunk and these terrible things keep happening and each one is worse than the last . . ." He waved his hand in a gesture of hopelessness. "Hell, it's no fun anymore—our luck's all running out at the same time."

When we got back to the office I thought about what he'd said, and I began to think that Sala might be right. He talked about luck and fate and numbers coming up, yet he never ventured a nickel at the casinos because he knew the house had all the percentages. And beneath his pessimism, his bleak conviction that all the machinery was rigged against him, at the bottom of his soul was a faith that he was going to outwit it, that by carefully watching the signs he was going to know when to dodge and be spared. It was fatalism with a loophole, and all you had to do to make it work was never miss a sign. Survival by coordination, as it were. The race is not to the swift, nor the battle to the strong, but to those who can see it coming and jump aside. Like a frog evading a shillelagh in a midnight marsh.

So, with this theory firmly in mind, I went to see Sanderson that night, meaning to leap from the bog of threatened unemployment to the high-dry branch of fat assignments. It was the only branch I could see within a thousand miles, and if I missed it, it meant a long haul to a new foothold, and I didn't have the faintest idea where it would be.

He greeted me with a fifty-dollar check, which I saw as a good omen. "For that article," he explained. "Come on out to the porch, we'll get you a drink."

"Drink, hell," I said. "I'm looking for unemployment insurance."

He laughed. "I might have known—especially after today."

We stopped in the kitchen to get some ice. "Of course you knew Segarra was going to quit," I said.

"Of course," he replied.

"Jesus," I muttered. "Tell me, Hal—just what does the future hold for me? Am I going to get rich, or go to the dogs?"

He laughed and started for the porch, where I could hear other voices. "Don't worry," he said over his shoulder. "Come on out where it's cool."

I didn't feel like dealing with a bunch of new people, but I went out to the porch anyway. They were young and they had all just come from somewhere exciting, and they were very very interested in Puerto Rico and all its possibilities. I felt successful and *au courant*. After days of being blown and buffeted in the rotten winds of life, it was nice to be back on the inside.

Seventeen

I WAS awakened the next morning by a tapping on my door, a soft, yet urgent tapping. Don't answer it, I thought, don't let it happen. I sat up in bed and stared at the door for a minute. I groaned, putting my head down in my hands and wanting to be anywhere in the world but here and involved in this thing; then I got up and walked slowly over to the door.

She was wearing the same clothes, but now she looked haggard and dirty. The delicate illusions that get us through life can only stand so much strain—and now, looking at Chenault, I wanted to slam the door and go back to bed.

"Good morning," I said.

She said nothing.

"Come in," I said finally, stepping back to clear the doorway.

She kept staring at me with an expression that made me more nervous than ever. It was humiliation and shock, I suppose, but there was something else in it—a shade of sadness and amusement that was almost a smile.

It was a frightening thing to see, and the longer I looked at it the more convinced I was that she'd lost her mind. Then she walked in and put her straw pocketbook on the kitchen table. "This is nice," she said in a quiet voice, looking around the apartment.

"Yeah," I said. "It's okay."

"I didn't know where you lived," she said. "I had to call the newspaper."

"How did you get here?" I asked.

"A cab." She nodded toward the door. "He's waiting outside. I don't have any money."

"Jesus," I said. "Well, I'll go out and pay him—how much is it?"

She shook her head. "I don't know."

I found my wallet and started for the door. Then I realized I was wearing nothing but shorts. I went back to the closet and pulled on my pants, half desperate to get out of the place and organize my thoughts. "Don't worry," I said. "I'll get it."

"I know," she said wearily. "Could I lie down?"

"Sure," I said quickly, hopping over to the bed. "Here, I'll straighten it out for you—it's one of those beds that turns into a couch." I pulled up the sheets and tucked the spread around them, snatching at the wrinkles like a charwoman.

She sat down on the bed, looking at me as I pulled on a shirt. "This is a wonderful apartment," she said. "So much sun."

"Yeah," I replied as I moved toward the door. "Well, I'll pay the cab now—see you in a minute." Then I ran down the steps to the street. He smiled happily as I came toward him. "How much is it?" I said, opening my wallet.

He nodded eagerly. "Sí, bueno. Señorita say you pay. Bueno, gracias. Señorita is not okay." He pointed meaningfully at his head.

"That's right," I said. "Cuánto es?"

"Ah, sí," he replied, holding up seven fingers. "Seven dólares, sí."

"Are you nuts!" I said.

"Sí," he said quickly. "We go all over, around and around, stop here, stop there . . ." He shook his head again. "Ah, sí, two hours, loco, señorita say you pay."

I gave him seven dollars, assuming he was lying, but believing him when he said the morning had been loco. No doubt it had been, and now it was my turn. I watched him drive off, then I went over to a spot under the flamboyan tree, out of sight of the windows. What the hell am I going to do with her? I thought. I was barefoot and the sand was cool under my feet. I looked up at the tree, then over to the window of my apartment. She was in there, already on the bed. Here the *News* was about to fold and suddenly I had a penniless girl on my hands—and a nut, to boot. What could I say to Yeamon, or even Sala? The whole thing was too much. I decided I would have to get her off my hands, even if it meant paying her way back to New York.

I went upstairs and opened the door, feeling more relaxed, now that I'd made up my mind. She was stretched out on the bed, staring up at the ceiling.

"Have you had any breakfast?" I asked, trying to sound cheerful.

"No," she replied, so softly that I barely heard.

"Well I have everything," I said. "Eggs, bacon, coffee, the whole business." I went over to the sink. "How about some orange juice?"

"Orange juice would be fine," she said, still staring at the ceiling.

I cooked a pan of bacon and scrambled some eggs, happy for something to keep me busy. Now and then I would glance back at the bed. She was lying on her back with her arms folded across her stomach.

"Chenault," I said finally. "Do you feel okay?"

"I'm fine," she replied in the same dull voice.

I turned around. "Maybe I should call a doctor."

"No," she said. "I'm fine. I just want to rest."

I shrugged and went back to the stove. I put the eggs and bacon on two plates and poured two glasses of milk. "Here," I said, taking her plate over to the bed. "Eat this and see if you feel any better."

She didn't move and I put the plate down on a table beside the bed. "You better eat," I said. "You look pretty damn unhealthy."

She kept staring at the ceiling. "I know," she whispered. "Just let me rest awhile."

"Fine with me," I said. "I have to go to work anyway." I went to the kitchen and drank two mouthfuls of warm rum, then I took a shower and got dressed. When I left, the food on her table was untouched. "See you about eight," I said. "Call the paper if you need anything."

"I will," she said. "Goodbye."

I spent most of the day in the library, taking notes on previous anti-communist investigations and looking for background material on people involved in hearings that were scheduled to start on Thursday. I avoided Sala, hoping he wouldn't come looking for me to ask for news of Chenault. At six o'clock Lotterman called from Miami, telling Schwartz to handle the paper and saying he'd be back on Friday with "good news." It could only mean that he'd found some financing; the paper would last a little longer and I still had my job.

I left about seven. There was nothing else to do and I didn't want to get caught in some movement to Al's. I went down the back stairs and slipped into my car like a fugitive. Somewhere in Santurce I ran over a dog, but I kept going. When I got to the apartment Chenault was still asleep.

I made some sandwiches and a pot of coffee, and while I was clattering around in the kitchen she woke up. "Hello," she said quietly.

"Hello," I said, not turning around. I opened a can of tomato soup and put it on to heat. "You want something to eat?" I asked.

"I think so," she said, sitting up on the bed. "I'll fix it, though."

"It's already fixed," I said. "How do you feel?"

"Better," she said. "Much better."

I took a ham sandwich and a bowl of soup over to the bed. The bacon and eggs from breakfast were still sitting there, looking cold and withered. I took the plate off the table and put the other food down in its place.

She looked up and smiled. "You're such a good person, Paul."

"I'm not good," I said on my way back to the kitchen. "Just a little confused."

"Why?" she said. "Because of what happened?"

I took my food over to a table by the window and sat down. "Yeah," I said after a pause. "Your . . . ah . . . your maneuvers of the past few days have been . . . ah . . . sort of obscure, to say the least."

She looked down at her hands. "Why did you let me in?" she said finally.

I shrugged. "I don't know—did you think I wouldn't?"

"I didn't know," she replied. "I didn't know how you'd feel."

"Neither did I," I said.

Suddenly she looked up at me. "I didn't know what to do!" she blurted. "When I got on that plane I hoped it would crash! I wanted it to blow up and sink in the ocean!"

"Where'd you get a plane ticket?" I said. "I thought you didn't have any money." I asked without thinking, and the minute the words came out of my mouth I regretted them.

She looked startled, then she began to cry. "Somebody bought it for me," she sobbed. "I didn't have any money, I—"

"Never mind," I said quickly. "I didn't mean to ask anyway. I was playing journalist."

She put her face down in her hands and kept crying.

I resumed eating until she quieted down, then I looked over at her again. "Look," I said. "Let's start everything from right now. I'll just assume you've had a bad experience and I won't ask any more questions, okay?"

She nodded, without looking up.

"All I want to know," I added, "is what you plan to do now." She looked like she was going to cry again and I quickly added: "Just so I can help out."

She sobbed, then said, "What does Fritz think?"

"Well," I said. "He wasn't real happy when I last saw him. Of course that was Sunday night and we were both in pretty bad shape—he might feel better by now."

She looked up. "What happened—did he get in a fight?"

I stared at her.

"Don't look at me that way!" she screamed. "I don't remember!"

I shrugged. "Well—"

"The last thing I remember is going into that house," she said, starting to cry again. "I don't remember anything else until the next day!"

She fell down on the bed and cried for a long time. I went to the kitchen and poured a cup of coffee. I was tempted to drive her out to Yeamon's and leave her on the road behind his house. I thought about it for a while, but decided I'd better talk to him first and find out how he felt. For all I knew he might break both her arms if she showed up out there in the dead of night with this malignant-sounding story. The little she'd said was enough to kill any hopes I'd had that it was all a mistake, and now I didn't want to hear any

more. The sooner I could get her out of here, the better. If I didn't
see Yeamon in town the next day, I would drive out to his house after work.

She finally stopped crying and went to sleep. I sat by the window
and read for a few hours, sipping the rum until I got sleepy. Then I
shoved her over to one side of the bed and very carefully stretched
out on the other.

When I woke up the next morning Chenault was already in the
kitchen. "It's my turn to do something," she said with a bright
smile. "You just sit there and be waited on."

She brought me a glass of orange juice, then a big omelette, and
we both sat on the bed and ate. She seemed relaxed and talked
about having the place cleaned up by the time I got back from
work. I had meant to tell her that I was going to see Yeamon and
have her off my hands by nightfall, but now the idea of saying it
made me feel like an ogre. What the hell, I thought. No sense telling
her—just do it.

She brought the coffee over on a little tray. "Right after this I'm
going to take a shower," she said. "Do you mind?"

I laughed. "Yes, Chenault, I forbid you to use the shower."

She smiled, and when she finished her coffee she went into the
bathroom and I heard the water turn on. I went to the kitchen for
another cup of coffee. I felt slightly indecent, wearing nothing but
my shorts, and decided to get dressed before she came out of the
shower. First I went downstairs to get the paper. As I came back
through the door I heard her call from the bathroom: "Paul, can
you come here a minute?"

I went over and opened the door, thinking she would have the
curtain pulled. She didn't, and greeted me with a big smile. "I feel
human again," she exclaimed. "Aren't I beautiful?" She stepped out
of the stream of water and faced me, lifting her arms like a model
demonstrating some new and unusual soap. There was such a
weird, nymphet egotism about her stance that I had to laugh.

"Come on in," she said happily. "This is wonderful!"

I stopped laughing and there was an odd silence. I heard a gong
somewhere in the back of my brain, and then a melodramatic

voice saying, "And this concludes The Adventures of Paul Kemp, the Drunken Journalist. He read the signs and saw it coming, but he was too much of a lecher to step out of the way." Then there was organ music, a sort of feverish dirge, and then I was stepping out of my shorts and into the shower with Chenault. I remember the feel of those soapy little hands washing my back, keeping my eyes tightly shut while my soul fought a hopeless battle with my groin, then giving up like a drowning man and soaking the bed with our bodies.

She was stretched out with a peaceful smile on her face, still wet from the shower, when I finally left for work. All the way into San Juan I drove blindly, muttering and shaking my head like a man who has finally been tracked down.

When I got to the office there were two things on my desk: one was a small book titled *72 Sure-Fire Ways to Have Fun*, and the other was a note saying Sanderson wanted me to call him.

I checked with Schwartz to see if there were any assignments. There weren't, so I went out for some coffee, walking several blocks down the waterfront to avoid any possibility of meeting Sala. I also expected Yeamon to come bounding into the office at any moment. It took me a while to compose myself, but finally I decided that the morning had never happened. Nothing had changed. I would see Yeamon and get her off my hands. If he didn't come into town, I would drive out there after work.

When I felt myself under control I went back to the office. At two-thirty I had to go to the Caribé to talk to one of the Congressmen who had come down for the anti-communist investigation. I drove over there and talked to the man for two hours. We sat on the terrace and drank rum punch, and when I left he thanked me for the "valuable information" I had given him.

"Okay, Senator," I said. "Thanks for the story—it's a hot one." Back at the office I was hard-pressed to get four paragraphs out of the entire conversation.

Then I called Sanderson. "How're you coming on that brochure?" he asked.

"Oh Jesus," I muttered.

"Damnit, Paul, you promised me a first draft this week. You're worse than this fellow Yeamon."

"All right," I said wearily. "I'm going nuts right now, Hal. I'll get it to you this weekend, maybe Monday."

"What's wrong?" he said.

"Never mind," I replied. "I'll be rid of it tonight—then I'll do the brochure, okay?"

Just as I hung up Schwartz motioned me over to the desk. "Big wreck on Bayamon Road," he said, handing me a page of scribbled notes. "Sala's not around—can you handle a camera?"

"Sure," I said. "I'll get a few Nikons from the darkroom."

"Good thinking," he said. "Take them all."

I raced out Bayamon Road until I saw the flashing red lights of a parked ambulance. I got there just in time to get a shot of one of the bodies, lying in the dust beside an overturned farm truck. For some reason that nobody understood, it had swerved out of its lane and slammed head-on into a bus. I asked a few questions, talked awhile with the cops, then hurried back to the office to write the story. I typed feverishly so I could finish the damn thing and get out to . . .

Suddenly I realized I was not going to Yeamon's. I was hurrying because I was anxious to get back to the apartment. I'd been anxious all day, and now, as the afternoon came to an end, I groaned inwardly as the truth slithered out in the open and stared me in the face.

I turned the story in and went down the stairs to my car, thinking I should probably check by Al's to see if he might be there. But the thing that drew me toward the apartment was huge and powerful. I started up toward Al's, then suddenly turned off toward Condado and tried not to think about anything until I pulled up in front of my apartment.

She was wearing one of my shirts and it hung on her like a short nightie. She smiled happily when I came in and got up off the bed to make me a drink. The shirt flapped lewdly around her thighs as she bounced into the kitchen.

I felt totally defeated. For a while I paced around the apartment, barely hearing her happy chatter, then I gave up entirely and went over to the bed and took off my clothes. I fell on her with such a violence that her smile quickly disappeared and it became a desperate business. She kicked her feet in the air and shrieked and arched her back and she was still trying when I exploded inside her and collapsed with total exhaustion. Finally she gave up and locked her legs around my hips and her arms around my neck, and started to cry.

I leaned on my elbows and looked down at her. "What's wrong?" I asked.

She kept her eyes closed and shook her head. "I can't," she sobbed. "I get so close, but I can't."

I looked at her for a moment, wondering what I should say, then I put my head down on the bed and moaned. We stayed that way for a long time, and finally we got up and she cooked dinner while I read the *Miami Herald.*

The next morning I drove out to Yeamon's. I didn't know exactly what I was going to say to him, so I kept thinking about his bad points so I could lie without feeling guilty. But it was hard to see a bastard at the end of that drive. The hot, peaceful beauty of the ocean and the sand and the green-gold palms threw me completely off balance, and by the time I got to his house I felt like a decadent intruder.

He was sitting naked on the patio, drinking coffee and reading a book. I pulled up beside the house and got out. He turned and smiled. "What's the score?"

"Chenault's back," I said. "I have her at the apartment."

"When?" he said.

"Yesterday—I meant to bring her out here last night, but I thought I'd check with you first."

"What happened?" he asked. "Did she tell you?"

"Just fragments," I said. "It didn't sound good."

He kept staring at me. "Well, what's she going to do?"

"I don't know," I said, feeling more and more nervous. "You want me to bring her out here?"

He looked out to sea for an instant, then back at me. "Hell no," he snapped. "She's yours—with my compliments."

"Don't give me that," I said. "She just showed up at my apartment—she was in pretty bad shape."

"Who gives a damn?" he said.

"Well," I said slowly, "she wants me to get her clothes."

"Sure," he said, getting out of the chair. He went into the hut and began throwing things out the door. They were mostly clothes, but some of them were mirrors and little boxes and glass objects that broke on the patio.

I went to the door. "Take it easy!" I yelled. "What the hell is wrong with you?"

He came out with a suitcase and threw it toward the car. "Get the hell out of here!" he shouted. "You and that whore make a good pair!"

The clothes were all in a heap and I loaded them into the back of my car while he watched. When I got it all packed in I opened the door and sat down. "Call me at the paper," I said. "But wait till you calm down. I have enough trouble as it is."

He glared at me and I quickly backed the car out to the road. It had been just about as bad as I'd thought it was going to be, and I wanted to get away before it got any worse. I pushed the accelerator to the floor and the little car bounced over the ruts like a jeep, throwing up a huge trail of dust. It was almost noon and the sun was glaring hot. The sea rolled in on the dunes and the swamp sent up a steamy mist that burned my eyes and blotted out the sun. I drove past the Colmado de Jesús Lopo and saw the old man leaning on his counter and staring out at me as if he knew the whole story, and was not at all surprised.

When I got back to the apartment Chenault was washing the dishes. She looked over her shoulder and smiled as I came in. "You're back," she said. "I wasn't sure you'd make it."

"He wasn't happy," I said, dumping a load of her clothes on the bed.

She laughed, but it was a sad sound and it made me feel even worse. "Poor Fritz," she said. "He'll never grow up."

"Yeah," I said. Then I went back down to the car for more clothes.

Eighteen

ON my way to work the next morning I stopped by Al's and found Sala on the patio. He was drinking a beer and thumbing through a new issue of *Life en Español*. I got a jar of iced rum from the kitchen and went out to his table.

"Are they in there?" I asked, nodding at the magazine.

"Hell no," he grumbled. "They'll never use 'em—Sanderson told me they were scheduled last fall."

"What the hell?" I said. "You got paid."

He tossed the magazine aside and leaned back in the chair. "That's only half of it," he said. "I can get paid anytime."

We sat for a while in silence, then he looked up. "Ah, this is a shitty place, Kemp—the shittiest place I've ever seen." He reached into his shirt pocket for a cigarette. "Yep, I think the time has come for old Robert to put his ass on the road."

I smiled.

"No, it won't be long now," he said. "Lotterman gets back today and I won't be surprised if he folds the paper by midnight." He nodded. "The minute they hand out those checks I'm going to run like hell for the bank and get mine cashed."

179

"I don't know," I said. "Schwartz said he got some money."

He shook his head. "Poor Schwartz, he'll still be showing up for work when they turn the place into a bowling alley." He chuckled. "What else? El Headline Bowling Palace, with Moberg tending the bar. Maybe they'll hire Schwartz to do publicity." He shouted toward the kitchen for two beers, then looked at me. I nodded. "Four," he yelled. "And turn on the goddamn air conditioning."

He fell back in the chair again. "I have to get off this rock. I know some people in Mexico City—I may give it a try." He grinned. "I know they have women there, anyway."

"Hell," I said. "Plenty of women around if you'd get off your ass."

He looked up. "Kemp, I believe you're a whorehopper."

I laughed. "Why?"

"Why!" he exclaimed. "I'm onto your sneaky ways, Kemp. I suspected it all along—and now you've lured that girl away from Yeamon."

"What?" I exclaimed.

"Don't deny it," he said. "He was in here earlier—told me the whole sleazy story."

"You bastard!" I said. "Chenault just showed up at my apartment. She didn't have anywhere else to go."

He grinned. "She could have moved in with me—at least I'm decent."

I snorted. "Christ, you'd have finished her off."

"I suppose you're sleeping on the floor," he replied. "I know that apartment, Kemp. I know there's only one bed. Don't give me this Christian crap."

"Christian hell!" I said. "You're such a sex-crazy sonofabitch that there's no sense telling you anything."

He laughed. "Calm down, Kemp, you're getting hysterical—I know you wouldn't touch the girl, you're not that way." He laughed again and ordered four more beers.

"Just for the record," I said, "I'm sending her back to New York."

"Probably the best thing," he replied. "Any girl that runs off with a pack of bushmen is bad news."

"I told you what happened over there," I said. "She didn't run off with anybody."

He shook his head. "Forget it," he said wearily. "I couldn't care less. Do whatever you want. I have my own problems."

The beers arrived and I glanced down at my watch. "It's almost noon," I said. "You don't figure on going to work?"

"I'll go when I'm drunk enough," he replied. "Have another beer—we'll all be gone by Monday."

We drank steadily for three hours, then we drove down to the office. Lotterman was back, but he'd gone out somewhere. He finally came in about five and called us all together in the middle of the room. Then he climbed up on a desk.

"Men," he said. "You'll be happy to know that that goddamn worthless Segarra finally quit. He was the worst goldbricker we've ever had in this place and on top of that he was queer—now that he's gone I think we'll be all right."

There were a few snickers, then silence.

"That's only part of the good news," he said with a big smile. "I suppose you all know the paper hasn't been making much money lately—well by God we don't have to worry about that anymore!" He paused and looked around. "You've all heard of Daniel Stein, I guess—well he's an old friend of mine, and as of Monday morning he's half-owner of this newspaper." He smiled. "I walked into his office and I said, 'Dan, I want to keep my paper alive,' and he said, 'Ed, how much do you need?' That's all there was to it. His lawyers are fixing up the papers and they'll be here on Monday for me to sign." He shifted nervously on the desk and smiled again. "Now I know you boys were expecting to get paid today, and I hate to cramp your style for the weekend, but under my agreement with Dan I can't give out any paychecks until I sign those papers—so you won't get paid until Monday." He nodded quickly. "Of course anybody who needs a few bucks to get by until then can hit me up for a loan—I don't want you boys getting thirsty and blaming it on me."

There was a ripple of laughter, then I heard Sala's voice from somewhere on the other side of the room. "I know about this guy, Stein," he said. "Are you sure he'll come through?"

Lotterman banished the question with a wave of his hand. "Of course I'm sure, Bob. Dan and I are old friends."

"Well," Sala replied. "I have a pretty big weekend coming up, and if it's all the same to you I'd just as soon borrow my whole pay-check right now, then you won't have to give me anything on Monday."

Lotterman stared down at him. "What are you trying to say, Bob?"

"I don't talk in swirls," Sala replied. "I just want you to lend me a hundred and twenty-five bucks until Monday."

"That's ridiculous!" Lotterman shouted.

"Ridiculous, hell," said Sala. "I worked in Miami, remember? I know Stein. He's a convicted embezzler." He lit a cigarette. "And besides, I might not be here on Monday."

"What do you mean?" Lotterman shouted. "You're not quitting?"

"I didn't say that," Sala replied.

"Now listen, Bob!" Lotterman shouted. "I don't know what you're trying to do here, telling me you might quit and you might not—who in hell do you think you are?"

Sala smiled faintly. "Don't shout, Ed. It makes us all nervous. I just asked for a loan, that's all."

Lotterman jumped down off the desk. "You can see me in my office," he said over his shoulder. "Kemp, I want to see you next." He waved his hand in the air. "That's all boys, let's get back to work."

Sala followed him into his office. I stood there and heard Schwartz saying: "This is a terrible thing—I don't know what to believe."

"The worst," I replied.

Moberg came running over to us. "He can't do this!" he screamed. "No salary, no severance pay—we can't stand it!"

Lotterman's door opened and Sala came out looking very unhappy. Lotterman appeared right behind him and called to me. He waited until I got inside, then closed the door behind us.

"Paul," he said. "What can I do with these guys?"

I looked at him, not sure what he meant.

"I'm on the ropes," he said. "You're the only one here I can talk to—the others are vultures."

"Why me?" I said. "I'm a hell of a vulture."

"No you're not," he said quickly. "You're lazy, but you're not a vulture—not like that stinking Sala!" He sputtered angrily. "Did you hear that crap he was giving me? Have you ever heard anything like it?"

I shrugged. "Well—"

"That's why I want to talk to you," he said. "I have to handle these guys. We're in real trouble—this guy Stein has me pinned to the wall." He looked up at me and nodded. "If I can't get this paper going, he'll close it and sell it for junk. I'll go to debtor's prison."

"Sounds pretty bleak," I said.

He laughed humorlessly. "You don't know the half of it." Then his voice became hearty and full of purpose. "Now what I want you to do is get these guys on the ball. I want you to tell 'em that we all have to pull together, or we'll sink!"

"Sink?" I said.

He nodded emphatically. "You're damn tootin'."

"Well," I said slowly. "That's sort of a hairy proposition, what do you figure Sala would say if I went out there and told him it was sink or swim with the *Daily News*?" I hesitated. "Or Schwartz, or Vanderwitz—even Moberg."

He stared down at his desk. "Yeah," he said finally. "I guess they can all run—like Segarra." He slammed his fist on the desk. "That greasy little pervert! He didn't just quit—he broadcast it all over San Juan! People kept telling me they'd heard the paper was bankrupt. That's why I had to go to Miami—I can't borrow a dime in this town. That mealy-mouthed lizard is out there screwing me."

I was tempted to ask him why he'd hired Segarra in the first place, or why he had put out a fifth-rate paper when he might have at least tried to put out a good one. Suddenly I was tired of Lotterman; he was a phony and he didn't even know it. He was forever yapping about Freedom of the Press and Keeping the Paper Going, but if he'd had a million dollars and all the freedom in the world he'd still put out a worthless newspaper because he wasn't smart enough to put out a good one. He was just another noisy little punk in the great legion of punks who march between the banners of bigger and better men. Freedom, Truth, Honor—you could rattle off a hundred such words and behind every one of them would gather a thousand punks, pompous little farts, waving the banner with one hand and reaching under the table with the other.

I stood up. "Ed," I said, using his name for the first time, "I believe I'll quit."

He looked up at me, his face blank.

"Yeah," I said. "I'll be back on Monday for my check, and after that I think I'll rest awhile."

He jumped out of his seat and rushed at me. "You cheap Ivy League sonofabitch!" he shouted. "I've tolerated your arrogance long enough!" He pushed me toward the door. "You're fired!" he screamed. "Get out of the building before I have you locked up!" He gave me a shove into the newsroom, then went back in his office and slammed the door.

I wandered over to my desk and started laughing when Sala asked me what happened. "He went off his nut," I replied. "I told him I was quitting and he snapped."

"Well," said Sala, "it's all over anyway. He promised me a month's salary if I'd tell people that he fired Segarra because he was queer—said he'd pay it out of his own pocket if Stein didn't come through."

"The cheap bastard," I said. "He didn't offer me a dime." I laughed. "Of course he talked like he was ready to give me Segarra's job—until Monday."

"Yeah, Monday's D-Day," said Sala. "He'll have to pay us if he wants to put out a paper." He shook his head. "But I don't think he does—I think he sold out to Stein."

He snorted. "So what? If he can't pay the staff, he's finished, no matter what he wants. I know one damn thing—he'll be running the greyest paper in the Western Hemisphere if I don't get my check on Monday. I'm coming in here tomorrow morning and clean out the whole photo library—about 99 percent of that stuff is mine."

"Hell yes," I said. "Hold it for ransom." Then I grinned. "Of course they'd get you for grand larceny if he pressed it—he might even remember about your thousand-dollar bail."

He shook his head. "Jesus, I keep forgetting about that—you think he really paid it?"

"I don't know," I said. "Probably a pretty good chance he got it back, but I'd hate to count on it."

"Ah, to hell with it," he replied. "Let's go up to Al's."

It was a hot, muggy night and I felt like getting drunk as a loon.

We had been there about an hour, swilling rum at top speed, when Donovan came roaring in. He had been out at the golf tournament all afternoon and had just heard the news. "Holy mother of jack-bastards!" he yelled. "I went back to the paper and there was no-body there but Schwartz, working his ass off." He fell down in a chair. "What happened—are we done in?"

"Yes," I said. "You're finished."

He nodded gravely. "I still have a deadline," he said. "I must fin-ish my sports section." He started for the street. "I'll be back in an hour," he assured us. "All I have to do is this golf story. To hell with the rest of it—I'll run a full-page cartoon."

Sala and I kept drinking, and when Donovan came back we stepped up the pace. By midnight we were all pretty wild and I be-gan thinking about Chenault. I thought about it for another hour or so, and then I got up and said I was going home.

On the way back, I stopped in Condado and got a bottle of rum. When I got to the apartment she was sitting on the bed, reading *Heart of Darkness* and still wearing the same shirt.

I slammed the door behind me and went to the kitchen to mix a drink. "Wake up and ponder the future," I said over my shoulder. "I quit tonight and got fired about two minutes later."

She looked up and smiled. "No more money?"

"No more nothing," I replied, filling two glasses with rum. "I'm clearing out. I'm tired of it."

"Tired of what?" she asked.

I took one of the drinks over to the bed. "Here," I said. "Here's one of the things I'm tired of." I shoved it into her hand, then walked over to the window and looked down at the street. "Mainly," I said, "I'm tired of being a punk—a human suckfish." I chuckled. "You know about suckfish?"

She shook her head.

"They have little suction cups on their bellies," I said. "And they attach themselves to sharks—when the shark gets a big meal, the suckfish eats the leftovers."

She giggled and sipped her drink.

"Don't laugh," I snapped. "You're Exhibit A—first Yeamon, then me." It was an ugly thing to say, but I was raving now and I didn't care. "Hell," I added. "I'm no better. If somebody came up to me and said, 'Tell me, Mister Kemp, just what is your profession?' I'd say, 'Well, you see, I swim around in murky waters until I find something big and bad to clamp onto—a good provider, as it were, something with big teeth and a small belly.' " I laughed at her. "That's the combination a good suckfish looks for—avoid the big belly at all costs."

She looked at me, shaking her head sadly.

"That's right!" I shouted. "I'm drunk and nuts both—no hope for me, is there?" I stopped pacing and looked at her. "Well there's not much hope for you either, by God. You're so damn stupid that you don't know a suckfish when you see one!" I started pacing again. "You said to hell with the only person down here without cups on his belly, and then you grab on to me, of all damn people." I shook my head. "Christ, I'm cups all over—I've been grabbing leftovers so long I don't know what the real thing looks like anymore."

She was crying now, but I kept on. "What the hell are you going to do, Chenault? What *can* you do?" I went back to the kitchen for more drink. "You better start thinking," I said. "Your days are numbered here—unless you want to pay the rent when I go."

She kept on crying, and I walked back to the window. "No hope for an old suckfish," I muttered, suddenly feeling very tired. I wandered around for a while, saying nothing, then I went over and sat down on the bed.

She stopped crying and sat up, leaning on one elbow. "When are you leaving?" she said.

"I don't know," I replied. "Probably next week."

"Where?" she asked.

"I don't know—someplace new."

She was silent for a moment, then she said, "Well, I suppose I'll go back to New York."

I shrugged. "I'll get you a plane ticket. I can't afford it, but what the hell."

"You don't have to," she said. "I have money."

I stared at her. "I thought you couldn't even get back from St. Thomas."

"I didn't have any then," she said. "It was in that suitcase you got from Fritz—I hid it, so we'd have something left." She smiled faintly. "It's only a hundred dollars."

"Hell," I said. "You'll need some when you get to New York."

"No I won't," she replied. "I'll still have fifty, and—" she hesitated. "And I think I'll go home for a while. My parents live in Connecticut."

"Well," I said. "That's good, I guess."

She leaned over and put her head on my chest. "It's horrible," she sobbed. "But I don't know where else to go."

I put my arm around her shoulders. I didn't know where she could go, either, or why, or what she could do when she got there.

"Can I stay here until you go?" she asked.

I tightened my arm on her shoulders, pulling her closer. "Sure," I said. "If you think you can stand the gaff."

"The what?" she asked.

I smiled and stood up. "The craziness," I said. "Do you mind if I get naked and drunk?"

She giggled. "What about me?"

"Sure," I said, taking off my clothes. "Why not?"

I made some new drinks and brought the bottle back to the table beside the bed. Then I turned on the fan and put out the lights while we sipped our drinks. I was propped up on pillows and she had her head on my chest. The silence was so total that the clink of the ice in my glass sounded loud enough to be heard on the street. The moon was bright through the front window and I watched the expression on Chenault's face, wondering how she could look so peaceful and content.

After a while I reached over and filled my glass again. In the process, I spilled some rum on my stomach and she leaned down to lick it off. The touch of her tongue made me shudder, and after a moment of contemplation I picked up the bottle again and spilled some rum on my leg. She looked up at me and smiled, as if I were playing some kind of an odd joke, then she bent down and carefully licked it off.

Nineteen

WE woke up early the next morning. I drove down to the hotel to get some papers while Chenault took a shower. I got a *Times* and a *Trib,* so we'd both have something to read, and then as an afterthought I bought two copies of what I figured was the final issue of the *San Juan Daily News.* I wanted to have one as a souvenir.

We had breakfast at the table by the window and afterward we drank coffee and read the papers. That morning was the only time I ever felt a sense of peace in the apartment, and when I thought about it I felt dumb, because that was the only reason I'd wanted it in the first place. I lay on the bed and smoked and listened to the radio while Chenault washed the dishes. There was a good breeze, and when I looked out the window I could see across the trees and the red-tiled rooftops all the way to the horizon.

Chenault was wearing my shirt again, and I watched it bounce and flutter around her thighs as she moved in the kitchen. After a while I got up and crept over to her, lifting the shirt and seizing her rump with both hands. She shrieked and spun around, then fell against me, laughing. I put my arms around her and playfully

jerked the tail of the shirt up over her head. We stood there swaying slightly and then I carried her over to the bed, where we made
love very quietly.

It was mid-morning when I left the house, but the sun was already so hot that it felt like mid-afternoon. Driving along the beach
I remembered how much I'd enjoyed the mornings when I first
came to San Juan. There is something fresh and crisp about the
first hours of a Caribbean day, a happy anticipation that something
is about to happen, maybe just up the street or around the next corner. Whenever I look back on those months and try to separate the
good times from the bad, I recall those mornings when I had an
early assignment—when I would borrow Sala's car and go roaring
along the big tree-lined boulevard. I remember the feel of the little
car vibrating beneath me and the sudden heat of the sun on my
face as I zipped out of the shade and into a patch of light; I
remember the whiteness of my shirt and the sound of a silk tie flap-
ping in the wind beside my head, the unhinged feel of the
accelerator and a sudden switching of lanes to pass a truck and
beat a red light.

Then into a palm-lined driveway and hit the rasping brakes, flip
down the Press tag on the visor and leave the car in the nearest No
Parking zone. Hurry into the lobby, pulling on the coat to my new
black suit and dangling a camera in one hand while an oily clerk
calls my man to confirm the appointment. Then up a soft elevator
to the suite—big greeting, pompous conversation, and black coffee
from a silver pot, a few quick photos on the balcony, grinning
handshake, then back down the elevator and hustle off.

On my way back to the office, with a pocketful of notes, I would
stop at one of the outdoor restaurants on the beach for a club sandwich and a beer; sitting in the shade to read the papers and ponder
the madness of the news, or leaning back with a lusty grin at all the
bright-wrapped nipples, trying to decide how many I could get my
hands on before the week was out.

Those were the good mornings, when the sun was hot and the air
was quick and promising, when the Real Business seemed right on

the verge of happening and I felt that if I went just a little faster I might overtake that bright and fleeting thing that was always just ahead.

Then came noon, and morning withered like a lost dream. The sweat was torture and the rest of the day was littered with the dead remains of all those things that might have happened, but couldn't stand the heat. When the sun got hot enough it burned away all the illusions and I saw the place as it was—cheap, sullen, and garish— nothing good was going to happen here.

Sometimes at dusk, when you were trying to relax and not think about the general stagnation, the Garbage God would gather a handful of those choked-off morning hopes and dangle them somewhere just out of reach; they would hang in the breeze and make a sound like delicate glass bells, reminding you of something you never quite got hold of, and never would. It was a maddening image, and the only way to whip it was to hang on until dusk and banish the ghosts with rum. Often it was easier not to wait, so the drinking would begin at noon. It didn't help much, as I recall, except that sometimes it made the day go a little faster.

I was snapped out of my reverie when I turned the corner into Calle O'Leary and saw Sala's car parked in front of Al's front door, and next to it was Yeamon's scooter. The day turned instantly rotten and a sort of panic came on me. I drove past Al's without stopping, and kept looking straight ahead until I turned down the hill. I drove around for a while, trying to think it out, but no matter how many reasonable conclusions I came to, I still felt like a snake. Not that I didn't feel perfectly right and justified—I just couldn't bring myself to go up there and sit down at a table across from Yeamon. The more I thought about it, the worse I felt. Hang out a shingle, I muttered: "P. Kemp, Drunken Journalist, Suckfish & Snake—hrs. noon to dawn, closed Mondays."

As I circled the Plaza Colón I got jammed up behind a fruit peddler and blew my horn savagely at him. "You stinking little nazi!" I shouted. "Get out of my way."

My mood was turning sour. My sense of humor was slipping. It was time to get off the street.

I headed for the Condado Beach Club, where I hunkered down at a big glass table on the deck with a red, blue, and yellow umbrella to keep off the sun. I spent the next few hours reading *The Nigger of the Narcissus* and making notes for my story on The Rise and Fall of the *San Juan Daily News*. I was feeling smart, but reading Conrad's preface frightened me so much that I abandoned all hope of ever being anything but a failure . . .

But not today, I thought. Today will be different. Today we will whoop it up. Have a picnic. Get some champagne. Take Chenault out to the beach and go wild. My mood swung immediately. I called the waiter and ordered two special picnic lunches with lobster and mangoes.

When I got back to the apartment, Chenault was gone. There was no sign of her, none of her clothes in the closet. There was an eerie sense of quiet in the place, a strange emptiness.

Then I saw the note in my typewriter—four or five lines on *Daily News* stationery with a vivid pink lipstick kiss above my name.

Dear Paul,

    I can't stand it anymore. My plane leaves at six. You love me. We are soul-mates. We will drink rum and dance naked. Come see me in New York. I will have a few surprises for you.

                             Love,
                           Chenault

I looked at my watch and saw that it was six-fifteen. Too late to catch her at the airport. Ah well, I thought. I'll see her in New York.

I sat on the bed and drank the bottle of champagne. I felt melancholy, so I decided to go swimming. I drove out to Luisa Aldea where the beach was empty.

The surf was high and I felt a combination of fear and eagerness as I took off my clothes and walked toward it. In the backlash of a huge wave I plunged in and let it suck me out to sea. Moments later I was hurtling back toward the beach on top of a long white breaker that carried me along like a torpedo. Then it spun me around like a dead fish and slammed me on the sand so hard that my back was raw for days afterward.

I kept at it as long as I could stand up, riding out with the riptide and waiting for the next big one to throw me back at the beach.

It was getting dark when I quit and the bugs were coming out, millions of diseased little gnats, impossible to see. I felt a thick black taste in my mouth as I stumbled toward my car.

Twenty

MONDAY was a crucial day and the tension was waiting for me when I woke up. I had overslept again and it was almost noon. After a quick breakfast, I hurried down to the paper.

When I got there I found Moberg on the front steps, reading a notice tacked to the door. It was long and complicated, saying in essence that the paper had been sold into receivership and all claims against the former owners would be duly considered by Stein Enterprises of Miami, Florida.

Moberg finished reading it and turned to me. "This is unconscionable," he said. "We should break in and loot the place. I need money, all I have is ten dollars." Then, before I could stop him, he kicked the glass out of the door. "Come on," he said, starting through the hole. "I know where he keeps the petty cash."

Suddenly, a bell began ringing and I jerked him backward. "You crazy bastard," I said. "You've triggered the alarm. We have to get away from this place before the cops get here."

We raced up to Al's and found the others huddled around a big patio table and jabbering feverishly. Drizzling rain forced them to hunch closely as they plotted the murder of Lotterman.

"That swine," said Moberg. "He could have paid us Friday. He has plenty of money, I've seen it."

Sala laughed. "Hitler had plenty of money, but he never paid his bills."

Schwartz shook his head sadly. "I wish I could get into the office. I have to make some calls." He nodded meaningfully. "Long calls—like Paris, Kenya, and Tokyo."

"Why Tokyo?" said Moberg. "You can get killed there."

"You mean *you* can get killed there," Schwartz replied. "I mind my own business."

Moberg shook his head. "I have friends in Tokyo. You'll never make friends—you're too stupid."

"You dirty little lush!" Schwartz exclaimed, suddenly standing up. "One more word out of you and I'll punch your face!"

Moberg laughed easily. "You're cracking up, Schwartz. I'd advise you to take a bath."

Schwartz took a quick step around the table and swung like he was throwing a baseball. Moberg could have dodged, if he'd had any reflexes, but he just sat there and let himself be bashed off his chair.

It was a tough show and Schwartz was obviously pleased with himself. "That'll teach you," he muttered, starting for the door. "See you fellows later," he called back to us. "I can't stand being around that lush."

Moberg grinned and spit at him. "I'll be back in a while," he told us. "I have to see a woman in Río Piedras—I need money."

Sala watched him go, shaking his head sadly. "I've seen a lot of creeps in my time, but that one takes the cake."

"Nonsense," I said. "Moberg is your friend. Never forget that."

Later that night we went to a garden party given by the Rum League and the San Juan Chamber of Commerce, to honor the spirit of American scholarship. The house was white stucco, ornate and sprawling, with a big garden in back. About a hundred people were there, most of them dressed formally. On one side of the garden was a long bar and I hurried toward it. Donovan was there, drinking heavily. He opened his coat discreetly and showed me a butcher knife tucked into his belt.

"Look at this," he said. "We're ready."

Ready? I thought. Ready for what? Slitting Lotterman's throat?

The garden was full of rich celebrities and visiting students. I noticed Yeamon standing off from the crowd with his arm around an exceptionally pretty girl. They were sharing a pint of gin and laughing harshly. Yeamon was wearing black nylon gloves, which I took as an ominous sign. Jesus, I thought, these bastards have gone through the looking glass. I wanted no part of it.

The party was dressy. There was a band on the porch, playing "Cielito Lindo" over and over again. They gave it a mad waltzing tempo and each time they finished, the dancers would yell for more. For some reason, I remember that moment as well or better than anything else I saw in Puerto Rico. A sensuous green garden, surrounded by palms and a brick wall; a long bar full of bottles and ice, and behind it a white-coated bartender; an elderly crowd in dinner jackets and bright dresses, talking peacefully on the lawn. A warm Caribbean night, with time passing slowly and at a respectful distance.

I felt a hand on my arm and it was Sala. "Lotterman's here," he said. "We're going to nail him."

Just then we heard a shrill scream. I looked across the garden and saw a flurry of movement. There was another scream and I recognized Moberg's voice, yelling: "Watch out, watch out... eeeeeeyahhaaaa!"

I got there just in time to see him getting up off the ground. Lotterman was standing over him, waving his fist. "You stinking little sot! You tried to kill me!"

Moberg got up slowly and brushed himself off. "You deserve to die," he snarled, "die like the rat you are."

Lotterman was trembling and his face was dark red. He took a quick step toward Moberg and hit him again, knocking him back on some people who were trying to get out of the way. I heard laughter beside me and a voice saying, "One of Ed's boys tried to hit him up for some cash. Look at him go, would you!"

Lotterman was shouting incoherently and flailing at Moberg,

driving him back into the crowd. Moberg was screaming for help when he bumped into Yeamon coming the other way. Yeamon shoved him aside and yelled something at Lotterman. The only word I caught was "Now . . ."

I saw Lotterman's face collapse with surprise, and he was standing straight as a wooden pole when Yeamon hit him in the eyes and knocked him about six feet. He staggered wildly for a moment, then collapsed on the grass, bleeding from his eyes and both ears. Then, out of the corner of my eye, I saw a dark shape come hurtling across the garden and strike the group like a cannonball. They all went down, but Donovan was first on his feet. He had a berserk grin on his face as he grabbed one man by the head and mashed him sideways against a tree. Yeamon dragged Lotterman out from under another man and began whacking him around the garden like a punching bag.

The crowd panicked and rushed to escape. "Call the police!" one man shouted.

A wrinkled old woman in a strapless dress went stumbling past me, shrieking, "Take me home! Take me home! I'm afraid!"

I edged away through the mob, trying to attract as little attention as possible. When I got to the door I looked back and saw a bunch of men staring down at Lotterman's body and making the sign of the cross. "There they go!" someone shouted, and I looked toward the back of the garden where he was pointing. There was a rustling in the bushes, the sound of snapping limbs, and then I saw Donovan and Yeamon scrambling over the wall.

A man came running up the steps to the house. "They got away!" he shouted. "Somebody call the police! I'm going after them!"

I slid out the door and ran along the sidewalk toward my car. I thought I heard Yeamon's scooter somewhere nearby, but I couldn't be sure. I decided to hurry back to Al's, saying that I'd ducked out of that unruly crowd and gone down to the Flamboyan for a few quiet beers. It would be a flimsy alibi, if anybody at the party had recognized me, but I had no choice.

I'd been there about fifteen minutes when Sala arrived. He was trembling as he hurried over to the table. "Man!" he said in a loud whisper. "I've been driving like a bastard all over town. I didn't know where to go." He looked around to make sure there was nobody else in the patio.

I laughed and leaned back in the chair. "Wasn't that a bitch?"

"A bitch?" he exclaimed. "Did you hear what happened? Lotterman had a heart attack—he's dead."

I leaned toward him. "Where'd you hear that?"

"I was there when they took him away in the ambulance," he replied. "You should have seen the place—women screaming, cops everywhere—they took Moberg." He lit a cigarette. "You know we're still out on bail," he said quietly. "We're doomed."

The lights were on in my apartment, and as I hurried up the stairs I heard the shower running. The bathroom door was closed and I pulled it open. The curtain jerked back and Yeamon peered out of the shower. "Kemp?" he said, peering through the steam. "Who the hell is it?"

"God damn you!" I shouted. "How did you get in here?"

"Your window was open. I'll have to stay here tonight—the lights failed on my scooter."

"You dumb bastard!" I snapped. "You might have a murder rap on your ass—Lotterman had a heart attack—he's dead!"

He jumped out of the shower and wrapped a towel around his waist. "Jesus," he said. "I better get out of here."

"Where's Donovan?" I said. "They're after him too."

He shook his head. "I don't know. We hit a parked car on the scooter. He said he was going to the airport."

I looked at my watch. It was almost eleven-thirty. "Where's the scooter?" I asked.

He pointed to the rear of the building. "I put it around the side. It was hell getting here with no lights."

I groaned. "Christ, you're sucking me right into jail! Get dressed. You're leaving."

It was a ten-minute drive to the airport and we had barely got under way when we ran into a tropical monsoon. We stopped and put up the top, but by the time we got it snapped down we were both soaking wet.

The rain was blinding. A few inches above my head it pounded on the canvas, and beneath us the tires hissed on the wet pavement.

We swung off the highway and started up the long road to the airport. We were about halfway to the terminal when I looked to my left and saw a big plane with Pan Am markings come hurtling down the runway. I thought I could see Donovan's face at one of the windows, grinning and waving at us as the plane lifted off the runway and went past us with a great roar, a winged monster full of lights and people, all bound for New York. I pulled over and we watched it climb and go into a steep turn above the palm jungle and then out to sea, until finally it was nothing but a tiny red dot up in the stars.

"Well," I said. "There it goes."

Yeamon stared after it. "Is that the last one?"

"Yep," I replied. "Next flight's at nine-thirty tomorrow morning."

After a pause he said, "Well, I guess we should head back."

I looked at him. "Back where?" I said. "You might as well give yourself up right now as come out here tomorrow morning."

He stared out at the rain and glanced around nervously. "Well goddamnit, I have to get off this island—that's all there is to it."

I thought for a moment, then I remembered the ferry from Fajardo to St. Thomas. As far as I knew, it left about eight every morning. We decided that he would go over there and get a cheap room at the Grand Hotel. After that he would be on his own—I had my own problems.

It was forty miles to Fajardo, but the road was good and there was no hurry, so I drove easily. The rain had stopped and the night smelled fresh. We put the top down and took turns sipping the rum.

"Damn," he said after a while. "I hate to have to take off for South America with one suit and a hundred dollars to my name."

He leaned back in the seat and wept. I could hear the surf a few hundred yards to the left of the road. To the right I could see the peak of El Yunque, a black outline against a menacing sky.

It was almost one-thirty when we came to the end of the highway and turned off to Fajardo. The town was dark and there wasn't a soul on the streets. We rounded the empty plaza and drove down toward the ferry dock. There was a small hotel about a block away and I stopped in front of it while he went in to get a room.

In a few minutes he came out and got into the car. "Well," he said quietly, "I'm okay. The ferry leaves at eight."

He seemed to want to sit for a while, so I lit another cigarette and tried to relax. The town was so quiet that every sound we made seemed dangerously amplified. Once the rum bottle banged against the steering wheel as he was passing it back to me, and I jumped like somebody had fired a shot.

He laughed quietly. "Take it easy, Kemp. You don't have anything to worry about."

I wasn't so much worried, as spooked. There was something eerie about the whole business, as if God in a fit of disgust had decided to wipe us all out. Our structure was collapsing; it seemed like just a few hours ago that I was having breakfast with Chenault in the sunny peace of my own home. Then I had ventured into the day, and plunged headlong into an orgy of murder and shrieking and breaking of glass. Now it was ending just as senselessly as it began. It was all over and I was very sure of it because Yeamon was leaving. There might be some noise after he left, but it would be orthodox noise, the kind a man can deal with and even ignore—instead of those sudden unnerving eruptions that suck you into them and toss you around like a toad in rough water.

I couldn't remember where it actually began, but it was ending here in Fajardo, a dark little spot on the map that seemed to be the end of the world. Yeamon was going on from here and I was going back; it was definitely the end of something, but I wasn't sure just what.

I lit a cigarette and thought about other people, and wondered what they were doing tonight, while I was here on a dark street in Fajardo sipping rum out of a bottle with a man who would tomorrow morning be a fugitive murderer.

Yeamon handed the bottle back to me and got out of the car. "Well, I'll see you, Paul—God knows where."

I leaned across the seat and stuck out my hand. "Probably New York," I said.

"How long will you be here?" he asked.

"Not long," I replied.

He gave my hand a final shake. "Okay, Kemp," he said with a grin. "Thanks a lot—you came through like a champ."

"Hell," I said, starting the engine. "We're all champs when we're drunk."

"Nobody's drunk," he said.

"I am," I said. "Or else I'd have turned you in."

"Balls," he replied.

I shoved the car into gear. "Okay, Fritz, good luck."

"Right," he said as I pulled away. "Good luck yourself."

I had to go down to the corner to turn around, and as I came back up the street I passed him again, and waved. He was walking down toward the ferry and when I got to the corner I stopped and watched to see what he would do. It was the last time I saw him and I remember it very clearly. He walked out on the pier and stood near a wooden lamppost, looking out at the sea. The only living thing in a dead Caribbean town—a tall figure in a rumpled Palm Beach suit, his only suit, now full of dirt and grass stains and bulgy pockets, standing alone on a pier at the end of the world and thinking his own thoughts. I waved again, although his back was to me, and gave two quick blasts on the horn as I sped out of town.

Twenty-one

O N my way back to the apartment I stopped to get the early editions. I was stunned to see Yeamon on the front page of *El Diario* under a big headline that said "Matanza en Río Piedras." It was from the shot of the three of us in the jail, taken when we got arrested and beaten. Well, I thought, this is it. The jig is up.

I drove home and called Pan Am to book a seat on the morning plane. Then I packed my bags. I crammed everything—clothes, books, a big scrapbook of my stuff from the *News*—into two duffel bags. I laid them side by side, then I put my typewriter and my shaving kit on top of them. And that was it—my worldly goods, the meager fruits of a ten-year odyssey that was beginning to look like a lost cause. On my way out I remembered to take a bottle of Rum Superior for Chenault.

I still had three hours to kill and I needed to cash a check. They would do it at Al's, I knew, but maybe the cops would be waiting for me there. I decided to risk it and drive very carefully through Condado, across the causeway and into the sleeping Old City.

Al's was empty, except for Sala sitting alone in the patio. When I walked to the table Sala looked up. "Kemp," he said, "I feel a hundred years old."

"How old are you?" I said. "Thirty? Thirty-one?"

"Thirty," he said quickly. "I was just thirty last month."

"Hell," I replied. "Imagine how old I feel—I'm almost thirty-two."

He shook his head. "I never thought I'd live to see thirty. I don't know why, but for some reason I just didn't."

I smiled. "I don't know if I did or not—I never gave it much thought."

"Well," he said. "I hope to God I never make forty—I wouldn't know what to do with myself."

"You might," I said. "We're over the hump, Robert. The ride gets pretty ugly from here on in."

He leaned back and said nothing. It was almost dawn, but Nelson Otto was still lingering at his piano. The song was "Laura," and the sad notes floated out to the patio and hung in the trees like birds too tired to fly. It was a hot night, with almost no breeze, but I was feeling cold sweat in my hair. For lack of anything better to do, I studied a cigarette burn in the sleeve of my blue oxford-cloth shirt.

Sala called for more drink and Sweep brought four rums, saying they were on the house. We thanked him and sat for another half hour, saying nothing. Down on the waterfront I could hear the slow clang of a ship's bell as it eased against the pier, and somewhere in the city a motorcycle roared through the narrow streets, sending its echo up the hill to Calle O'Leary. Voices rose and fell in the house next door and the raucous sound of a jukebox came from a bar down the street. Sounds of a San Juan night, drifting across the city through layers of humid air; sounds of life and movement, people getting ready and people giving up, the sound of hope and the sound of hanging on, and behind them all, the quiet, deadly ticking of a thousand hungry clocks, the lonely sound of time passing in the long Caribbean night.

ABOUT THE AUTHOR

HUNTER S. THOMPSON was born and raised in Louisville, Kentucky. His books include *Hell's Angels, Fear and Loathing in Las Vegas, Fear and Loathing on the Campaign Trail '72, The Curse of Lono, Songs of the Doomed, Better Than Sex,* and *The Proud Highway.* He is a regular contributor to various national and international publications. He now lives in a fortified compound on an island near Puerto Rico.

A History of the Type

The text of this book is set in Berthold Walbaum, a typeface based on the 1800 design by Justus Erich Walbaum of Weimar. In 1919 the Berthold Foundry of Berlin acquired Walbaum's original punches and matrices, and in 1976 it reissued a new version of the face designed by Günter Gerhard Lange. In 1991 Adobe Systems introduced the digital rendering, which is used here.

Walbaum is a direct relative of Firmin Didot's and Giambattista Bodoni's roman type designs, as evidenced in the thin, unbracketed serifs; in the contrast of stroke weight, which makes for a visually vibrant page; and in the equalized height of the capitals and ascenders. Walbaum also demonstrates the condensed letterform and increased x-height introduced in the *romain du roi* type cut by Phillippe Grandjean for the Imprimerie Royale of Louis XIV in 1702. These types represent a significant break with the humanist calligraphic tradition in typography born from the types of Nicholas Jenson and Aldus Manutius in the fifteenth century. Henceforth, printing types began to be understood as stylistically independent from the written hand.

J. E. Walbaum was a contemporary of Beethoven, Novalis, and Goethe, who also lived in Weimar around 1800. The year 1800 is notable as the year Napoléon's army conquered Italy; the United States capital was moved from Philadelphia to Washington, D.C.; Alessandro Volta invented the zinc-and-silver battery cell; German physician F. J. Gall founded the science of phrenology; in England Humphry Davy published *Researches, Chemical and Philosophical, Concerning Nitrous Oxide;* and Eli Whitney designed a musket with interchangeable parts.

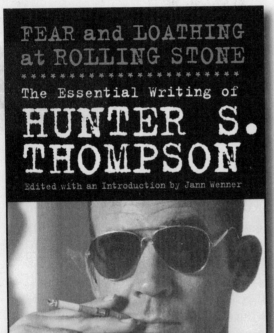